royally lost

Also by
A n g i e   S t a n t o n

rock and a hard place:
A Jamieson Brothers Novel

snapshot:
A Jamieson Brothers Novel

Angie Stanton

royally lost

An Imprint of HarperCollinsPublishers

Library of Congress Control Number: 2013958344
ISBN 978-0-06-227258-4 (pbk.)

Typography by Andrea Vandergrift
14 15 16 17 18   CG/RRDH   10 9 8 7 6 5 4 3 2 1

❖

First Edition

For Kevin

You have the heart, soul, and integrity of a prince.

1

Crown Prince Nikolai forced a print-worthy smile as he exited the antiquities museum. The flash from a sea of cameras blinded him as onlookers called his name. He nodded through the bright glare. In the two months since he finished school, every day had been filled with tedious dedications, droll speeches, and royal appearances. He paused as his mother, Queen Elana, and his sister, Princess Alexandra, entered the limo.

The demands of the monarchy—and his parents—threatened to suffocate the life right out of him. As each day passed, he lost more of himself.

Nikolai entered the vehicle last and eased back against the leather seat as the door closed. He released a polished brass button at the collar of his uniform, and finally drew a deep breath as the limo smoothly eased away.

"Nikolai, at tomorrow's events, would you please act more interested in the proceedings?" The queen frowned while removing her long white gloves. Her stylish blonde hair framed her smart blue eyes and porcelain face. "The last thing we need is for you to show up at the dedication of the new hospital wing with a perfunctory look on your face."

His sister, Alexi, kicked off her heels and sat on her legs, crushing her gown.

"Alexandra, sit like a lady!" the queen exclaimed.

"Why? My feet hurt from those stupid shoes. It's not like anyone can even see inside the car."

"It doesn't matter if the press sees you, I see you." The queen pursed her lips.

As their mother looked away, Alexi rolled her eyes.

"Mother, give her a break. She's not hurting anything," Nikolai said.

"You have no room to talk. Your behavior of late has not been helpful to the image of the royal house. You do realize the press will be covering all of the events, and the people expect a regal young man, not a bored teenager."

"The press has photographed my every move since the day I was born."

He gazed out the window as his mother droned on about the next day's schedule and his attendance at the annual placing of flowers on the tomb of his ancestor, the centuries dead King Nikolai. At least his namesake was a real royal and not a holdover from archaic traditions that should have been put to rest decades earlier.

"Nikolai! Pay attention. At the state dinner tomorrow evening, I want you resplendent. Your father will be introducing you to the leaders of the European Union as well as foreign policy makers."

Alexi shot him a sympathetic look. He grimaced. These important political figures would be respectful to him, protocol demanded they do so, but they knew what Nikolai's parents and the Mondovian government refused to acknowledge. Nikolai would have no more power in the political future of Mondovia than the homeless people who dined at the government-funded soup kitchen he'd recently visited.

Nikolai was no more than a handsome face to keep the masses distracted from the real problems troubling his country. How could his parents not see this?

He couldn't take it anymore. He'd been their puppet. He'd gone to the schools and the military academy they demanded. But he was eighteen now.

The queen continued on. "It is essential we ensure that the political leaders of Mondovia continue to honor the importance of the monarchy."

He turned to her. "Why is it so important they honor us? What have we done for them?"

"Nikolai! What has gotten into you? I don't know who your friends were at the academy, but clearly it's good you are finished so you can think straight again."

The limo pulled down a long, oak-lined lane, into the circular drive, and stopped before the marble pillars of Mersch Palace.

"This has nothing to do with who my friends are. I'm allowed to have a mind of my own. You may be able to dictate everything else in my life, but you can't control my thoughts."

"In a few weeks, none of that will be an issue because you'll be installed into the royal officers' academy," she stated matter-of-factly.

"What?"

The palace doorman opened the limo door.

"Nikolai, don't act surprised. You knew this day was coming." His mother stepped gracefully from the vehicle.

He scrambled after her. "No, actually, I did not. You can't force me into the military. This is a free country!"

"It's a free country *because* we have a strong military. Your father entered the armed forces at your age as did his father before him."

"Yes, but we were at war then. We aren't now."

"It's time you take your place in history. This is just the first step."

He followed his mother through the mammoth-sized double doors into the Grand Hall. Alexi made a quick dash past them.

"Mother. I will not join the military! I can't!"

There, he'd said it. The idea of carrying a gun, let alone shooting one, went against everything he believed in.

She turned on her heel. "You can and you will. You are Crown Prince of Mondovia, Nikolai. It is time you grow up and show the people that they can have faith in their future king."

Nikolai fought the urge to scream out his frustration. He looked around the opulent room filled with gilded chairs and priceless paintings. A massive chandelier made of Austrian crystals hung from the ceiling. From his parents' point of view, this was normal, but they lived in the Dark Ages. This was the twenty-first century, for crying out loud.

"You are living in the past, Mother. The people of Mondovia don't need a king. How can you not see that?"

"That is enough!"

"And they sure as hell don't need a crown prince." He whipped the medal-adorned sash over his head and tossed it on a teak side table next to a crystal lamp.

"Nikolai, whether you like it or not, the blood of the most powerful rulers in European history runs through your veins."

The queen approached him with the grace and poise that had been instilled in her from the moment she could speak. She grasped his chin with her delicate hand and lowered his gaze to hers.

"You are of age. It is time to put aside your childish

ways and step into the role you were born to."

"And what is that? To dress up like a fairy-tale character and spend the next forty years with people bowing and curtsying to me as I parade around acting as if I'm better than the rest of the world? That might work for you and Father, but I'm a realist, Mother. The monarchy is dead!" He stepped away from her hold.

His mother gasped, a rare occurrence for Her Royal Highness.

"And I refuse to sacrifice my life to play some antiquated figurehead who possesses no actual power beyond that of an artificial title. I'm sorry to disappoint you but I didn't choose this. I will not live my life to suit your schedulers. I can't stay here another minute."

"You may disagree and you may walk away, but one thing I can guarantee. You have a responsibility to your country, to your king. You cannot deny your birthright."

"Yeah? We'll see about that." He stormed up the wide marble steps of the winding staircase, past the paintings of former Mondovian rulers. Perhaps they didn't have a choice in their destinies, but he did.

Nikolai stalked into his suite of rooms and tossed his uniform jacket over the Louis XV armchair as he entered his closet. He changed into jeans, pulled on a dark T-shirt, and ran his fingers through his neatly combed hair, mussing it back to the way he liked it.

Finally he could breathe freely. Rummaging around, he pulled out a backpack and stuffed a few items inside, essentials to get him by for a while.

"Sir, may I assist you?" Dmitri, his personal secretary, asked from the doorway.

"No, Dmitri, thank you. The less you are involved, the better off you'll be." He dropped a pair of sunglasses into the pack. "My mother may think this is just a sign of me acting out or trying to get a moment of her attention, but it isn't."

"You misunderstand, sir. I wish to help in whatever way you need."

"My plans will only get you into trouble. Trust me when I say you should walk away now, while you can. I've seen what this life did to my parents and grandparents. They were not happy people. This cannot be my life."

Dmitri stepped closer. "Sir, if your plans are to leave the palace grounds, I will not stop you. However, I do wish you to go prepared."

Nikolai stopped packing and looked with fresh eyes at the man. "Why would you risk your reputation, possibly your job? I expect to make a bit of a stir, and anyone who helps me will likely go down at my side."

In his early thirties, Dmitri had been Nikolai's personal secretary since the king and queen increased Nikolai's royal duties three years prior. Today Dmitri looked at him with a compassion and understanding he'd never noticed before.

"Sir, you've been patient with your parents. Perhaps you are correct to deliver your message in a new way. You are the future of Mondovia, and I support your belief that change is needed. This is my way of helping the cause."

Nikolai grinned. "Well then, what am I overlooking?"

"I imagine you plan to travel light, but one thing you'll need is cash. You won't get far with empty pockets."

"Of course, I'd hate to have to come running back in two hours like a wayward child. I need to disappear for as many days as possible. Have we got much in my safe?" God, he hoped so. This was one more reason their system was archaic. If you were royal, you never needed money. Unless you were on the run. His lip curled in anticipation.

"I'll see what there is." Dmitri disappeared into the office of Nikolai's private quarters and soon returned with a stack of bills. "There is just over three hundred euros. If we add what I've got in my wallet, that will bring you to over four hundred. That should provide for a couple days' holiday."

Nikolai stared as his only confidant pulled out his wallet and handed over all its contents. "Dmitri, I can't take your money. Thank you, but it would be wrong."

"I'm a betting man, and I bet that your act of dissent makes an impact with the king."

Nikolai saw the sincerity in Dmitri's eyes. "I'll pay you back. I promise." He accepted the cash and put it in his wallet.

"Don't forget your phone, Your Highness. I'm here in case anything goes awry."

"It won't," Nikolai said, sliding the phone and charger into the nearly full pack.

"I'm sure you are right, and what car were you planning to take?"

"Whatever is the least noticeable."

"Might I suggest the motorbike gifted to you on your last birthday?"

Nikolai had totally forgotten about the motorbike he'd received from the shah of Borganistan. He'd enjoyed two rides through the countryside before his father's security detail deemed it too great a safety risk. "Dmitri, you're a genius!"

"I do my best."

Nikolai scanned the room one last time; his desk, used by every Mondovian prince before him; the formal sitting area; and the fireplace so large he could walk into it, a centuries-old clock on the mantel. He was happy to leave it. There was nothing drawing him to stay.

Alexi popped into the room, now wearing jeans and a tank top, and her blonde hair in a ponytail. "What are you doing?"

"Nothing," he answered, then glanced at Dmitri. "I'm set, thank you."

Dmitri nodded and discreetly departed, closing the door behind him.

Alexi plopped onto the edge of his bed. "I wish I were you."

He grabbed the book he'd meant to start reading and stuffed it into his pack. "No you don't. You'd hate it."

"If I were a boy, I could say what I felt and tell Mother and Father I didn't want to go to another stinking charity dinner. I hate it. I hate them!"

Nikolai stopped packing and sat next to her. He took her hand in his. "You don't mean that. They are old-fashioned and live on tradition, but they love us very much."

"You hate them."

"No, I don't hate them. I just don't want to live my life for them. I need to get away from here before they brainwash me."

Alexi noticed his backpack. "You're leaving?" She aimed her bright blue eyes on him. "Take me with you! Please!"

He sighed. "You know I can't do that."

"Why not? I'm just like you! I can't stand it here. I don't want to be Princess Alexi. I want to shop at the mall, eat fast food, and go to a rock concert. Please take me with you."

"It's bad enough what they'll do to me. I can't ruin your life, too." He stood up, knowing he'd better leave now, before Alexi dissolved into a puddle of tears and changed his resolve.

"It's not fair. You get to have all the fun. Where are you going to go?"

This wasn't about fun. This was about taking back his life. He bumped her shoulder with his.

"I'm not sure where I'm going yet, but I have to leave now while I still have the nerve. I'll call you while I'm gone, promise."

"When are you coming back?" Her eyes turned watery.

"I honestly don't know." He gave her a quick hug. "Be good while I'm gone." He slipped on a hoodie, grabbed his pack, and walked to the door.

Now why did he tell her to be good? He sounded just like his parents. He turned in the doorway. "I take that back. Don't be good, give 'em hell."

Alexi grinned. "I will. I'll tell Mother that you were angry and snuck out to that little pub on the edge of town. That should buy you some time."

"Thanks. You're the best."

Satisfied he'd cheered Alexi up and given her new purpose, he disappeared down the corridor and out a servants' side door.

2

If there was a fate worse than death, Becca knew for sure that this was it. She'd been sentenced to a week on a riverboat cruise through Europe, with people older than fossils and who smelled like stale coffee.

The only upside was that it got Becca out of Madison, Wisconsin, after her boyfriend dumped her for her best friend, Kelly.

It really sucked that Ethan broke up with Becca in a text message right before graduation. It made the grad gift she bought him of a vintage Graphite Angels T-shirt kind of pointless. She gave the shirt to her brother, Dylan, whose chair next to hers sat empty.

"Are you sure you told him dinner was at six?" Vicky, her stepmother, asked. Vicky wore her hair in a sleek black bob. Silver drop earrings accentuated her crimson lipstick.

"Dylan knows. He was unpacking. I'm sure he's on his

way," Becca fibbed. Her laid-back brother was usually up to something. Dylan possessed no more interest in this trip than Becca, but their dad and Vicky decided that quality family time, in the form of a multi-country river cruise, would keep Dylan out of trouble. However, her brother saw this as an opportunity to party in the beer drinking capital of the world and hook up with European girls.

"There he is," her father said, glancing up from his cell phone. In an effort to conform to the casual dress code, her dad wore a navy golf shirt with his dress khakis.

"Bill, put that phone away. We're on vacation. This trip is about family time, not work," Vicky chided, pretending they even knew how to behave as a family.

Vicky could try all she wanted, but there was no way they'd ever be a family. She was an outsider and always would be. Becca wished Vicky would give up trying so hard and accept the fact.

Dylan wandered over wearing a faded T-shirt, cargo shorts, and flip-flops. He slid into the seat next to Becca as the waiter arrived with wine.

"Good evening, my name is Melenka. I will be serving you this evening. May I offer you wine, sir?" he asked her dad.

He nodded. "Cabernet."

"Chardonnay. Thank you, Melenka." Vicky smiled as he poured.

The waiter glanced at Becca.

"No, thank you. I'm only eighteen." Becca answered his question before he could ask.

"Can I get a beer?" Dylan asked the waiter.

"I think you can refrain from drinking beer during dinner. We're in Europe, not at a frat party," their dad said.

"Are you kidding me? We're going to Hungary, Austria, and Germany. This is the holy grail of beer. So no, I won't be refraining. Plus, the brochure said free beer at lunch and dinner."

Her dad frowned and Vicky sighed. Melenka seemed unsure if he should listen to the college kid or the rich parent funding the highbrow trip.

"Fine, but control yourself and don't embarrass me," her dad warned, setting the trip off on a familiar, stressful note.

"I never do." Dylan grinned. Becca bit back her smile as the waiter scurried off to fetch Dylan's beer.

Dinner was a drawn-out, painful affair, complete with extra forks and palate cleansing. At least the exotic new foods tasted good. Who knew she'd enjoy snails? They tasted like a buttery, garlic mushroom.

Vicky worked hard to keep the conversation flowing. Becca was pretty sure her stepmother kicked her dad under the table at least once to keep him talking. He wasn't used to seeing his kids this much, let alone speaking to them. Apparently, when you're a bigwig president of an important technology company, you have to pick family or business. He picked business.

"You know, during college, I spent a month touring Europe and staying at hostels," Vicky said, trying to keep them talking.

Becca nodded, since Dylan and her dad didn't respond at all.

"It was one of the best times of my life. I hope you and Dylan get a chance to do that sometime. Every young person should."

"Here you are, crème brûlée," Melenka said, setting before her a dessert dish garnished with a raspberry and mint leaf. "So where have you traveled from?" he asked.

"Madison, Wisconsin," Becca answered.

The waiter looked confused.

"We're from the United States, near Chicago," her father said.

"Ah, Chicago! Yes, I've heard of Chicago." Melenka served the remaining desserts. "Enjoy."

Becca tapped her spoon through the crunchy top of her dessert and tried a bite. Heaven.

The next morning, Nikolai sipped his cappuccino at an outdoor café in Budapest. The air smelled of overnight rain, fresh-baked pastries, and flowers from nearby hanging baskets. Tourists milled about, peeking into store windows. For the first time in a long while, Nikolai's parents' expectations weren't a crushing vise.

He sank his teeth into a warm croissant and savored the freedom and independence he'd been forced to steal. While at boarding school, his parents had left him alone, but since his return, the pressures of living up to their outdated expectations had become unbearable. And now they expected him to join the military.

His grip tightened on the cup. He was far more interested in saving the planet from pollution than plotting invasions in war-torn countries. How could his parents not see that? Nikolai hoped that by disappearing for a while, they would understand he was serious about not following their laid-out plans for the rest of his life.

He'd always wanted to ride along the Danube. No one would look for him in old river towns. They'd expect him to fly to Paris, London, or someplace more metropolitan and grand.

Last night, he'd ridden his motorbike until late, putting as many miles as possible between himself and Mondovia. Just when fatigue set in, luck provided a youth hostel. The dorm-style lodging offered the sense of anonymity he'd been craving. Tourists weren't likely to recognize the Crown Prince of Mondovia. Whereas the British royalty were splattered over every worldwide media venue, Mondovian royalty was a small blip. Europeans might recognize him, but they were used to seeing him on magazine covers, not disappearing among the locals and tourists.

He took another sip of coffee as a group of tourists walked along the cobblestone street while their guide spoke into a headset. "And here we have Váci Utca. A popular spot to enjoy a cup of coffee or pick up a few souvenirs. Remember this was the city of Pest before three cities joined in the 1870s. This street dates to medieval times when it was the border of the walled city. Look closely and you will see remains of the Váci gate."

Nikolai watched the group of twenty or so people wander past. Most were older couples with fascinated expressions and wearing comfortable shoes. They obediently turned in each direction the guide indicated, soaking in Budapest's history.

As the last of the tour group shuffled past, Nikolai spotted a stylish couple and two teenagers at the back. The man appeared to be in his mid-fifties and sported thinning gray hair, a golf shirt, and perfectly creased pants. His wife looked a bit younger with striking good looks, red lips, and inappropriately high heels.

Lagging behind them were a girl and a guy who both appeared to be about Nikolai's age. The guy wore earbuds hooked into his iPod and ignored the tour guide in favor of checking out every young woman who passed by.

The girl was obviously his sister, as they shared the same high cheekbones and shade of light brown hair, but the similarities stopped there. Her hair had been kissed by the sun and lay in soft waves past her shoulders. The shorts she wore showed off long tan legs and hugged her hips nicely.

Suddenly, the dark-haired woman slipped on the cobblestone and stumbled. Her husband took her arm. "Vicky, are you okay?"

"Yes, but these streets are terrible. They should blacktop them like we do in the U.S."

Nikolai shook his head. Why were American tourists so ignorant? He noticed the girl roll her eyes at the mother, and he laughed to himself. The girl and the mother looked nothing alike and apparently thought differently, too. She reminded him of Alexi.

The girl wandered around the corner to peek in a shop window. The rest of the tour moved forward. He watched as she became transfixed at whatever was in the shop. The group rounded a corner and disappeared a block farther down.

Nikolai watched to see what the girl would do when she realized she'd been left behind. After a minute, she glanced up and returned to the main street. She looked in both directions, her brow furrowed.

She examined the street signs and slowly turned around, searching in each direction. She ended up walking in the opposite direction of her group.

Nikolai chuckled. Should he call out and tell her she was going the wrong way? It wasn't as if she was in any danger, plus, she was great morning entertainment.

Before she passed more than a few shops, Nikolai made up his mind to step in and help, but then the girl's brother appeared.

"Hey, Becca! Where are you going?" he called.

The girl, Becca, turned, realization dawning, and headed back. They met right in front of Nikolai's table, oblivious to their audience.

"I was looking for some place to buy a soda," she said.

"Sure you were. Don't think you can take off and leave me stranded with those two. If you leave, I do, too."

"That goes both ways," she said.

"Deal."

The pair retraced the steps of the group and disappeared around the corner. Nikolai felt a strange kinship to the two. He wasn't the only one who didn't want to be with his parents.

"I'm going outside to look around," Becca said, bored of watching Vicky and her dad shop for overpriced porcelain figurines.

"That's fine, but don't go far—we meet up with the guide in ten minutes," her dad said.

"I won't."

"And see if you can find your brother. I don't want you two holding up the group again," Vicky added.

"Okay." Becca wandered out of the brightly lit expensive boutique that looked like it belonged in New York City instead of exotic Budapest.

Outside, quaint sidewalk cafés and colorful souvenir shops of every kind dotted the cobblestone street. Displays of paprika, collectible dolls, and T-shirts occupied every inch of shelf space. She paused to look at an arrangement of painted plates, snow globes, and refrigerator magnets. Did people really buy this stuff? She moved on, occasionally glancing back at the boutique to keep track of her location. What she really wanted was a cold Diet Pepsi.

Becca discovered a narrow store with stacks of newspapers in languages that looked like gibberish. She peeked inside the door to discover the Budapest version of a convenience store. The walls were packed with everything from magazines and paperback books, to batteries, tobacco, candy, and chips. She entered the store.

While many of the items were familiar brands, she couldn't decipher the names as all the packaging was printed in a foreign language. The clerk waited on a customer. Becca spotted a refrigerated cooler. *Yes!*

Her eyes dashed over the chilled bottles. "No Diet Pepsi?" she muttered. But there was a bottle called Coca-Cola Light, which looked a lot like a Diet Coke from back home. Not exactly the beverage she wanted, but she grabbed the soda anyway and brought her purchase to the checkout counter.

"Oh! I'm sorry," Becca said, nearly bumping into a guy as he turned to leave. She peered up at a guy with dusty blond hair and the most interesting shade of sapphire eyes.

"Excuse me," he said with a light accent and surprised look.

Becca stood dumbfounded, wanting to lose herself in those gorgeous eyes, but then she snapped out of it and stepped to the side. At the exact instant he did the same. *Oops.*

She stepped the other way, and he mirrored her move. He paused and smiled, a lazy, confident one, as if he knew she was checking him out.

"Sorry. I'll stand still so you can pass." She gripped the soda bottle and tried not to embarrass herself further.

"No problem. I should have looked where I was going." His warm eyes were kind, with a hint of humor. She liked the low timbre of his voice and smiled as he slipped past.

When Becca reached the counter, she turned around and discovered him paused in the entryway, looking back at her. She turned away, flustered to be caught watching him, when in reality he was watching her, too.

Becca paid for her soda. When she turned to leave, hoping to get another glimpse of the cute guy, he was gone.

3

Later that afternoon, Becca stared out the tinted windows of the tour bus as they passed by historic buildings of Budapest. She pulled the strap of the radio receiver from around her neck. The riverboat company had the tourists all wired with receivers and earbuds so they wouldn't miss a word of the guide's endless droning. She tossed it on the seat between her and Dylan.

"Aw, come on. It's not that bad," he said, while fiddling with his iPod.

"Ten days of this. Shoot me now. Everything here is a gabillion years old. The palace of this, the castle of that. Seriously?"

"You're jet-lagged. We'll find lots of ways to have fun."

"You're joking, right? It would be a different story if I were here with a bunch of friends, but this whole *let's play happy family* scene is a load of bull."

"True, but did you notice the tour guide? She totally wants me."

"Dylan, not every girl with a pulse is interested in you."

"Just the hot ones."

Great. Dylan, the man whore, was already targeting his prey. "You are not shacking up with some girl in our room. I swear I'll kill you. You want to hook up, go to her place."

The bus pulled up to a stoplight. Becca noticed a young guy walk across a parking lot to a motorcycle. Something about the way he walked captured her attention. Was it the careless confidence in his stride, or maybe the way his T-shirt stretched across his chest as his arms moved? She couldn't get a good look at his face. He probably had a great body to compensate for a big nose or eyes that were too close together.

"You're just jealous," Dylan said, interrupting her thoughts.

"Not even close. I'm a little anti-men right now, if you haven't noticed."

"Ethan is an idiot. You were too good for him. I always wondered what you were doing with that jerk."

The guy outside put something into the pack strapped to the back of his cycle, then turned and she saw his face. The cute guy from the shop!

She sat up and strained for a better view. He swung his leg over the cycle, leaned the machine upright, and started it. The insulated tour bus muffled the sound. Despite the fact a helmet was strapped to the back of the cycle, he didn't put it on.

He rode into traffic in the lane next to the bus, and Becca was able to get a good look at him. He was easy on the eyes, and his sunglasses provided an air of mystery. Becca liked the way he gripped the motorcycle handlebars, so strong and in control. He gently revved the engine. She could hear the soft purr of the bike. His shirt stretched across his back and shoulders; the light breeze toyed with his hair and blew it off his forehead.

"Sure. You're not interested in guys right now," Dylan interrupted in a knowing tone.

"It doesn't hurt to look." When she turned back, the light had changed and the guy on the motorcycle sped off. *Dang.* She watched to see if the bus would catch him, but he was long gone.

She leaned back in her seat, quickly bored again, and wishing she were home. Other than the couple of moments of eye candy, Becca hated Europe.

That night, Becca ate as fast as she could to end the incessant questions from their dinner companions, a nosy retired couple from Philadelphia. All during the meal, the topic had been Becca's future. They quizzed her with questions about college, her hobbies, pretty much anything except the date of her last menstrual cycle.

To make it worse, her dad chimed in that she was going

to be pre-law, which was totally not what she wanted. She couldn't bear the idea of being stuck in a stuffy office for the rest of her life. The only thing she knew was that she loved nature.

"Do you have a boyfriend who will be pining for you when you go off to college this fall?" asked the older woman, who sported a brassy red dye job and earlobes that hung low due to her heavy earrings.

Becca took a bite of asparagus so she wouldn't have to answer. Unfortunately, her dad spoke for her.

"Both Becca and her boyfriend are going to Northwestern. He's a very bright young man. What's his name? Eric?"

She wanted to slide under the table and hide.

Vicky dabbed her mouth with a napkin. "No, honey, it's Ethan, remember? But he broke up with her a few weeks ago."

"That's right," her father said. "Becca never seems to keep a boyfriend for long. Anyway, she'll be too busy this fall studying to have time for boys."

What was wrong with these people? So she'd been dumped. No need to tell the world.

"Look there," Vicky pointed, abruptly changing the subject. "We're going through our first lock."

They all looked out the windows as the boat floated slowly into the long narrow passageway.

Becca turned to Dylan and silently pleaded with him

to get her out of there, and save her from this slow torture.

Dylan fought back his laughter. "Hey, Dad, you don't mind if Becca and I skip out early, do you? We want to go up on the top deck and watch the locks."

"Don't you want to stay for dessert?" Vicky asked.

Becca wiped her hands. "No, I don't think I could handle another bite."

Her father nodded and waved them away. Dylan grabbed his beer. Becca couldn't escape the dining room fast enough. She wanted to explode.

Once in the lobby, Dylan said, "Come on, tiger, let's go up on deck. No one will hear you yelling up there."

Becca marched up the narrow metal steps to the empty top deck of the boat while the rest of the guests lingered over dinner. She walked past the comfortable chairs and went straight for the railing, wishing she could jump off.

"Oh my God! They are such idiots!" she yelled.

"That's good. Let it out." Dylan leaned back against the rail.

"Don't they have anything better to talk about? I mean, seriously!"

"I know."

She gripped the railing and screamed. "Arrrrgh!"

Dylan took a drink of beer. "Feel better?"

"A little," she said as the boat cruised slowly through the open doors of a giant lock. "I feel like my life keeps getting worse. My boyfriend cheats on me with my best friend. In six weeks I'm supposed to start college, when I have no idea what I want to do with my life. And, Ethan will be on the same dorm floor as me."

"That does suck."

"How am I going to survive hanging out with Dad and Icky Vicky every flippin' day? They're killing me! This trip is like water torture."

"Don't sweat it, Becs. I have a feeling things are going to turn around for you."

"And why's that?"

"Because tomorrow we're in Vienna, the city of love." He grinned.

"Yeah, great for you, sucks for me." She leaned on the railing as the last light of her crummy day disappeared.

Dylan was wrong. Vienna was even worse. They spent an hour on an overly air-conditioned tour bus, riding around something called the Ringstrasse. Apparently it was a loop around the center of Vienna, but all Becca knew was that the tour guide droned on endlessly about long dead musicians, old buildings, and more history than anyone should ever have to hear. From what Becca could gather, some family named Habsburg seemed to be tied to everything. It's not like she'd ever need to know any of this stuff. She needed fresh air, trees, and grass.

She tugged the earbud out of Dylan's ear.

"What?" he said.

"The kids in Europe must hate history class. These countries go back so freakin' far. At least the U.S. is barely two hundred years old."

Dylan grunted and put the earbud back in. She slumped in her seat and watched the buildings go by.

Finally they were let off the bus and allowed to breathe warm summer air and stretch their legs. After a walk down narrow roads where they heard about the Hofburg Palace, the war of this, and the king of that, they entered a large open square.

"Here we are at the St. Stephen Cathedral, built between 1263 and 1511. It is the symbol of Vienna, and its tower stands four hundred and fifty feet tall, making it one of the most impressive churches in all of Europe."

The guide blathered on about the old church, which, if Becca wasn't so annoyed, she'd admit was impressive, but how much was she expected to put up with? She'd rather live life in the here and now.

"That concludes our walking tour this morning. For those of you who are taking the afternoon tour of the Schönbrunn Palace, we'll depart here in a few minutes. Those of you who want to spend the rest of the day exploring the heart of Vienna on your own, be sure you have your walking map back to the pier."

Becca groaned. She couldn't stand one more tour. Her dad and Vicky were talking to a couple from Austin, while Dylan scoped out girls in the square.

She sidled up to her brother and said, "You have to get me out of that palace tour. If I have to hear any more flippin' history, I'm going to turn into a zombie. Do you think Dad will believe me if I say I'm sick and need to go back to the boat?"

"Chill. You don't want to be cooped up on the boat all day. We're in Vienna, the home of apple strudel, Wiener schnitzel, and hot women. If I can play this right, we'll be free for the afternoon and can skip the concert tonight, too."

"Oh crap, I forgot about the concert." Two hours of sleep-inducing classical music. No thank you.

"Come on. I've got this."

They approached their dad and his new friends. Dylan waited for a break in the conversation.

"Hey, Dad, I know there's that palace tour this afternoon, but Becca and I were really interested in the Habsburgs and wanted to explore more here in the city."

"Really?" Her dad glanced at Becca, who nodded like a bobble head, hoping he'd buy Dylan's story.

"Plus, there's so much history right here. We thought it would be fun to tour the Imperial Apartments of the Hofburg." Dylan lied like a pro.

"Well, I think it's great that the two of you want to spend more time together," their dad said.

"See, vacation is the perfect thing to bring families closer," Vicky said with a satisfied smile, as if her grand plan to make them a functioning family had actually worked.

"All right then, we'll see you at dinner," he said.

"Thanks," Dylan said, and Becca echoed him.

Dad and Vicky headed off with their new best friends. Dylan waited until they were out of earshot. "Piece of cake. Now I think I'll go grab myself one of those strong coffees served in a tiny cup."

"But you told Dad we were going to take that tour. Shouldn't we do that first?"

"We don't need to actually take the tour."

Becca chewed at the side of her lip. "But what if he asks? I don't think I could look Dad in the eye and lie."

"I thought the point of this was to avoid taking another tour. If you're that worried about it, you could go buy tickets for the tour as proof. He won't ask for details."

"Okay. Which way is it?" Becca looked around at all the streets.

"Take that street there." Dylan pointed down one of the many streets that led off the square. "The entrance was about three blocks down on the left. You can't miss it. Do you have your cell in case you get lost?"

"I'm fine. I have a map." She waved it at him. "I saw a McDonald's back that way. I'm going to grab something to eat, too," she said, indicating another side street.

"Okay. I'll catch ya later." He beelined for a café where pretty girls sipped fancy coffees.

Becca was glad to be off on her own while Dylan plied his charms on unsuspecting girls.

People milled about the square, their cameras dangling in one hand, and locals walked with cells phones planted to their ears. Everyone seemed to buzz with the excitement of a bright summer day. Becca didn't share their enthusiasm.

As she stood alone among the bustling crowd, all she wanted was something familiar, like an icy cold, American Diet Pepsi, french fries, and music that wasn't three hundred years old. She checked out the streets jutting off the square and chose the street where she saw the McDonald's.

After a few minutes Becca knew she'd picked the wrong street. She'd been positive this was where she'd spotted the miniature-sized golden arches. Not ready to give up, she walked a couple of blocks in each direction until she became hopelessly lost in a maze of narrow cobblestone streets peppered with gift shops, restaurants, and the occasional business office.

Standing on a corner, she pulled out her city map. If she could locate St. Stephen's church, where she'd started from, and then the Hofburg Palace, she should be able to figure out how to get from one to the other. But she had one major problem. She didn't even know where she was standing.

She considered asking for directions, but everyone looked either totally unapproachable, like the businessmen speaking rapidly in a foreign tongue, or totally clueless, like the four middle-aged women wearing fanny packs and visors.

Chewing on her lip, she checked the map's jigsaw

puzzle of streets, deciding to focus on the large area on the map that read Hofburg Palace. She'd walked by that area on the tour. It covered several blocks, so it should be easy to find again. Except that she'd taken about twenty-seven turns since then. She squinted at the confusing labyrinth, wishing for an internal GPS. She refused to call Dylan and ask him for help. He'd probably be mad he had to come find her again. She would figure this out.

"Excuse me, do you need some assistance?"

Becca looked up, startled. A familiar face with a traffic-stopping smile and bright blue eyes gazed at her. Her breath caught.

4

This was the guy she'd seen in the store yesterday and later on his motorcycle.

She offered him a stunned smile. He wore a dark gray T-shirt with foreign words written on the front, a couple days' beard growth, and a backpack. His sunglasses were hooked over the neck of his T-shirt.

This was definitely the same guy she saw yesterday, but that was in Budapest. Now they were in Vienna. Austria.

"Oh, ah." She smiled politely as if not totally flustered by his presence. "I'm just trying to find the Hofburg Palace." She didn't want to admit that until he showed up, all she really wanted was to find some french fries, close her eyes, and fantasize she was back home. Instead, she offered him the map.

The edge of his mouth curled and her stomach turned a little flip. "It's okay. I know where it is. It's that way." He

33

pointed in the direction behind Becca.

She followed his gaze. "No," she said, sure he was mistaken. "Look." She pointed at the map. "St. Stephen's church, where I started from, is here. I came from this direction, so the palace has to be that way." She indicated the opposite direction.

Laughter lit his eyes. "No. I'm sorry, but it's not." He placed a long finger where the church was labeled on the map. "Here's the St. Stephen's Cathedral, and the Hofburg is here." He slid his finger to the palace. "And we are standing right here." He indicated an area several blocks away from the two historic landmarks.

Her brow furrowed as she tried to figure out how she ended up so far off track.

"Look here." He lowered his head as he examined the map. "We're at the corner of Teinfaltstrasse and Schreyvogelgasse."

She enjoyed the close-up view of him. The way his hair lay at the nape of his neck, and he smelled good. All guy.

"See?" He raised his gorgeous eyes to hers and she wanted to dive in.

"Oh," she answered. She couldn't give a flip about the names of the streets or the map.

He looked at her for a long moment, his eyes warm and inviting. He checked his watch. "Would you like me to take you there?"

Hell, yes!

"Sure. That is, if you don't mind. I don't want to keep you from anything." Shivers of excitement ran up her arms.

He laughed. "Not at all. My schedule is wide open. Oh, and by the way, I'm Nikolai."

Becca took his outstretched hand. "Hi, I'm Becca." His grip was firm, yet gentle. She noticed the softness of his skin and the light tan of summer on the back of his hand.

"Hi, Becca. Nice to meet you." He released her hand and gestured in the direction of the palace.

"I don't know if you remember, but I'm pretty sure I bumped into you yesterday," she said.

"In Budapest." He smiled.

"Yes! I thought you were the same person."

"The palace is this way. It won't take but a few minutes to get there." He indicated the direction and they began walking.

"So yesterday you were in Budapest and now you're in Vienna, same as me. You're not following me, are you?" she asked, thinking of the movie where the young girl is taken.

Considering the number of tour buses and the riverboat she'd been on since yesterday, it didn't seem possible he was a stalker. Plus, everything about him oozed nice guy. Not that she hadn't been wrong about guys before.

"No. I'm not following you." Nikolai laughed. But he might like to. She seemed nice and was certainly beautiful.

He was used to being stalked by the press, and the last

two days without them had been so relaxing. No scheduled appearances, no advisors, and no cameras.

"So, what are you doing here in Vienna?" she asked.

Nikolai slid his hands into his pockets as they walked; there was suddenly a lightness in his step. "I'm on sort of a holiday. I'm traveling up the Danube."

"Sort of a holiday? What does that mean?"

"Well," he sighed, trying to decide how to explain it without actually telling her. "Long story short, I took off without my parents' permission."

"Really? I wish I had the guts to do that."

"I don't recommend it. There'll be hell to pay when they catch up with me."

"Your parents don't know where you are?" Becca brushed a lock of silky hair behind her ear, revealing her sun-kissed cheek.

"Not yet. I figure they're giving me a couple days of freedom before they try to track me down and order me home, but that's not going to happen." He glanced at the sidewalks, crowded with tourists. At least he hoped that was the case and that they hadn't already sent a security detail after him.

Becca laughed. "No? Why is that?"

"Because I'm living off the grid, you know, like Jason Bourne."

"Are you telling me you're an international spy or, oh no, an assassin?" She feigned a shocked expression.

"Hardly. I'm just another derelict kid avoiding family responsibilities and disappointing my parents."

He wondered what she'd think if he confessed he was the Prince of Mondovia and had run away like a spoiled child.

"That's a drag. I take it they're pretty demanding."

He nodded, the weight of his birthright pressing on his conscience. "You have no idea."

"Where is home?"

Nikolai considered lying, but surprised himself when he didn't. Something about Becca made him relax, not that she'd put two and two together. He couldn't put his finger on why he trusted Becca, but Americans didn't really pay attention to European royalty unless it was Prince William or Prince Harry.

"I'm from Mondovia."

"It sounds familiar. . . ."

"It's okay, we're a small country, and not nearly as glamorous as Austria. Most Americans don't know much about Mondovia. They confuse us with Monaco, Luxembourg, and Montenegro."

"How do you know I'm American?"

"Besides the fact you're wearing an American Eagle shirt? You sound American." He also gestured to the telltale audio box hanging around her neck.

"Oh my God! I forgot I was still wearing this thing." She whipped the cord over her head, sweeping her thick mane of hair off her shoulder in the process. She stuffed the device in her bag. "Yeah, I guess I scream, 'American tourist.' I feel like such an idiot. I mean, I didn't even want to come on this trip. My dad made me. He said it would be good family bonding, which is such a joke. So far, the bonding has consisted of strained dinner conversation and trying to avoid a retired art history professor on our boat who talks constantly about the history of neoclassical, Rococo, or Baroque styles."

"And where are your mom and dad now?"

"It's my dad and my stepmom," she corrected. "Right about now they are probably downing their second glass of chardonnay with lunch. After that they're going to some summer home or fourth residence of the eighteenth King of 'I Couldn't Care Less,' and then a classical concert designed to put even the most caffeinated history fanatics to sleep."

Nikolai laughed. "And they left you to fend for yourself?"

"No. My brother is around here somewhere. He maneuvered my dad into letting us skip out of their afternoon of torture. I was on my way to the Hofburg Palace to get tickets, just in case my dad checks, which is unlikely. Unless my brother, Dylan, lands another speeding ticket or I fail to make the honor roll, Dad wouldn't know we're on the same continent."

A tour group approached on the crowded sidewalk. Their guide carried a tall pole with a bright yellow flag at the top so the distracted tourists in her group could spot her from a distance and wouldn't get lost.

Nikolai touched Becca's arm. "Here, let's step out of the way. These groups are known to take over the streets." They ducked into a store entryway to avoid the crush. A rack of magazines lined the wall with several stacks of popular newspapers and gossip publications.

His eye was drawn to a picture of himself across the front page of the German paper, *Daily Snoop*. Nikolai stared at the image of himself laughing after a polo match last month in Monaco.

He read the headline. *Prince Nikolai of Mondovia Skips Out on State Dinner*, with a caption, *The palace is tight-lipped on the prince's mounting list of canceled appearances.*

Crap.

Becca appeared beside him. "Hey, that guy in the paper looks a lot like you."

5

"*What?* Oh, you think so?" He really didn't want to go into detail about his identity. For once in his life couldn't he be a normal guy?

"Who is he?" Becca tried to translate the paper.

Nikolai realized she couldn't read the German words. "No one important, just a polo player who won the match. Hey, look." He pointed across the store. "Baseball caps. I need one." He crossed the shop to the shelf of caps, distracting her from the newspaper. He wouldn't be flying under the radar for long with his picture plastered on magazine covers.

Becca selected a dark blue cap with *Vienna* stitched across the front. She handed it to him, and he placed it on his head and looked at her. "What do you think?"

She gazed at him, and their eyes met. "It looks good." Her cheeks blushed and she looked away.

Nikolai hid his grin as he took the cap to the checkout counter. So she liked him, at least a little. It surprised him how much he enjoyed that fact. "Want anything?"

"No, I'm fine," she said, but he noticed her checking out the candy display. He tossed a bag of M&M's on the counter, and a couple of candy bars. After paying, he put on the cap and ripped open the bag of candy as they stepped onto the sidewalk. "Want some?"

Becca hesitated, which he found amusing. "What? Afraid to take candy from a stranger?"

"No," she laughed. He held her hand and poured candy into her palm.

"Before we got sidelined, you were talking about your brother."

"Oh yes, Dylan. He pretty much does only what he feels like doing. One time my dad set up an interview for an important internship, and Dylan didn't show. He didn't cancel it or let my dad know. He just didn't go. I think the only job he's ever had was when he was sixteen and wanted to get to know a girl. He got a job at the movie theater where she worked so he could get close to her."

Nikolai liked how her eyes lit up when she talked. "Did he end up going out with her?"

"Of course, for a month, until he got bored and became interested in someone else. He quit the theater job and started hanging out at the pool to get to know a girl named Tess."

"Don't tell me, he faked drowning."

"How'd you guess?" She popped a candy into her mouth.

"I think I'd like your brother."

He guided her around a mother who'd stopped her stroller in the middle of the sidewalk.

"So what's he doing now?"

"Hitting on girls."

Nikolai didn't like that her brother left her alone in a big city when she clearly couldn't find her way around the block.

"Well, I'm glad I saw you. It's a shame to spend the day in Vienna by yourself."

He poured more candy in her palm as they passed under an archway. A gathering of people was peeking into an arena.

"What's everyone looking at?" Becca asked.

"That's the Spanish Riding School where they house and train the Lipizzan horses. They're sort of the royalty of horses here in Austria."

Becca stepped closer to see the majestic white horses trot through their exercises.

"They're beautiful. But why are there royal horses if there isn't a king anymore?"

"I don't know. Tradition, I guess. So much of Europe is anchored in the past."

"Does your country, Mon . . ." She fumbled over the word.

"Mondovia," he offered.

"Right, does Mondovia have a king?"

Nikolai's chest tightened at the mention of his father. "Yes, it does."

"Really? Does he live in a castle?"

"Sometimes. There are a few palaces around the country, but his main residence is a palace in our capital city, Genoa."

They continued walking.

"Is he a good king or a bad king?"

"If you're asking if he chops off people's heads, no. He doesn't do anything bad like that."

"But you don't like him," she stated, popping the last candy in her mouth and wiping her hand on her shorts.

He startled. "I never said that."

"You didn't have to. I can tell from your tone that you're not a fan."

"It's not that I don't like the man, because I do. He's honorable. I guess it's just the whole system of having a king and royalty in this day and age."

This was the oddest conversation he'd ever had, talking about his father as though he didn't know him.

"But doesn't he run the country?"

"No. We have parliament with elected officials. It's a lot like England."

Becca wrinkled her brow. "So what does the king do?"

"Exactly!" Nikolai crumpled the candy wrapper and tossed it in the trash. "Mostly the king makes appearances. He attends formal dinners, he awards medals, and recognizes achievements."

Nikolai pictured his future all mapped out before him in a carbon copy of his father's. "I guess he's just there to make people feel that Mondovia is something special."

"That sounds like the most boring job I've ever heard of."

He sighed. "Yes, it is. They hold on to the old traditions even when it no longer makes sense."

"See, that's what I hate about history. People hang on to it like the old ways were the best. Can you imagine if we did that with medicine or technology? Progress, people!" she said, raising her hands in the air.

"I like the way you think. Some countries have embraced the changing times better than others. Here in Vienna, they honor their history of music, art, and some of the most powerful rulers of their time, and still manage to keep a strong economy based on industry and technology."

If only Mondovia could learn to honor its past, and yet live in the present, Nikolai's life would be much better.

Becca stepped around a man lighting a cigarette. "How do you know all this stuff?"

"You mean the history? School, I suppose." Or maybe living it every day.

"But you're not even from here! I don't know how you

can remember the history of other countries. I can't tell you a thing about Canada other than they play a lot of hockey there. History is my worst subject. I barely pulled off a B last semester."

"I guess I have a natural gift. Come on, the Hofburg is up ahead."

They approached the grand entrance to the palace. Nikolai had been here a couple of times over the years for some formal dinner or event but never as a tourist. The Hofburg was still considered the heart of royalty in this part of the world.

Being surrounded by so many people would normally drive him crazy, but now he realized they didn't know or care who he was. He didn't act or dress royal, so he blended in with the rest of the tourists.

When they reached the ticket booth, Becca stepped forward and bought admission for two. She slipped the change in her pocket and waved the tickets. "My free passes for the day."

"So now that you are officially free, what do you plan to do?" he asked, not ready to say good-bye to this quirky, opinionated girl.

"I hadn't really thought that far ahead. I don't know."

"We could take the tour. I mean, you've got the tickets, and then maybe we could spend the afternoon together. If you want to." His pulse raced as he waited for her response. He wasn't used to worrying if a girl might turn him down.

"I'd like that." She smiled, and he found himself mesmerized by her doe eyes and long lashes. "Hopefully it doesn't suck too much."

"How about we do the speed version of the tour and then go find something to eat?"

"Okay."

"And maybe a little Habsburg history will rub off on you."

"Nah, I doubt it," she laughed. "Hang on a sec while I text my brother and tell him what's going on."

After Becca sent her message, they entered through the gigantic doors of the palace and came upon two large portraits, one of a woman, the other a man. Below, a plaque commemorated Maria Theresa, Holy Roman Empress and her son, Joseph, Holy Roman Emperor of the Habsburg Dynasty.

"So what's the big deal with this Maria Theresa chick I keep hearing about? I've never heard of her before today."

"Seriously? Maria Theresa's power touched most of Europe. She was one of the most influential European rulers, in part because she married her sixteen children off to other powerful royal families."

Including his.

"Huh. So you're saying there is a lot of inbreeding going on with royalty."

Nikolai laughed. "I wouldn't go that far. I can tell you that Marie Antoinette was one of her daughters."

Becca cringed. "There's proof that arranged marriages don't work out."

"Come on," he said with a chuckle.

They walked down long halls filled with tapestries and stucco ceilings, and through the offices of former rulers. Becca glanced at the ancient paintings adorning the walls, but seemed unimpressed.

Nikolai didn't blame her, yet this was the home of his forefathers. As his ancestors stared down from their high-framed perches, they seemed to be asking him the big, important question. Would he follow in their footsteps and hold up his part of the family dynasty? Or would he let them down and become a brief footnote in Mondovian history?

"Look at all those dishes," Becca said as they entered a room with floor-to-ceiling shelves filled with dishes, pulling his attention back to the present. "No one needs that many plates, and why did they save them? Because honestly, who cares about three-hundred-year-old plates?"

"Becca, you have a gift for stating the obvious. Let's get out of here." He led her past the remaining rooms and directly to the exit.

She sighed. "Thank you. I know history is important, but jeesh. Live for today, people! I can't believe I have another week of this stuff."

Nikolai wasn't sure if he agreed with her or wanted to defend his heritage. "Okay, no more history. You've paid your dues and have duly suffered, but I must tell you that Vienna, heck, all of Europe, is actually quite modern. It's not all old."

She raised an eyebrow.

"What?" he asked.

"So modern that you need to pay every time you want to use a bathroom? That sounds like something out of the Middle Ages."

He laughed. "I know something that will prove my case." He led them down the street, away from the Hofburg.

"Where are we going now?"

"You'll see." They walked a couple of blocks and took a left turn. He stopped before a small restaurant with large windows and bright golden arches on the sign. "I offer you the modern day, universal symbol of goodwill."

"French fries!" She laughed, her face lighting up with a gorgeous smile. Nikolai had never seen someone so happy over something so simple in a very long time.

After snacking on french fries and sipping sodas in the most Americanized restaurant on the planet, they headed over to the Naschmarkt. Nikolai had never been there himself, but he saw a flyer for it posted on the wall of the hostel where he'd stayed last night.

They walked through a myriad of local vendor booths that sold everything from pickles and stuffed peppers, to scarves and jewelry.

"So where does your river cruise stop next?"

"I don't know. We're at a different port each day. My dad told me, but I'd never even heard of any of the cities." Becca stopped and ran her hands over the colorful scarves. "If he'd said Paris or Rome, I'd have remembered."

"I'm afraid Paris and Rome are nowhere near here, so it's not likely."

She wrapped a green floral scarf around her neck. "I wish I did remember. Maybe it would be where you're going. That would be pretty wild. What do you think?" She struck a pose.

He shook his head no to the scarf and handed her a purple one. Considering he had no definite itinerary, and didn't know her next stops, they would soon be saying good-bye. Becca had been a bright light during this short jaunt of his, and he didn't really want to say good-bye.

"Aw, I'm sure you'll find a new guy in every port," he teased, but hoped it wasn't true.

Becca tossed the scarf artfully around her neck and peeked in a small mirror hanging on a post.

"Yeah, I'll get pictures of every new guy. That ought to show my ex-boyfriend." She turned to the woman running the booth. "I like this. I'll take it."

"Allow me," Nikolai said.

"What? Why?" She looked dumbfounded.

"As a souvenir of our afternoon together." He handed the euros to the saleswoman. "And for the record, your boyfriend was a fool to let you go."

Becca dipped her head and spoke softly. "Thanks."

They walked on in silence until she pointed up ahead. "There's my brother."

Nikolai swallowed down his disappointment that they'd found him so soon.

"Hey, Dylan," Becca said as they caught up.

Dylan sat on a high stool at an open-air pub talking to two attractive blondes, one with a mass of loose curls framing her porcelain face, the other with long straight hair that she twirled around her finger. Neither appealed to Nikolai like Becca.

"Hey, Becs." Dylan's eyes wandered to Nikolai and gave him a quick once-over.

"Hey. This is Nikolai," she said.

"Hi." Nikolai offered his hand.

"Hi." Dylan stood and gave him a firm handshake. "This is Aneka and Hannah. They're from Denmark."

Nikolai pulled his cap lower as they exchanged greetings. To his relief, the European girls paid him no attention.

"So tell me, Becca. You got lost and this poor guy had to help you," Dylan teased in a brotherly tone familiar to Nikolai.

"Actually," Nikolai spoke up before Becca could. "I was trying to find the Hofburg and she helped me."

Becca looked at him in confusion. He lowered his

sunglasses for a moment and winked at her.

"No kidding. That's got to be a first." Dylan drained his beer. "Well, I hate to say it, but I suppose we should be getting back before the boat takes off without us." He turned to the Danish girls and said his good-byes.

Nikolai pulled Becca aside. "Thanks for a great afternoon. I had a wonderful time."

"I doubt that. Showing an American tourist around can't be that fun."

"Unless it's this American tourist." He smiled and squeezed her hand.

They gazed at each other with unspoken words hanging in the air. Why couldn't she be staying in Vienna for the week? They could have so much fun. She had helped him feel alive again.

"Becca," Dylan interrupted.

"One sec," she said and turned back to Nikolai. "I wish I didn't have to go."

"Me too." He pushed back his regret. "Enjoy the rest of your trip. You only have a couple dozen more churches and a few rambling old castles to visit. You'll be on your way home before you know it."

"Thank you again for the beautiful scarf." She caressed the delicate fabric. "And enjoy the rest of your trip. I hope your parents don't catch up to you for a while."

Nikolai saw Dylan waiting. He turned back to Becca. "I guess this is good-bye." He leaned forward and kissed her cheek before he could overthink it.

Surprised, her eyes lit up. "I better go."

He smiled, wishing for more time.

"Thanks again," she said, joining her brother.

Nikolai nodded to Dylan. As they walked away, his heart sank, which seemed stupid, since he barely knew her. But something about Becca and this day were the best time he'd had in a long time. He'd like to think it was because she liked him. After all, she laughed at his lame jokes. And she didn't even know about his royal title.

6

Becca gazed back at Vienna from the top deck as the boat pulled away. She touched the soft scarf draped around her neck. She still couldn't believe he'd bought it for her.

Today had turned out to be the best day ever. Nikolai had been the nicest, funniest guy she'd ever met. Suddenly all the pain she felt over Ethan dumping her for Kelly evaporated as if he'd never even mattered.

Unfortunately, the perfect guy had to be from some obscure European country. If she had been able to tell him their next stop, maybe he would have wanted to meet her there. Heck, she didn't even know the name of the boat. She glanced across the deck and saw a decorative life ring with the ship name, *Bolero*, painted on it.

She should have asked for his email address or if he was on Facebook. But if he didn't want to give his address, that would have been awkward. Maybe it was better this way.

She leaned on the railing and watched the city grow distant. Either way, Nikolai had been so charming and nice, not to mention really good-looking. He was the best thing to happen in longer than she could remember.

"Oh no. Sulking over your European hottie?" Dylan joined her.

"Hardly. I just met the guy," she said in a cheery voice, belying her real mood.

"Yeah, I saw how he looked at you."

"How was that?" She hadn't noticed him looking at her in any special way.

"The same way you were looking at him. Like he was a chocolate ice cream cone and you couldn't wait to take a lick."

"Dylan! Shut up!" She swatted him.

"I'm just saying, the guy was totally into you."

Tingles fluttered in her stomach at Dylan's comment. "I finally find a guy who's interested and then I have to leave. What did I do to deserve such rotten luck?"

"Maybe it's a sign that there are better guys out there, and you should stop settling for self-centered losers. Take me, for example. I am constantly testing the laws of attraction. The more you put yourself out there, the more awesome people you'll cross paths with."

Dylan might have a point, but the only person she wanted to cross paths with would be miles away by morning.

* * *

The next afternoon, surrounded by a mass of tourists who moved like zombies, Becca resigned herself to the fact that she'd have to tolerate having ancient history crammed down her throat for the rest of the trip. After that, she could go home to her familiar life of hanging with friends on State Street, boating on the lake, and getting ready for college. She couldn't wait to escape the daily annoyance of spending time with her dad and Vicky. They were not a family unit and never would be.

Their tour group meandered through the quaint village of Melk, Austria, adorned with its shuttered windows, pastel-hued buildings, colored planters bursting with flowers, and the occasional sidewalk café. The sun glared brightly, so she pulled on a baseball cap along with her sunglasses. She wore a tank top and her hair up in a knot, in hopes of surviving the hot day. Small groups of tourists wandered in the opposite direction, having finished their tours of the abbey. Becca wished she belonged to the departing crowd.

The guide paused to point out an ancient fresco painted on the side of a building. As most of the group stared upward, mesmerized by the refurbished painting of a mythic God, Becca's eyes wandered down the side street where a middle-aged man swept the cobblestones outside his shop. Across from the man she noticed a simple painted sign, *Hostel*.

That's what Vicky had been talking about the other night, cheap lodging for students as they backpacked through Europe. At that moment, the door opened and a guy stepped out. His tall, lean frame reminded Becca of Nikolai, even though he faced the opposite direction. Then he turned and glanced in her direction, and she noticed that his blue baseball cap was embroidered with the word *Vienna. Nikolai!*

But Nikolai looked away and began to walk in the other direction. Didn't he see her? She could swear he looked right at her. She stepped away from her group. "Nikolai!"

He paused in his steps and turned. She removed her hat and sunglasses. Nikolai did a double take, and broke into his megawatt smile. Becca laughed and fought the urge to squeal her excitement. He shook his head in disbelief and headed toward her. The familiar gait of his step set her heart racing.

"I didn't plan this. I swear it." He grinned, looking as surprised as she.

"What are the odds?" She feasted upon his gorgeous face, broad shoulders, and the shorts that hugged his hips in an Abercrombie kind of way.

"A million to one. At least. Nice scarf," he said.

"Thanks. It's from an old friend."

The tour started to move on without them. Becca desperately wished she could disappear with Nikolai, but what lame excuse could she give her dad for skipping the tour?

Nikolai gestured to the departing group. "Let's go. We don't want to be left behind."

"You're coming with?" she asked, still dumbfounded by his sudden appearance, and now thrilled he planned to stick around.

"Well, yeah. It's a free country. I assume your tour is going to the Melk Abbey. I hear it's the hottest ticket in town."

"But you're not part of our group," she said, afraid he'd be discovered and land in trouble.

"Haven't you heard? The abbey is open to anyone, not just American riverboat passengers who hate history."

He winked and she thought she might self-combust right there. *Thank you, fate. I don't know how you pulled this off, but I'm glad you did!*

They followed the crowd to the huge open courtyard of the Melk Abbey. The massive building was painted the shade of straw at harvest time and looked like a combination of a Spanish hacienda and a castle.

Becca couldn't help but wonder how Nikolai had ended up here. Had he somehow followed their boat up the river all through the night? "So, what made you stop in Melk?"

"Apparently, you." His blue eyes twinkled. "After you left yesterday, Vienna wasn't much fun, so I decided to head out. I planned on riding a lot farther, but I kept seeing signs for Melk. When I was a kid, my parents brought me here for a—a tour. I took the turnoff and spotted a sign for the hostel. And look, you're here, too!"

As everyone gathered in the courtyard, Becca wondered how she'd explain Nikolai to her dad and Vicky. There were groups from several boats, so it was easy to stay out of their sight, but then Dylan appeared. When he spotted Nikolai at her side, he raised an eyebrow, smiled, and disappeared back into the crowd.

"So you're really planning on taking the tour?" she asked.

"Of course, isn't that why we're here? And you obviously need some serious education in European history. You Americans are too ignorant about the rest of the world," he teased.

"And you're going to teach me?" she challenged.

"Yes, ma'am, I am."

"But what if the guides figure out you're not with our group?"

"What are you afraid of? That they'll call the police?" He grinned as if relishing the idea.

"No. Maybe. I don't know. I just don't want you to get in trouble."

"Becca, I have spent most of my whole life doing the right thing. I think breaking a few rules is exactly what I need. And it sounds like you could use a little rule breaking yourself." He bumped her shoulder with his. She had to agree, since all she'd been doing lately was whatever her dad or Vicky said. Breaking rules sounded pretty good right now.

Their tour guide, Luis, a self-confessed professor of history with shaggy brown hair, round-rimmed glasses, and a rumpled wool jacket led them into the Melk Abbey. He spoke into a small microphone that relayed his voice to the audio boxes that each cruise passenger wore.

"Here, want to share?" Becca held out one of the tiny speakers.

Nikolai looked at the small device. "Sure."

Becca pulled the earbuds farther apart so that his could reach him. He accepted the earpiece. In order to stay connected, they walked close together, which Becca didn't mind at all.

They listened through the earbud to Luis's fluent English tinged with a thick German accent.

"The abbey was founded in 1089 when Leopold II, Margrave of Austria, gave one of his castles to Benedictine monks from Lambach Abbey."

Becca ignored Luis. She was only aware of Nikolai, who shuffled alongside her, his shoulder brushing hers as they tried to stay connected. She glanced over and found him listening intently. Was he really this into history?

Luis droned on. "Today's impressive Baroque abbey was built between 1650 and 1700 to designs by Johann Prandtauer."

Nikolai leaned down as they walked and whispered in her ear. "He's wrong."

"What?" she asked, noticing the bow shape of his

mouth and his perfectly straight teeth.

"He's wrong about the dates. They didn't start building it until the early 1700s. And the designer wasn't Johann; it was Jakob."

Becca stopped short and the earbud pulled out of her ear. "How do you know that? Are you some sort of freak?"

Nikolai handed her earpiece back, grinning. "I wrote a term paper on the architectural design of Melk Abbey for school, and I have an excellent memory."

"I'm impressed." She placed the earbud back in her ear.

"Here, let's stay together." Nikolai put his arm around her shoulder, so they stood closer, and the earbuds had less chance of falling out again. Becca held back a grin as her stomach did a flip. She enjoyed the scent of Nikolai's shaving cream or maybe it was his shampoo.

The tour led them down a long corridor and into a room different from the rest, lit in a neon-blue low light. A Plexiglas display case housed a suitcase-sized Bible, so old the relic could have been written by Jesus himself.

"This looks more like a New Age nightclub than an abbey," Becca whispered. "I feel like a deejay's going to start playing and monks are going to dance in." Nikolai caressed her bare shoulder with his thumb, sending shivers through her. She hoped he didn't stop.

Becca giggled. "Not too much history in here."

"And I'm so disappointed. I really wanted to teach you a few things." He whispered close to her ear, his breath tickled her neck.

"Did you now?"

"What? I'm talking about history. What are you think-ing about?" he said, his blue eyes all wide and innocent, but she knew better.

They moved from the blue room into a green-hued room filled with centuries-old papal robes. The next room was lit bright yellow, and held encased gold crosses and Communion chalices. Nikolai appeared to be interested, but Becca wondered if he even listened to the guide dribble on about this eight-hundred-year-old trunk or that six-hundred-year-old rosary. Becca was tempted to turn the speaker off, but didn't want to risk losing Nikolai's arm, which he draped comfortably around her. He occasionally whispered something in her ear that made her laugh.

Next they entered a richly adorned library, so huge that it spanned two stories. Narrow walkways led to the books. Old tomes occupied every inch of the richly hued wooden shelves. The guide rattled on about how this was only a small percent of all the tens of thousands of books in the abbey collection, and that several other rooms hosted even more. Bringing up the rear, as the group shuffled over the marble floors, Becca and Nikolai passed a narrow wind-ing staircase with a *No Admittance* sign blocking the entry. Becca leaned over and looked up. A spiral staircase went up several stories.

"Look at that. It's amazing." Becca leaned over the

railing and pointed up. The staircase wound skyward and the banister created an artistic view leading to the painted ceiling several stories above.

"Let's check it out." Nikolai unhooked the velvet rope blocking the stairway.

"Are you out of your mind? We can't go up there!"

"Sure we can. Come on." He pulled her along and reattached the rope behind them.

"Oh my God. We are going to get in so much trouble." And she never got in trouble, but she didn't want to miss a moment of Nikolai.

"Only if we get caught." He smirked.

7

They heard the monotone voice of the next tour group entering the library.

"Someone's coming! Hurry up!" Becca rushed up the stairs and out of the next group's sight.

At the top of the first landing, they ducked into another room of books. Becca's heart pounded. The dim light in the cozy study revealed a few old chairs, and tables with reading lamps. The room smelled dusty and musty, like old books.

"I like this room. It's more personal, as if people actually came in here to read." She stepped to a shelf and touched the spine of an ancient volume. "I can't believe we're in here."

The edge of the bookshelf was intricately patterned with inlaid wood, and crystal lamps sparkled in the low light.

"Everything is so beautiful." Her fingers glided over the age-old wood.

Nikolai appeared at her side, totally relaxed, as if trespassing in a foreign land was no big deal. "Yes, it is," he answered with a playful glint in his eye, moving so close to Becca that the heat of his body warmed hers.

Nikolai took her hand and turned her toward him. He slid his hand under Becca's hair and caressed her neck, causing little shivers of excitement to tingle up her spine.

Becca's pulse raced. Nikolai leaned down and brushed his lips against hers, his kiss soft and intoxicating. He paused, then kissed her some more and gazed into her eyes.

"I couldn't resist. You're different from any other girl I've met."

"Oh." She didn't know what to say. She'd never been kissed like that before and was ready for another.

"Come on, I want to show you something." He took her hand and led her out of the room and down a long hallway.

"Where are we going now?" She stumbled after him, disappointed. Why not more kisses?

After two turns and another long hallway they approached an ancient door with a medieval-looking handle.

"Shh," Nikolai whispered. It wasn't like she was going to do anything to alert security. He turned the handle and slowly opened the door.

Becca wasn't sure what she expected, maybe another

library room or an office. But she was not prepared for the sight before her, as she shaded her eyes from the brightness.

"Oh my!" she uttered as they stepped onto a second level alcove and entered the most spectacular church she'd ever seen. Everything before her seemed to be dipped in gold: the cornices, statues, trim work, and window edging. What wasn't gilded was creamy white. Becca glanced up to find the ceiling a massive fresco of cherubs and symbols she couldn't begin to understand. Below, clusters of tourists meandered by gold columns that supported the high arches.

"Impressive, isn't it?" Nikolai said, guiding her along.

"How did you know about this?"

"It's hard not to know about this when you live where I come from."

"Is that real gold?" she asked, pointing to the massive golden pulpit that wound majestically around a column and overlooked the pews.

"Oh yeah, it's all real." He led her down narrow side stairs to the marble church floor worn with age.

"This is insane. I've never seen so much gold in my life. There must be millions of dollars' worth in here."

"I wouldn't doubt it."

"All this for a bunch of monks, and it's been here all this time?"

"Yes, it's been here for hundreds of years."

"During all the wars and droughts and famines. The

people must have hated this place. One gold leg from the altar would have probably fed the whole village."

"I never thought of it that way before." His brow furrowed.

"Oh no! There's my dad," Becca said.

"Where?"

"By the church doors. Hang on. I'll be right back." She headed over to her dad and Vicky. She preferred not to explain Nikolai. Vicky or her dad would ask annoying questions and it wasn't any of their business who she talked to.

"There you are. I thought I told you not to wander off and get lost," her dad said.

"I wasn't lost."

"We're going to stop by the abbey restaurant and have a coffee and pastry with the Martins," Vicky said, indicating the annoying couple they sat with at dinner last night.

"Where's Dylan?" Becca scanned the area, but didn't see him.

"He's playing his disappearing act again. I swear, he better be back to the boat in an hour for departure or I'll make him walk to the next port. Becca, you should join us and the Martins."

Becca took a step back. "No. I'd rather not. I'll look around on my own."

"Nonsense. Let's stay together. We've already lost

Dylan. It will save time trying to meet up later," her dad said.

"Dad, I'm eighteen, not four. I'll be starting college soon and can handle getting back."

He sighed in annoyance. "Fine, but don't be late."

"I won't," she answered as he walked away. She returned to Nikolai with a bounce in her step. "Guess what? I've got another hour before I have to be back at the boat. Let's get out of here."

He linked his fingers with hers in a way Becca wished would last for more than the next hour. As they passed through the abbey grounds, a string orchestra played in the courtyard. They took steep stairs away from the abbey and wound by homes with laundry waving from a clothesline in the breeze. She spied small vegetable gardens, and Nikolai pointed out a couple of backyard chickens.

They ended up in the village below the abbey on a cobblestone street lined by shops and cafés. It looked the same as most of the other cities she'd visited, except that Melk was much quieter and less populated. She noticed a lot of tourists pushing bicycles along the street.

"I don't suppose you know where your boat will be tomorrow," Nikolai asked.

She wanted to squeal like a little girl because he'd mentioned the next day, which meant he must want to see her again. "I do," she said, trying to mask the fact that she actually read her itinerary.

Nikolai stopped suddenly, pulling her back. "Really? Look who's paying attention to more than where the next McDonald's is."

Becca fought back her smile.

"So where will you be?"

"Some town called Passau. Do you know where it is?"

He smiled. "I do. It's only a couple of hours away. In fact, it has a pretty Old Town with an amazing—" He paused, waiting for her to finish his sentence.

Becca rolled her eyes. "Church! I know! What would a day in Europe be without visiting another church?"

Nikolai laughed. "Sorry, you just can't escape it here. But that's not why I asked." He leaned against the edge of a fence that overlooked a park. He took her hand gently in his. She loved the touch of his skin against hers. "I was hoping you might want to get together again. I don't know how long you're in port, but maybe we could take off for a while on my motorbike. See a little of the countryside."

Becca tried to act cool.

After spending the past couple of hours together, Nikolai wanted to see her again!

"Yeah, I'd like that."

"Good," he said, seeming satisfied, and not making a big deal about it.

Becca's insides churned with nervous joy.

"Let's meet outside St. Stephen's Cathedral at eleven. It's at the top of the hill in Old Town and is the easiest place to find."

"Isn't that the name of the church in Vienna?"

"See, you are paying attention. Yes, there is a St. Stephen's church in practically every town."

"Well, in that case, meeting at St. Stephen's sounds great."

As their time ran short, Nikolai walked her back to the pier where the *Bolero* was docked next to two other riverboats. She hated to say good-bye.

"So how come it takes my boat all night to get to Passau, and you said it only takes you a couple of hours? I know the boat isn't very fast, but still, that doesn't seem right."

"This section of the Danube River has a lot of locks. You'll be going through quite a few from here on out. Boats get backed up waiting their turn. Your boat probably spends half the night idling until they get through lock after lock."

They approached the pier, located next to a park with wooden benches and bright yellow playground equipment.

"Which cabin is yours?" he asked, looking at the giant boat.

"The last one on the top floor in the back. Right there." She pointed to her cabin, wishing she didn't have to go soon.

"Looks like you have a great view," he said and tugged

her behind a large tree, out of sight of the boarding *Bolero* passengers. "I'm so glad I ran into you today." His gleaming eyes locked with hers.

Her heart beat with excitement. "Me too." She couldn't help stare at his mouth, and recall his amazing kiss at the abbey. She licked her lips. He slid his hand behind her neck, lowered his mouth to hers, and kissed her softly.

"I'll see you tomorrow." Nikolai's gaze captivated her. She could stay like this all day, but then he released her.

"Tomorrow," she said, not trusting herself to say more. She headed for the *Bolero*, surprised at how alone she felt as soon as she left his side. As she reached the gangway, she turned to find Nikolai watching as she boarded. She gave him one last wave.

Once on board, instead of returning to her small cabin, she bounded for the top deck.

The afternoon sun shone down and a swift breeze blew across the bow. At the railing, her eyes scanned the park for Nikolai.

He was gone.

Her heart sank. Foolishly, she had hoped he'd stay until the boat left.

"Have fun today?" Dylan appeared next to her.

She looked at him and grinned.

"That good?" He leaned his forearms on the railing and laughed.

"I'm going to meet him again tomorrow."

Becca watched as the crew worked below and unhooked the giant ropes that anchored the boat to the dock. With a light rumble of the engines, the boat drifted smoothly away from land.

"Look at you! Hooking up with guys in Europe."

"I'm not 'hooking up.' We're just hanging out."

"Well, watch out. He seems like a nice enough guy, but I don't want some self-centered jerk using you. We're only in Europe for another week. I swear if he hurts you, I'll break his legs."

"Like you could ever hurt a fly. Sounds to me like you're talking about yourself," she teased. The boat cruised upriver.

"You know what I mean. He seems pretty sure of himself and you still haven't gotten over the last asshole that broke your heart."

"Don't worry, he's not like that. Anyway, I can take care of myself."

Dylan raised an eyebrow. Becca pushed thoughts of her recent breakup out of her mind. Nikolai was totally different. He carried himself with such confidence, yet was sweet and kind.

"Looks like this guy is as whipped as you are."

"What do you mean?"

Dylan pointed to the hillside.

Nikolai sat on a grassy hillside as the boat passed by.

"Oh my God!" She waved frantically. He hadn't left.

He'd moved upriver to wave good-bye one last time.

Becca couldn't believe her luck. Maybe she was supposed to come to Europe to find a decent guy.

She waved back as the boat went around a bend in the river. Until tomorrow.

8

Nikolai entered the hostel smiling. Something about this beautiful American girl kept him from thinking about anything else. It didn't make sense. Becca was ignorant of the historic cities she toured. Her sense of direction was so bad she could probably lose her own shadow, and her quirky sense of humor made him constantly want to kiss her.

He nodded hello to a couple guys he recognized from breakfast that morning. He'd been lucky to score a private room. While another night sleeping in a dorm room would have been an adventure, a private room seemed a smarter way to stay unrecognized.

Nikolai unlocked his door and entered the small room, which featured little more than a full-sized bed, a nightstand, a chair, and a small dresser with a mirror. The bathrooms were shared. A glance out the window to the street revealed a smattering of tourists. He dug into his backpack, fished out his phone, and sat back against the headboard.

He turned on the phone for the first time since his mad dash several nights ago. There were too many missed calls and messages to be counted. Nikolai ignored them all and pressed Alexi's number, feeling a little guilty that he hadn't called her since he left.

Mostly he'd been afraid to hear what kind of trouble he had stirred up. If he stayed in the dark about the uproar he'd created, he wouldn't feel so terrible. It was a bad sign that he'd spotted his picture in the gossip paper.

Alexi's phone rang and rang. Just as he was about to hang up, she answered.

"Oh my God, you are in so much trouble! I've never seen Father's staff freak out so much! Are you having fun? Where are you?" She fired questions so fast, Nikolai could barely keep up.

"Whoa! Alexi, slow down."

"Sorry, but this is the most excitement I've ever seen around here. I don't think Father and Mother have ever been disobeyed."

"No, I suppose they haven't. Is everything okay? They didn't give you a hard time, did they?"

"They did, but I told them I was glad you left. You deserve to have fun while you still can."

"Stirring the pot, are you? You might want to stay out of the line of fire." He kicked off his shoes.

"No way. I figure you're paving the way for me. They aren't going to like it when they find out I want to be an actress."

Nikolai laughed. "No, that will not go over well. So what's happening?"

"Father has been in meetings with his advisors several times a day. He's called in all his top security people. They are trying desperately to find you, so you better be careful."

The sound of his sister's voice gave him a twinge of homesickness. But only a twinge. Chances to get away like this never happened. This was a one-shot deal.

"Where are you, anyway? No! Don't tell me. They'll try to torture it out of me."

"You're being a little dramatic, don't you think?" Nikolai said, smiling.

"Did you know that the press thinks something horrible has happened to you? There are reports that you're really sick, you eloped with one of the maids, and my favorite, that you died, but the palace doesn't want the truth to get out, so they aren't saying anything."

"I had no idea. I saw a paper yesterday, but didn't take the time to read it."

"It's much worse today. This morning's paper speculated that you've been kidnapped by rebel forces."

"That's ridiculous." He reached for a water bottle from the nightstand and opened it.

"I know! Mother was really upset when you missed the

state dinner, but it's good you did. She had you seated next to the King of Kudan's elderly mother. She smelled like adult diapers."

He missed Alexi's babble. She could brighten any moment.

"So is it fun? You know, being on your own?"

"Yeah, it is. I've met a couple of really great people." He pictured Becca and the dreamy look in her eyes after he kissed her.

"Do they know who you are?"

"God, no. The less they know about me, the bet—"

"Uh-oh!" she whispered, cutting him off. "Here comes Mother and the head of security, and they look mad. I don't know how they figured it out, but I'm pretty sure they know it's you on the phone."

Nikolai pictured the stern stare of his father's chief security officer, Visar, as he came for Alexi's phone. Dammit.

Then he overheard his mother. "Alexi, give me that phone."

"I gotta go. Have fun!" she blurted.

"No! Don't you dare hang up, young lady."

The call clicked off. Nikolai worried about the trouble Alexi was in. Suddenly, his phone rang. Caller ID indicated Alexi's number, but he knew it was his mother. He bristled at the inevitable conversation, so he did what he knew he shouldn't.

He powered off his phone.

He was making things worse for himself, but he needed this. He swept his hand through his hair. He needed a chance to discover who he really was, and so far, he liked what he was finding.

It made sense that his father put a trace on his phone. He didn't know if they could locate him if the phone was off or not, but decided not to take a chance. Nikolai opened the back of the phone, pulled out the SIM card, and crushed it under the leg of a chair like he'd seen in movies.

A smile lit his face as he tossed the phone in the trash and joined the other travelers in the common room.

"Anybody want to join us for dinner tonight?" a young guy with curly brown hair and wearing a Stanford University T-shirt asked. His friends checked out a city map on the wall for local restaurants.

"What'd you have in mind?" said a tall, skinny guy wearing frayed shorts and flip-flops. "I'm Mitch, by the way."

"Hi. I'm James. I heard about a little place on the east side of town that has the best Wiener schnitzel for cheap and it includes your first beer and dessert."

Nikolai weighed his choices. He could stay here and hide out. But he'd end up spending the night wondering what drama was happening at home and worrying about Alexi. Or he could take this chance to do something he'd never done before, hang out with American college kids and be treated like an average student.

"I'm in. How about you?" Mitch asked Nikolai.

They appeared to all be Americans, which meant they weren't likely to recognize him.

"Sure, sounds great," Nikolai answered. If his excursion was going to be cut short, he better make the most of it while he could. Nikolai would enjoy dinner with people his age. And tomorrow, he'd spend the day with Becca, free from the crush of the city. He'd have her all to himself, and after that kiss today, he couldn't wait for more.

Even if his father's security could trace his earlier phone call to Melk, he'd be long gone before they arrived.

Becca arrived early to St. Stephen's Cathedral. Thanks to the spires towering so high in the sky like a homing beacon, the church was easy to find. The huge cathedral featured a courtyard with entry doors, steps to the main entrance in the front, and more doors on the other side. Nikolai hadn't said exactly where to meet, but she assumed he meant the front entrance. She didn't see him, so she perched on a ledge next to the front steps where she'd be easy to spot.

Who would have guessed, even a week ago, that she'd be skipping tours and meeting up with a cute guy she barely knew? She must be totally insane to cruise off to the countryside with him, but she loved it.

The bright sun warmed her skin, a welcome contrast against the cool stone of the ledge. Wearing strappy silver sandals, white shorts, and her cutest top, she crossed her legs and tried to appear relaxed.

The square outside the cathedral bustled with street vendors, tourists, and the occasional bicycle rider, but no sign of Nikolai. The clock tower struck eleven, their meeting time. She scanned the crowd, nothing, but then finally she heard the rumble of a motorcycle, or as Nikolai said, motorbike.

She hopped off the ledge as the cycle turned onto the square.

Instead of Nikolai, the rider was a heavyset man with curly hair. She slumped against the stone wall and waited, trying not to appear disappointed.

Ten minutes passed and then twenty.

At eleven thirty, Becca tried not to be discouraged. Tourists asked her to take their picture in front of the cathedral, so she did. The sun rose high, beating down on her as temperatures soared. She moved into one of the few shady spots, under an overhang, but a pigeon decided to mark its territory, some of which splattered on the side of Becca's shorts.

Crap.

She cringed and wiped at the disgusting goo with the edge of her Passau map. Couldn't anything go smoothly today? She glared at the offensive bird and moved back into the sun. Her perfect date outfit ruined.

As noon approached, tourists arrived in droves, entering the cathedral for a concert. Her dad and Vicky would be there, but probably not Dylan. He was most likely chatting up a pretty German girl in a gift shop somewhere. At least he wasn't here to witness Becca getting stood up.

Another motorcycle roar reverberated off the cathedral's stone walls. *Finally.* She warned herself not to get excited, but still, her heart leapt as she turned to see two motorcycles ridden by a couple of guys who pulled up to a tobacco shop and parked.

Had Nikolai really stood her up? If he had, she was a fool to keep waiting. No, she wouldn't let herself believe that. She'd only known Nikolai for a couple of days, but he seemed so nice. He hadn't put the moves on her.

Okay, that wasn't true. He'd totally made out with her in the library, but it was spontaneous. It wasn't like he was trying to hook up. *Was he?* And she'd loved that quick, hot kiss and had hoped for more of them today. Heck, that was half the reason she was still sitting here waiting.

She battled with her emotions. If he showed, he'd have a really good excuse about why he was late. And if he didn't show, well, that proved what? That she was a terrible judge of character? That he didn't really like her at all? One more guy on a long list who grew bored with her. But in two days? That would be a record. She frowned.

Loud classical organ music drifted out from the cathedral.

Becca scanned the mostly empty square. She sighed, not wanting to admit defeat. Sweat beaded down her forehead. Thirsty, she walked across the square to a shop. They didn't even have her Diet Pepsi. She bought a bottle of Coca-Cola Light.

Returning to the ledge, she imagined Nikolai showing up all apologetic. She knew she'd act like it was no big deal.

After a while, the concert let out and hordes of sightseers poured from the cathedral like kids after a rock concert, except that these concertgoers wore sensible shoes and prescription sunglasses.

Someone tapped her on the shoulder.

She whipped her head around with a huge smile.

9

"*Becca,* what are you doing here? We thought you were going to the Bohemian Glass Museum with Dylan," Vicky said, dressed in pressed navy slacks, a white designer blouse, and silver earrings.

Becca's heart dropped. She fought to keep the shocking disappointment off her face.

"Oh. Um, hi. Yeah, I was. We did. But now we thought we'd see what all the talk about the cathedral was. We were just waiting for the concert to let out."

The lies flew from her mouth without thought or hesitation.

Her dad looked around. "Where's Dylan?"

Becca looked around the square, searching for an answer. "Ah, he's in the bathroom. He'll be right back."

"Oh good, let's get a family picture here in front of

the cathedral. Maybe we can use it for a Christmas card," Vicky suggested.

Becca didn't know which part she abhorred more—the idea of doing a family Christmas card when they weren't a real family, or the idea of Nikolai suddenly appearing with her dad and Vicky here. Plus, unless Dylan showed up by some sort of miracle, they'd be waiting for him a long time.

"That would be fine." Her dad checked his watch. "But we're supposed to meet the Hebels for lunch at the Altes Bräuhaus."

"It'll only take a minute," Vicky answered, checking the area for Dylan. "Becca, you're getting red. Did you put on sunscreen today?"

"No. I guess I forgot."

"You can't afford to forget. Good skin is your best asset when you get older. Look at my skin, it's still porcelain perfect. Here, I've got some in my bag." Vicky dug around in her bag until she pulled out a travel-sized tube.

Becca accepted the tube and applied sunscreen to her arms, shoulders, and neckline. "Thanks."

"Don't forget your face," Vicky nagged.

Becca sighed and gave in. She'd worked hard on her makeup so it looked perfect. Now she smeared sunscreen over her blush. She handed the tube back.

"When did you say Dylan was coming back?" Vicky asked.

"I thought right away, but maybe he stopped for something to drink," Becca lied.

"I don't think we should wait any longer," her dad said in predictable fashion. He couldn't be inconvenienced by his kids, even for a lousy picture on a trip they didn't want to take.

"I suppose you're right," Vicky replied. "Becca, tell Dylan he shouldn't leave you alone like this. It's not safe. Be sure you two stick together."

"I will." Becca crossed her fingers behind her back.

Finally her dad and Vicky wandered away down a side street toward the beer garden where they would taste different beers for the next two hours and then stagger back to their cabin for a nap as the boat departed.

Becca spent those two hours with her stomach grumbling, waiting for Nikolai. If she didn't take a chance and wait for him now, she'd never see him again. They'd met several times by fate and she was sure they'd used up all their luck.

At two o'clock, she bit back her pride and accepted the fact that Nikolai didn't want to see her again. That or a terrible accident had happened and she refused to believe that. He probably met some other girl on vacation and took her for a ride on his cycle. Or maybe, he was kissing her in a dark museum library somewhere.

The only thing that made this day less humiliating was that no one would know about it, except Dylan. Hopefully he wouldn't rub it in her face too much, because she really couldn't bear it.

When Ethan dumped her the day of graduation, the whole school knew, which made going to grad parties pure torture.

Hungry and needing a bathroom, she stopped first at the public restroom and begrudgingly paid the attendant the required euro. As she washed her hands, the mirror revealed her sunburned face. She groaned. On the way back toward the boat, she stopped at a little grocery store and bought Cheetos and a Snickers bar. Even though the packaging was written in a foreign script, the food tasted familiar and comforting, like home.

She wandered back to the ship, burying her disappointment in her junk food snacks.

Back on board, she locked herself in her bathroom in case Dylan showed up. She didn't want him to know what a fool she'd been, falling for a guy with dusty blond hair, eyes deep like the ocean, and kisses that made her forget herself.

She held her head in her hands. How could she be so gullible and think some random hot guy would be interested in her? Had he been laughing at her all along? She didn't think so. She truly felt she'd found a nice guy.

The cabin door creaked open and shut. Dylan was back. Great. He'd want to know how her day went and then, even if he didn't speak the words, his eyes would say, *I told you so.*

He knocked on the bathroom door. "Becca, hurry up. I've got something to show you," he called.

She sighed. Might as well get it over with. She looked into the mirror. Sad eyes stared back from her sunburned face. She forced a smile and looked like an idiot. Her frown returned.

"Yeah, what is it?" She left the privacy of the bathroom and plopped down on her single bed, avoiding looking at Dylan or the sunny day outside the open balcony door.

"So how was your date?"

Becca glared at him.

"Uh-oh. Did he stand you up?" Dylan held a rolled-up magazine.

She frowned, frustrated and angry that she'd been so easily played. "Yeah, you could say that."

"Well, I think you should see this." Dylan held the magazine under her face, forcing her to look at the glossy picture of a guy who looked exactly like Nikolai. She took the magazine and examined it closer.

Her breath caught in her throat.

"That's Nikolai!"

On his motorcycle and wearing the same dark gray T-shirt he'd worn two days ago with his baseball cap on backward. She'd recognize him anywhere. She couldn't read the foreign headline, but it ended with an exclamation point.

Becca looked at Dylan. "Where did you find this?"

He grimaced and shrugged. "It was at every newspaper stand I saw today."

"Why is he on the cover? Did he do something wrong?" She paged through the magazine, holding her breath. Confusion turned to shock when she saw a two-page spread filled with pictures of Nikolai.

Nikolai at the beach with other guys and girls; a picture of him playing polo; a picture of him in a tuxedo with another girl wearing a gown. Then Becca's eyes landed on a formal picture of Nikolai in uniform, with a sword at his belt, standing next to a young girl. A stern man and austere woman sat in gilded chairs; both adults wore crowns.

Her jaw dropped open.

"Why is Nikolai in that picture with people wearing crowns? Who is he?" she asked. And who were the girls laughing and smiling with him in those photos? Her heart pumped so fast she could feel the blood pulse through her temples.

"I don't know, but it looks like he's related to some royal family."

He wasn't an average guy. He was . . . she didn't know who he was. Important? Royal? Rich? "Why did he lie about his identity?"

"I don't know. Based on all the pictures of him with girls, he doesn't need to do it to pick up women. No offense."

No, it appeared he had plenty of gorgeous women in his life. Becca stared at the glossy photos of stunning young women. She needed to find out who he was, but she couldn't read the foreign words.

"I've gotta get out of this room. I can't breathe." She stood, leaving the magazine on her bedside table.

Dylan picked up the magazine and held it out to her. "Becs, try asking one of the crew members. I bet they can read it."

She snatched the magazine and escaped the suffocating room.

Becca snuck in early to the dining room and found their waiter, Melenka, setting tables. With one quick glance at the magazine, he answered her question. "That's Prince Nikolai."

"A prince?" Becca looked to Melenka for confirmation. "As in, the kind who becomes king some day?"

"Yes. He is Crown Prince of Mondovia. He is very well-known, or how do you say in America? Famous for the ladies."

She took a hit in the gut. "Can you tell me what this says?" She pointed to the headline.

"It says, 'Nikolai, the Runaway Prince.'"

So, when he said he took off without his parents' permission, he wasn't lying. Becca couldn't believe it. She'd been hanging out with a real prince who was hiding from his parents—the king and queen. She shook her head, struggling to digest it all.

"Does it say how long he's been missing?" She recalled the sadness in Nikolai's eyes when he flippantly said he was just another derelict kid avoiding family responsibilities. It had sounded so normal at the time, but now she knew it wasn't. He was different.

Melenka scanned the article. "It says here, since last Saturday, so that makes it four days. Oh, the picture was taken outside Budapest." Melenka glanced up. "And we were just there! But this publication is gossip. It isn't real news."

"Thank you, Melenka. I appreciate it." Becca took the magazine and headed for the top deck.

Once there, she looked out over the Danube as the ship cruised by picturesque farmland and vineyards that grew along the hillside. A road ran parallel to each side of the river.

She tried to get her head around Nikolai's true identity—royal prince. Why would a prince randomly wander the streets of Budapest and Vienna? The magazine reported he was on the run. What could possibly make a prince run away?

She sipped lemonade and nibbled on snack mix when Dylan showed up later with a beer. He sank into the chair across from her and glanced at the magazine.

"Hot damn, Becca. You've been stood up by a prince. Not too many girls can say that."

"Gee, thanks. I feel so much better now." She gazed

ahead, noticing another bridge in the distance.

"I'm just sayin', when it comes to picking 'em, you have a special knack."

"Do you think he planned to stand me up all along? I mean, why would he go to the trouble of setting a time and place and then not show?"

Dylan popped a sesame stick into the air and caught it in his mouth. "Truth? If it were me and I'd made plans with a chick, I wouldn't purposely try to hurt her, but face it. The odds of me ever seeing any of these girls again is zero. If someone prettier, easier, or more fun stepped into my path, you bet I'd be onto her like foam on beer." He raised his glass in the air and took a drink.

"You're a real jerk, you know that?"

"But I'm a lovable jerk." He grinned.

As they approached an older bridge, sporting decorative arches, she noticed a figure standing in the center. He seemed to be watching the enormous boat approach.

The guy waved a cap in the air. She set down her lemonade and looked closer. "Dylan, look! That's him!"

Dylan looked up. "Well, I'll be damned. Prince Charming is back."

10

As the boat sailed closer, Becca recognized his ruffled blond hair and broad shoulders.

She wanted to yell to him, but a couple dozen people were scattered around the deck, enjoying the late afternoon sun. She stood and waved back, her pulse racing.

Nikolai seemed to visibly relax knowing she'd spotted him. As they neared the bridge, she didn't know what to do. She couldn't get off and he certainly couldn't jump on, not without breaking his neck.

"Dylan, what do I do?" she asked in a panic.

"I don't think you need to do anything. He came to you." Dylan smiled and propped up his feet on an empty chair.

The bridge loomed huge. Nikolai stood a good fifteen feet above them. Passengers on board the *Bolero* waved, but Nikolai only had eyes for her. As soon as they were within hearing distance, he yelled.

"I'm sorry!"

She didn't know what to say. It wasn't okay, but he was sorry, so he must not have meant to skip out on her. The boat floated under the bridge and blocked Nikolai from sight.

And then the sun broke out again as they came to the other side. She turned, hoping desperately to see him, but Nikolai wasn't there. Then suddenly he appeared.

"I'll see you at the next stop," he yelled.

Becca turned to her brother in a panic. "Where's our next stop? Where are we going to be tomorrow?"

He was mid-swallow of his beer.

She smacked his arm. "Dylan! Where?"

He choked on his beer. "Jeez, Becs, I don't know. Some German town, I guess."

She turned to Nikolai, who was quickly being left in their wake. "I don't know where we'll be!" she yelled back, but he didn't hear her. She shrugged in frustration.

Nikolai leaned on the railing and pounded.

"Dammit," she sighed as Nikolai and the bridge faded into the distance. Now that she knew he was sorry for not showing up today, she really wanted to see him again. "What do I do? I didn't even get to talk to him."

"Don't worry, if he's into you enough to wait for you from a bridge, he'll figure out where we're docked tomorrow."

Nikolai became a tiny dot on the horizon.

Dylan continued. "What was it Mom used to say? 'If you worry about the future, and dwell on the past, you can't enjoy the present.'"

"Yeah, well that doesn't help me much now." She plopped into her chair and sighed.

"Come on, let's go in to dinner. I hear they're serving something chocolate for dessert. You can eat away your troubles."

Becca didn't want to go to dinner. She wanted to stay on deck and watch for Nikolai at every bridge, but looking ahead, there were no more in sight. She didn't know when there would be another bridge or if Nikolai could reach it in time. Her stomach grumbled from missing lunch.

"Fine." Becca reluctantly got up and followed her brother down to eat.

Vicky spent the entire time during dinner talking about the benefits of international travel for young people, and studying abroad. She included a long dissertation on an extensive education in art history, political science, and international business studies.

Dylan cracked jokes the whole time, which eventually wore on Vicky's cool exterior until she pressed her thin red lips so tightly that they seemed to disappear. She gripped her steak knife like a potential weapon. Becca wanted to hug her brother.

With dinner over, Becca climbed to the top deck, wishing Nikolai would magically appear. He didn't.

After an hour, she retreated from the lonely night and returned to her empty room. Dylan had snuck off below deck with a cocktail waitress named Ursula. Becca envied his ability to find a good time no matter the circumstance.

She turned her bedside light on low, slipped out of the dark jeans she wore to dinner, and into loose shorts and a T-shirt. She sank onto her bed, leaning against the headboard. The magazine with Nikolai's pictures lay on the bedside table.

A glance out the door revealed they were entering another lock. Earlier in the trip she might have rushed onto the deck to watch the iron lock doors open as the enormous boat maneuvered into the tight space, but now, well, she just didn't care.

She sighed and picked up the magazine, examining each picture of Nikolai, from the laughing pictures of him with other girls, to the staid, formal picture of him with his family.

His sister seemed poised, her hands clasped as she stood beside their mother, a regal beauty with rigid posture and a graceful smile. His father, a handsome gentleman with Nikolai's looks, wore an unyielding expression, as if he were a high court judge about to impose a sentence. He reminded Becca of her dad.

Nikolai appeared stoic in a decked-out navy blue

uniform with gold sash and colorful adornments. He stood behind his father's shoulder. None of Nikolai's good-natured personality shown through.

Who was Nikolai really? The fun-loving guy who spent the day with her or a royal prince from the house of Mondovia? She sighed and tossed the magazine aside.

Outside her balcony, the smell of algae from the wet, slimy wall of the locks permeated her room through the open door. She considered getting up to close the door, but was too lazy. In a moment the boat would rise and in a few minutes, they'd be floating even with land again.

Becca turned on the TV and clicked through the channels. She found nothing but news channels, most of them European. They didn't even have the American version of CNN, let alone a music station.

She landed on the cruise ship's channel, which aired a program about the history of the Habsburg Dynasty. Jeez, could she never escape this stuff?

Becca set down the remote and rubbed her face. When she looked up, she saw a tall, imposing figure lurking on the other side of her balcony railing.

Becca screamed and scrambled back into the corner of her bed.

11

"*Becca,* it's me, Nikolai," he called out, hoping he didn't fall into the Danube as he clung to the outside of the moving boat.

She froze and studied his shadowed form across the dimly lit room. "Nikolai?"

His tightened his grip on the balcony railing. "Yeah."

"Oh my God! How did you get there?" She shot across the cabin to his side.

"I figured the only way to see you was to board the boat. Can I come in?" he asked from his precarious perch high above the water.

"Yes, of course. How did you get up here?"

"I waited at the lock. You told me your cabin is the top, last one on the end. When the boat rose in the lock and started moving, I took a chance and jumped for it."

"You're insane, you know that?" She giggled. He felt

a surge of relief and knew he'd been right to risk leaping aboard.

"I feel that way a lot lately."

"Hurry up. Get in here before someone sees you," she said.

Becca gripped his upper arm while he scrambled over the rail, and they came face-to-face in the tiny cabin. He noticed the light dusting of freckles on her sunburned nose and resisted the urge to kiss her.

"Hi." He grinned, glad to lay eyes on her after the day he'd had.

"Hi," she answered, then looked away, suddenly acting shy, as if she didn't know him. He could hardly blame her. Standing in her tiny stateroom, which was smaller than his closet, was a lot different from talking on a public street.

"So this is your cabin." Nikolai glanced around. Two nightstands separated twin beds. One bed was a cluttered mess of clothes and tangled sheets, the other was tidy with only a magazine and TV remote. He had a good guess which bed belonged to Becca.

"I can't believe you're actually here." She studied his face as if searching for something.

"I hope you don't mind that I, you know, barged in."

"No, I'm glad you did, but what if the door had been locked and I wasn't here?"

"I hadn't actually thought that far ahead." He dipped his head, suddenly realizing how crazy desperate he must look to climb aboard her boat.

"You've got something in your hair." Becca reached up, her face so close he kissed her. She smiled as a small leaf fell to the floor.

"I was hiding in the bushes. I didn't think the lock operators would welcome someone planning to stowaway. I waited till the last second and made a run for it. I don't think anyone saw me."

Becca's smile held such sweet adoration, he knew he'd been right to chase down her boat. "Come sit down. I'll get you some water," she said, opening a small fridge built into the cabinetry.

He sat on her brother's bed, pushing some clothes to the side. "Water would be great," he said.

She handed him the bottle and faced him from her bed, their legs stretched out to each other.

Becca's eyes darted around the room, to the magazine on her bed, then back to him. "So, what happened today? You didn't show up." She watched him carefully.

Now he understood her odd behavior. She was mad he stood her up.

"I'm so sorry I wasn't there. Today has been the biggest mess. It started when I prepared to leave Melk. My motorbike was gone."

Concern replaced her earlier cautiousness. "Was it stolen?"

"That's what I thought at first, but then I found out I'd

parked in a tow-away zone. It never occurred to me that I'd have to move it." He unscrewed the water bottle cap and took a swig, glad for the refreshment.

"After that I had to find out where they took it, and then I had some problem with the . . . uh . . . with getting my motorbike out of the holding lot." He almost blurted out his problem with the paparazzi, who'd somehow picked up his scent and camped out waiting for him. He'd have to be a lot more careful moving forward.

"But you got your bike back okay?"

"It took a while, and I had to jump through a few hoops, but I got it back."

"That's good, where is it now?"

"Hiding in said bushes, waiting for me to return."

"How are you going to get back? How are you going to get off the boat?"

"The same way I got on." He shrugged. "I figure there will be another lock soon enough. I'll walk back or catch a cab." He doubted cabs would actually operate this late at night in small villages. It would be a long walk.

"I can't believe you did all this just to see me."

"I had to. I didn't want you to think I'm a jerk. Plus, I really wanted to see you again and if I didn't try to now, you might slip away." He nudged her foot. Becca blushed.

"I don't understand you. You make no sense." Becca stared down at her painted toenails.

Something was still wrong and he couldn't imagine

what it was. "What don't you understand? Ask me and I'll tell you."

"It's just . . . I don't get it." She hesitated. "I'm nobody, just an American girl stuck on vacation with her family."

Nikolai shook his head. "First off, you're not a nobody. You're funny and irreverent and beautiful. Plus, you make me laugh. You are far from nobody."

She raised her eyes in doubt. He moved next to her. Becca took a measured breath as if nervous about something. He captured her hand, noticing her pretty, oval fingernails. "What's wrong?"

Becca tugged her hand away, reached for the magazine, and dropped it in his hands. His image filled the cover.

Dammit.

Nikolai heaved a sigh. The walls of his freedom were closing in and he hated it. The paparazzi were hot on his trail, his parents were tightening the noose, and now, Becca knew his true identity. How would she react?

He scrubbed his hands over his face.

She opened the magazine to a photo spread of him, including the most recent official royal family photo.

"So, who *are* you?"

He gazed into her innocent, amber eyes. She hadn't been ruined by the realities of the political world he lived in.

As he began to answer, the cabin door opened.

Becca's brother strolled in. Dylan stopped short when he spotted Nikolai.

"Whoa! How'd you get here?" he asked.

Nikolai stood.

"He came in through the balcony door at the locks," Becca answered for him.

"Impressive." Dylan nodded, his eyes still trained on Nikolai. "So what's the plan? You come here to hop in the sack with my sister?"

"Dylan! Shut up!" Becca said, as a flush crept across her cheeks.

Nikolai moved a step away from her. "No. I came to talk."

"Yeah?" Dylan seemed to weigh the situation. "I bet you have a lot to talk about." He gestured to the incriminating magazine.

Nikolai wondered if Dylan would toss him overboard or report him.

"Well, I've gotta use the can. I don't suppose you need me hanging around for your little chat. And just so you know, Becca will tell me everything you say after you're gone." Dylan turned and disappeared into the bathroom.

Becca's eyes were full of questions.

Before he could explain, a loud knock sounded at the cabin door. Becca turned in alarm. "Who the heck could that be? One of Dylan's girlfriends?" She held up a finger and gestured to Nikolai to stay silent. She spied through the peephole in the door and rushed back.

"It's my stepmother!" she whispered. "Quick, hide!"

"Where?" He scanned the tiny cabin. Other than the two twin beds, set against each wall, all the cabin contained were the small side tables, built-in dressers for their clothes, and a half closet, big enough for no more than a small child.

Becca looked frantic. "Get in his bed."

"You mean under his bed?"

"No, his suitcases are under it, you won't fit."

Another loud knock sounded.

"Hurry up. She won't go away until I let her in."

Becca dragged back the sheets and practically shoved Nikolai into the narrow bed. She yanked the covers over his head and tossed dirty clothes on top.

He faced the wall and struggled to slow his panicked breathing. He'd never stowed away on a cruise ship, let alone hid in a girl's bedroom before.

He heard the cabin door open and some mumbling. The voices came closer.

"I didn't hear the door at first, I was in the bathroom," Becca said softly.

"Where's Dylan?" a cultured voice asked.

"Sleeping," Becca whispered.

"Already? That's got to be a record," the stepmother said in a low voice. "I wanted to see if you and Dylan want to join your father and me for the extended walking tour tomorrow in Regensburg. It's an hour longer than the other tour, but includes the Imperial Chamber at City Hall and the old bishop's residence. The tour comes highly recommended, and I think you would get a lot out of it."

Nikolai fought the urge to scratch his itchy nose. Becca's stepmother sounded so close. All she'd have to do was pull down the covers, and she'd see he wasn't Dylan. He feared the covers shook from his nerves.

"Nah, I'll pass, I'm kind of historied out."

Becca's voice sounded right next to him. She must have stepped between her stepmother and him. He prayed that Dylan wouldn't suddenly appear from the bathroom.

"Becca, I know you weren't very happy about this trip, but you really should make more of this opportunity. We're in such an important part of the world, and you're missing out."

"You're right. I'll think about it. Can I let you know at breakfast?" Becca asked, speaking fast.

"That would be fine. You won't regret joining us. Oh, what's this?" her stepmother asked.

"It's just a magazine I picked up."

"Really? You don't speak German. How did you expect to read it?" He heard the sound of pages turning. "I see. You picked it up for the guy on the cover. It says here he's Prince Nikolai of Mondovia."

"You can read German?"

"I mentioned it before we left the States. I majored in German and spent a year abroad in Germany during college."

"Oh."

"He's heir to the Mondovian Dynasty. His family descends from some of the most influential royal families in history, including Tsar Nicholas of Russia and the Habsburg Dynasty."

"I had no idea." Becca sounded dumbfounded.

So much for him having the chance to explain.

"Well, my master's in European history is good for a few things. If I knew all it took for you to get interested in Europe was a good-looking young man, I'd have picked up a few celebrity magazines at the start of the trip."

"I'm sorry, Vicky. I'm kind of tired. If you don't mind, I think I'll go to bed." Becca yawned loudly.

"Oh. Of course. I'll see you in the morning then."

A few seconds later the door clicked shut.

"Prince Nikolai, you can come out now," Becca said sarcastically.

He lifted the covers and rolled to a sitting position.

She stood with her arms crossed and her head cocked, her expression a mix of cynicism and disbelief.

He grimaced. "Can we get out of here and go someplace to talk?" He didn't want to be interrupted by any more of her family members. Next thing he knew, her father would walk in.

"I think that's an excellent idea."

12

After allowing Vicky time to retreat to her cabin on the lower deck, Becca led Nikolai to a secluded area on the top deck. Most people had gone to bed, other than a small group at the front of the boat.

Becca's mind bounded with unasked questions, but she fought her urge to blurt them out. They sat facing each other on chaise lounges. The warm evening air smelled lush from dew as they cruised along the Danube.

"I didn't mean to lie to you," he said.

Becca frowned. "Really?"

"Okay, I did, but only to protect myself."

"Now that at least sounds honest."

"But I didn't lie when I told you about being on my own or leaving without my parents' permission. I didn't want anyone to know who I was or where I was going. I just needed to escape my life for a while."

"So, you really are the Prince of Mondovia."

He sighed. "I am."

He said it with such defeat. What had been going on in his life to cause him to leave his country? "And you wish you weren't?"

Nikolai shook his head and ran his hand through his hair. "It's so much bigger than that. To answer your question, I can't even wish I were someone else, because there is no escaping who I am." He stared up at the stars, unhappiness clouding his eyes.

"Why would you want to? I mean, from looking at those pictures, your life looks pretty sweet. Fancy parties, rich friends."

"An outsider would see it that way."

Becca bristled. "I'm sorry, but finding out you're a prince and not a regular guy has hit me out of left field. I'm not sure what to think about it." She fidgeted with the edge of her T-shirt. "I thought you were one person, but you aren't him at all. You're someone completely different. You're a damn prince! And that sucks, because I really liked the other guy."

Nikolai reached for her hand, cupping it between his, and her stress evaporated with the touch of his skin. "I'm still the guy you met. I just have one hell of a lot of baggage."

"So, what makes your life so horrible? I want to understand."

Nikolai blew out his breath. "I guess the thing that makes it so difficult is my lack of choices. There is very little I get to decide for myself. My parents have picked my schools, my activities, who I associate with. They and their advisors decide who I sit next to at formal events, who I speak to at a grand opening, who I take photos with at fund-raisers, what charities I must support, even what horse I'll ride."

Becca was awestruck by his caliber of activities. She thought she had it bad with her dad insisting she go to Northwestern instead of the University of Wisconsin, Madison, where her mom went. "What do you do for fun?"

"I just told you." He grimaced. "But, when I was away at school, I felt free."

"They sent you away?" She stretched her legs out near his and resisted the urge to touch him.

"Of course, to private boarding school. It was actually the happiest time in my life. But now that's over. I used to be okay with all the ceremony and traditions of our family, but the older I get, the more aware I am of my parents' true expectations. They want to send me to the military academy."

"And you don't want to go?"

"No! I understand that the military is an important aspect of every society, but it's not for me." He smiled weakly.

"But my father insists that as crown prince I must serve

in our military. That's how it's done in our family."

"What do you mean when you say 'crown prince'?"

"It means I'm the heir apparent, the next in line to inherit the throne."

"So you're going to be King of Mondovia someday." Whoa. That was a reality check. She lay on a chaise lounge chatting it up with a future king. Unreal.

"That's my parents' plan."

Becca pictured Nikolai with a gold crown and long red cape like a fairy-tale king. But the image didn't mesh with the sweet, funny Nikolai she knew. "If you do become king, you could never hang out with me."

"Nope. Not unless you were my queen." He smirked.

Becca nearly choked. The idea of her as a queen was . . . insanity. She was still trying to get her head around him being a prince. "Don't you have to marry a royal somebody, a princess? Not a commoner."

"Why? You want to marry me?" he asked with a devil-ish twinkle in his eye that made her stomach flip.

She couldn't tell if he was teasing. . . . Of course, he was teasing! "You offering me the job?"

"Not today." He smiled, but then turned serious. "This whole royal family thing is a joke. The Mondovian govern-ment hasn't been a monarchy run by the king in over fifty years. Parliament and the government run the country. It's a lot like how England is run. All my family is anymore are figureheads. We don't actually do anything, except parade around like we're something special and live off of taxpayers' money to fund our lavish lifestyle."

"Oh, that's terrible!"

"Exactly."

"And what was that you said about serving in the military? Other royal families, like in England, they don't have to go into the military, do they?"

"The direct heirs to the throne have all served." He frowned.

"So what are you going to do?"

"Run away." He leaned back in his chair and smiled, revealing his perfect white teeth.

Becca mulled over all the things he'd said. "Can I ask you something else?"

"Of course."

"Why are you hanging out with me? I don't have a fancy boarding school education, and Europe really isn't my thing."

While part of her longed for him to confess it was because he'd fallen for her and couldn't stand to be apart, she really did wonder what the heck a crown prince was doing slumming with an average American girl.

Nikolai laughed. "I don't know. I guess it's a way to be spiteful against my parents by hanging out with an American commoner." He grinned.

"You jerk." Becca threw him a dirty look, but couldn't hide her amusement.

"Come here." He reached for Becca and she let him pull her onto his chair. He scooted over and she climbed next to him, wondering what alternative universe she'd landed in to be cozied up to a prince.

"I didn't want to like you. Not at first," he confessed.

She craned her neck up to see his face. "No?"

He caressed her arm, sending shivers all the way up her neck. "Nope. You were walking through the marketplace in Budapest with your tour group. I found the whole flag carrying, headphone speaker system annoying. But then you hung back. I watched as the group moved on. When you realized you were alone, you went the wrong direction."

"I can't believe you saw that." She covered her face with her hand until he eased it away. She rested her hand on his chest, feeling it rise with each breath he took.

"I was debating whether to help you out, but then this tall, good-looking guy came looking for you."

She laughed. "Dylan."

"You two looked so much alike, I knew he must be your brother."

"What I don't understand is why you're with me when you could have any girl on the planet."

"But I don't want any girl on the planet. I never really have. Until I met you."

Becca wanted to believe his words, but knew a cheesy line when she heard one. "Nice try. I'm not falling for it."

He laughed and his chest bounced beneath her hand,

causing her to giggle. He pulled her close and brushed his lips against hers. "That's what I like about you, your honesty."

"You know, I saw you in Budapest, too," she said.

"At that small market."

"Yeah, but also later that day when you were on your motorcycle. You were leaving a gas station and I was on the tour bus heading back to the ship." She remembered his confident gait and how hot he looked even then.

"Really? I guess fate wanted us to get together."

"I guess it did." She sighed in contentment. The ship slowed and the engine groaned a low rumble. "We must be coming to another lock."

"That's my cue to leave."

"I don't want you to." She sat up, not ready to let him go. What if he didn't come back?

"I don't want to, either, but I have to get back to my motorbike. It's my only transportation. I can't rent a car, and I need to be able to get around. As it is, the paparazzi are on my tail, and I bet my parents aren't far behind."

"You didn't mention that."

"You don't need to worry about it." He brushed a strand of Becca's hair behind her ear. She looked ahead to see they still had a while yet before reaching the locks.

"But when will I see you again? I mean, do I get to see you again?"

"Of course. I'll see you tomorrow, which is probably

today already, so in a few hours. Can you sneak away from your parents?"

"You mean my dad and Vicky." She couldn't wait to get away from them. She amazed herself at how easy it had been to lie.

"Sorry, your dad and Vicky. She said that you'll be in Regensburg. I'm not familiar with that city, so how about I meet you where your ship docks? That should be the easiest place for us to find each other."

"We need a backup plan in case you get delayed again. Do you have a phone?"

"Actually, I did, but I dumped my phone in Melk. I need to pick up a new disposable phone tomorrow. I'll get your number then."

"Sounds good. But in case something happens, I want you to know how much fun I'm having. You've made this horrible trip the best time of my life."

"Nothing is going to happen, and if it did, now I know the name of your boat, the *Bolero*. I can always find you. I'll see you in the morning, and so you know, you've made my escape from reality far better than I ever dreamed."

He gently tilted her head back and kissed her. Becca relaxed in his arms and lay under the stars. She couldn't believe she was in the arms of the Crown Prince of Mondovia. She had never been as happy as she was at that moment.

After a few minutes of Nikolai's amazing kisses, he

spoiled the whole thing by stopping.

"I hate to say this, but I've got to go." He leaned his forehead against hers.

"I don't want you to," Becca protested. His arms felt so good around her and the way he kissed made her delirious.

"Becca," he groaned and held her tight for another moment. "If I don't jump off this boat while I have a chance, I'll be swimming back to where I left my bike, and I need it so I can take you away tomorrow."

"I know. You're right, but I hate this. I finally get to see you and you have to turn around and leave." Despite her feelings, she peeled herself away from him and stood. She looked around the deck, but didn't see anyone else. "It must be really late."

Nikolai stood and walked to the railing. The water that filled the locks had floated the boat level with the higher ground. A concrete walkway bordered the locks. A small operations building was located in the center.

He would need to climb over the boat's railing and jump to the walkway. It was only a couple of feet, but still, it wasn't something people were supposed to do.

"Are you going to be okay getting back? It's the middle of the night." She didn't like him leaving like this. She wished he'd wait until daylight and take a cab or bus back. She didn't even know how far they'd gone.

"I'll be fine. Don't worry. You go get some sleep and I'll see you soon." Nikolai pulled her close, molding her body to his and kissed her hungrily, awakening all of her nerve endings.

As quick as it started, he ended it. They gazed at each other, his glistening eyes filled with longing.

Before she realized what he was doing, he gripped the ship's railing and vaulted over like an Olympic athlete, landing smoothly on the other side. He shot her a sexy grin, and disappeared into the darkness.

Becca touched her mouth. She couldn't believe Nikolai had spent the past couple hours with her here on the boat. She must be dreaming, because there was no way a real live prince would go to all this trouble to spend time with her and then jump off so easily. It didn't make sense. Except that it really did happen!

She hugged herself and did a little happy dance. Turning back toward land, she looked up, and in the control room of the operations building, a guy peeked out from a window and smiled. Had he seen Nikolai jump off the boat? If he did, he hadn't sounded any sort of alarm. She waved at the man, then floated happily downstairs to her cabin.

Inside, Dylan sprawled out on his bed, deep in slumber. She was so happy she wanted to squeal, but knew it wouldn't go over very well. The last thing she felt like was sleep, so as she lay in bed, she replayed everything that had happened tonight. Nikolai, a gorgeous guy, not to mention the heir to the Mondovian throne, jumped aboard her river cruise boat and made out with her on the top deck.

Who would possibly believe her? She barely believed it herself.

Nikolai whistled as his feet crunched on the gravel road running alongside the river. This was the most time he'd spent on his own in his entire life, and he'd never been happier. Chasing after Becca was impulsive and maybe even stupid, since he was miles away from his cycle and bag, but something about her made him feel alive. Even now that she knew who he was, he could still be himself, and that hadn't happened in a long time.

He thought of his parents. They must be having a fit. He'd never acted out like this before. Ever. Earlier he'd felt a bit guilty about leaving, but now that he had Becca, he didn't care at all. Of course, he'd need to go back eventually, and he'd have to figure out how to convince them to release him from joining the military, but he could figure all that out later.

His thoughts returned to Becca and her shock when he appeared at her cabin. Each time they were together, he had more fun than the time before. He grinned. And, man, could that girl kiss! Being the Prince of Mondovia allowed him access to a lot of pretty girls, most of whom wanted to kiss a prince. But none drove him crazy like Becca.

Up ahead lay a small village and tavern. If there wasn't a cab on duty, maybe he could pay someone to drive him back to the last locks and his motorbike. Hopefully he'd hidden it well enough that it was still undisturbed.

If he lost his motorbike, he'd lose the chance to see Becca again. And that was the worst thing that could happen right now.

13

Becca wanted to fling her eggs Benedict across the linen-covered table. "Dad, I'm not going on some stupid extended tour."

"I've had enough of your lip, Becca. Since when do you talk back? We brought you on this trip for family time and so far we've barely managed to share meals. Keep it up and you can join us on this afternoon's monastery tour, too."

"Dylan isn't going with you today, so why do I have to?"

Vicky intervened. "Dylan is in bed sick. He even went to bed early last night. He's too ill to come."

Hardly. Dylan caught wind of her conversation with Vicky last night and jumped at the chance to skip out on a day of torture. Becca wanted to throw him under the bus, but never would.

"Please, Dad, just let me go on the regular tour."

"No, and that's final. We will have one day together."

"Oh my God, you don't get it!" She tossed her fork down. It clattered loudly on her plate. Other diners looked over at them.

Vicky smiled as if nothing were amiss. "Becca, Regensburg is fascinating. There is the historic bridge that allowed merchants to trade wares, there's the Imperial Chamber, and amazing architecture."

"This sucks." Becca threw her napkin in her eggs, and stormed off.

Back at her cabin, she found Dylan lounging in bed and playing games on his phone.

"This is all your fault, you know!"

"What did I do?" he asked without looking up.

"You're backing out today, so now I've become Dad's project. They're forcing me to go with them, but I'm supposed to meet Nikolai."

"Come on, Becs. You're smart enough to get out of it."

"No, Dylan, I'm not. I begged, I complained, I demanded, and he ignored me. I can't exactly claim I'm sick. You already pulled that one."

"You could be a no-show."

"They'd be in here in a second."

He lowered the phone. "You could disappear. Just take off. I've done it plenty of times."

"As much as I'd like to, that would be going too far. I couldn't do that to Dad. I don't want to go with him, but I don't want to freak him out either."

Dylan returned to his game. "I guess you'll just have to be a good little girl and do what Daddy says."

"You're such a jerk." She slumped on the edge of her bed.

He grinned. "Don't I know it."

"So why is it so easy for you to do what you want even if it means letting people down? I don't get it. You used to be the perfect child."

Dylan stopped messing with his phone and looked up. "You're right. I used to be perfect. When Mom was alive, she was sick for so long that I made a bargain with God."

Dylan didn't talk about their mom very often. Neither of them did.

"If God let her live, I'd be perfect and do everything expected of me. And I did for a long time."

"But then she got worse," Becca whispered.

"And died," he said. "I think that's the last day I ever cared what authority figures said." Dylan stood and tossed his phone on the bed. "Life's too short. It's not worth doing what other people want, just to please them. Sorry, but it's how I feel." He disappeared into the bathroom.

Becca realized she had acted the opposite of Dylan. While Dylan behaved before their mom died, she started behaving after.

On her deathbed, her mom had held Becca's hand and told her how proud she was of Becca. She told her to have a great life and always be good. And so Becca did.

In honor of her mom, she did whatever was expected, no matter how much she hated it. At school, she took all the higher-level science classes she hated because her dad insisted upon it. She'd been the good girlfriend, even though Ethan stood her up and forgot to call her all the time.

But since this trip started, something inside her had changed. Somehow she'd woken up and started living her own life, and despite feeling a little bad about lying and breaking the rules, Becca loved it. Could it have anything to do with meeting Nikolai? A warm happiness filled her.

She had to get out of this tour. But she couldn't think of any way to do it.

A few minutes before the group was to meet on the dock, she gathered her sunglasses and audio box and left the boat to break the bad news to Nikolai. Maybe he'd come up with a way to get her out of it.

A warm breeze welcomed her on the docks. It would have been a perfect day to take off with him. Four other boats were docked at port, lined up end to end. People from various boats milled around the long, wide walkway, searching for their group, or heading off for a day on their own. Becca envied their freedom.

Lining the port walkway was a tall brick wall with shops and buildings beyond. She couldn't see where Nikolai might have parked his motorcycle.

What if he wasn't even here? What if he couldn't find

the dock? What if he had trouble getting all the way back to his motorcycle? It was so late last night. She shouldn't have let him leave. Maybe he'd changed his mind and didn't want to see her again. Or, what if something had happened to him?

Becca frantically pushed through the congestion of clueless tourists.

Up ahead, she saw couples and small groups loaded up for the day with their water bottles and knapsacks. She suddenly spotted Nikolai, and her heart leapt. His tall, lanky frame leaned back with his foot and shoulders against the stone wall. He wore his baseball cap and a backpack. Today he wore a muted green T-shirt and cargo shorts that rested low on his hips. He looked good.

But of course he did. He was a prince. She'd actually forgotten about that for a minute. Nervous jitters ran through her.

Nikolai glanced up and aimed his megawatt smile in her direction. She regretted even more what she had to tell him.

He pushed off the wall and walked toward her. "Good morning." He grinned and kissed her cheek.

"We have a problem," she blurted as people passed them by.

"What's wrong?" He took her arm and led her away from the crush.

"My dad's making me go on some stupid tour."

She saw the disappointment on his face and wanted to cry. "I've tried everything. I can't even get Dylan to help me."

He considered the situation. "Well, then I'll just have to come with you."

"What? You can't come on the tour."

"Why not? Look at all these people. Do you really think they know who is supposed to be with them? Plus, no one noticed me at Melk Abbey."

She watched the hordes of nameless, faceless tourists pass by. "This is different from the abbey where we were mixed in with the public. Today's group will be a lot smaller. I don't know what we should do."

"You don't want me to join you?" he asked with a smirk.

She laughed. "Well, you are kind of a know-it-all on tours." She looked into his eyes. Today they resembled the color of an ocean on a sunny day.

"Come on, where do we meet?" He guided her back toward her ship.

Becca held up. "What about Vicky? She knows who you are! She recognized you in the magazine last night."

"That ought to make it even more fun. I'll just have to stay in the back and keep my head down."

"You, not stand out in a crowd? I don't think so. Just don't let Dad and Vicky see us together too often. They'll wonder who the guy is I'm talking to and start asking questions."

"Got it. I'll blend in." He winked at her, and the butterflies in her belly fluttered.

Her nerves danced as she approached their boat. Becca couldn't believe he was going to sneak onto their tour. The crowds had thinned and she easily spotted her dad. She glanced at Nikolai and tilted her head, indicating he should join the other side of the group. He grinned as they parted.

She caught up with her dad and Vicky. "I'm here. Are you happy?"

"Right on time, good," her father said, as if checking off something on his agenda.

Becca scowled. He ignored her and turned to the couple next to him, a man with bushy eyebrows and a protruding belly, the woman wearing a floppy hat, capri pants, and tennis shoes with ankle socks. No doubt Dad and Vicky met them last night while in the lounge at a wine tasting. Becca huffed and walked away.

She looked over at Nikolai, a few people away. He'd put on sunglasses. Now she couldn't see his sapphire eyes or read his thoughts. Becca had to admit that with his sunglasses and unshaven face, he was much harder to recognize. The stubble had grown since she first met him in Vienna three days ago. It gave him a laid-back vibe.

"Please, gather around," said their tour guide, a woman

with a thick German accent, in a raised voice. "Tune your headsets to Channel 10.3."

Becca tuned the audio box that hung from a cord around her neck, but Nikolai didn't have one. She looked at him and frowned. He shrugged and smiled.

"Mine isn't working," said a white-haired, wrinkly woman as she fumbled with the knobs. She reminded Becca of her grandma.

"Let me see." The guide reached for the device. She examined and adjusted it. "You're right. It's not working. I'm sorry. I don't have any extra audio boxes. If you follow me closely, you'll be able to hear me."

"She can use mine." Becca stepped forward, slipping the cord from her neck.

"Oh, that's so sweet. Are you sure?" the older woman asked.

"Absolutely. I don't mind at all." Becca smiled at the appreciation in the woman's eyes. "You take it."

The woman accepted the device. "Thank you so much."

As Becca walked past her father and Vicky on the way back to her spot, they both frowned.

"I told you I wasn't interested in the tour. She'll appreciate hearing it a lot more than I would." A glance at Nikolai showed him fighting back a smile and shaking his head.

"All right then, hello everyone. My name is Lena

and today we will be doing an in-depth walking tour of Regensburg. At the end of the tour, I will bring you back here, so you can either board the ship, or a bus, which will take you upriver for the optional river gorge ride to a centuries-old monastery and a brewery tour." Lena walked, and the group followed like cattle to slaughter.

Becca huffed her resignation, reconsidering Dylan's idea of just walking away. What could her dad do if she did?

"Welcome to Regensburg, the former capital of Bavaria, home of a medieval stone bridge built in the twelfth century. But to the locals the city may be most popular for its Regensburg mustard."

Letting the more enthusiastic tourists pass, Becca lagged to the back of the crowd until she and Nikolai carried up the rear. "Bored yet?"

"I'll never be bored with you around," he said. The corner of his mouth curled.

The group left the dock behind and walked on a wide cobblestone pathway. An occasional bicyclist sped by. The group stopped in front of a building with open-air dining, and their guide spoke again.

"Here is the world's oldest sausage kitchen dating back to the twelfth century. Be sure to stop by and try some before you go. . . ."

Becca rolled her eyes. "I'm sorry our day didn't work out the way we planned."

Nikolai gave her shoulder a warm squeeze. "I don't mind."

The guide continued. "The stone bridge, which is now closed to vehicle traffic, is one of the oldest landmarks in Regensburg. It features sixteen arches and is more than three hundred meters long. There is a beautiful view of the city from the bridge. We'll walk to the center for some spectacular photo opportunities."

The bridge bustled with tourists snapping pictures, joggers, and bikers whizzing past.

Becca focused on the cobblestones as she stepped, but her senses were really only aware of Nikolai standing a few inches away, pretending he didn't know her. Their group had spread out, and her dad and Vicky posed for a picture near the stone railing. Becca imagined them falling into the river. She was still mad and couldn't shake it. She wanted to disappear when they weren't looking and pay the price later.

Reaching the side, Becca placed her hands on the ancient stones and looked out over the Danube. Nikolai joined her.

"Think anyone would notice if we jumped off and swam away?" she asked.

"Somehow I don't think that would work out. But it sure is a nice view," he said.

Becca looked out at the panorama. Across the river, church spires shot tall into the sky. "Yeah, the city does look pretty awesome."

"I wasn't talking about the city."

Becca glanced over to find him gazing at her. "You and your lines, do they work on all the girls?" She laughed and stepped away to look off the other side.

Nikolai grabbed her hand. She yanked it away in case her dad and Vicky were watching.

"Becca! Look out!"

14

She turned her head to look.

Wham!

A bike ran into her at full speed, hitting her first with the tire and then the handlebars slammed into her stomach.

Becca and the bicyclist crashed to the cobblestones.

She lay still. Stunned. The bright blue sky shone above. With the rider and his bike on top of her, she fought to catch her breath.

Her legs felt tangled in the wreckage. Suddenly, the pressure eased as the biker climbed off her and spoke rapidly in a foreign tongue.

People appeared, staring down at her and asking questions she couldn't immediately register.

Someone lifted the bike away, and she sucked in a deep breath.

"Miss? Are you hurt?" a balding man asked.

She started to move. Was she hurt? *Crap.* She better not be.

Nikolai's glorious face appeared and the rest faded away. "Becca, are you okay?" He sounded so worried.

She nodded and whispered, "How's this for a nice view?"

He took her hand in his. "I like the idea of a girl falling at my feet, but this wasn't what I had in mind."

"Rebecca, are you all right?" Her father appeared on her other side and kneeled. Vicky hovered above.

Becca stole a quick glance at Nikolai. "Yeah, I think I am." She released his hand and sat up.

Her dad glared at the biker, who tried to straighten his bike. "That imbecile should know better than to ride through a congested area as if he's in the Tour de France."

She wiped her hands off and noticed a heavy scrape on each of her palms from sliding across the rough, gritty stones. "I wasn't looking where I was going. It was my fault."

"No, it wasn't. There is no reason to be riding that fast. I have a mind to have him ticketed."

Becca tried to stand.

"Here, let me help you." Nikolai held out his hand and gently guided her to her feet, concern etching his face.

"Thanks." She brushed dirt off her shorts. The others gave her a little breathing room. The side of her right leg had a long, red scrape from her impact with the road. She shook out each leg. Her hip hurt where she landed on it. She felt sore, but okay.

"Perhaps we should get you to hospital and have you checked out," Lena said, assessing Becca's injuries.

"No! Seriously, I'm fine."

No way was she going to a hospital. She'd be forced away from Nikolai, and that was not going to happen. She stepped back, stretched her limbs, and shook off the stiffness. "See? Totally fine."

"Becca, you're bleeding," Vicky said.

"Huh? Where?" Becca looked down and, other than some bad scrapes, saw nothing.

Vicky pointed to a trickle of blood on her arm. "Here, on your elbow."

"It's nothing bad. See, it's already stopped. I'm good to go."

"Well, she certainly can't continue the day like this," Vicky insisted.

"You're absolutely right. We'll have to get her back to the ship," her father said, which was about the most concern she'd ever heard out of him other than keeping her grades up and finding a respectable internship.

Then the lightbulb turned on and she saw her chance.

"I would hate for you to miss the day here. You've both been so excited about it. I can get back on my own." She looked at them expectantly and avoided looking at Nikolai, who watched from two steps away.

"What kind of parents would we be if we didn't take you back and make sure you're okay?" Vicky asked.

Becca swallowed back her retort that Vicky wasn't her parent. "Dylan's there. If I need anything, he can help. It'll actually be fun. I should probably relax and lay low anyway. He and I can watch some movies together."

Her father seemed to weigh the options. "Vicky's right, we can't just set you off on your own in this condition."

"Excuse me, sir?" Nikolai stepped forward. "I'd be happy to take your daughter back to the boat. I really don't mind."

Her dad looked at Nikolai as if he'd just sprouted from the ground.

Holy crud. So much for keeping the friendship on the down low. Nikolai angled his body so Vicky couldn't get a good look at him.

"I'm also on the *Bolero*, so it would be no trouble." Nikolai acted the concerned young man out to do a good deed rather than a lovesick teenager wanting to sneak off with the man's daughter.

Becca fought to keep a grin off her face.

Her father studied Nikolai as if he were an ax murderer. "Is that so? I don't recall seeing you. I think it best I escort her."

"Oh my God, Dad! Are you serious? He was at the table across from us at breakfast this morning!"

"He was? I didn't realize." Her father's stance relaxed.

131

Apparently he was now more at ease with the idea.

"Dad. It's not that big of a deal. We're only like a couple of blocks from the boat. I can see it from here. Plus, Dylan will be there."

Vicky touched her father's arm and nodded consent.

"Well, if you both think it's all right, that will be okay."

"I'm glad to help." Nikolai unleashed his charming smile.

Becca turned to Nikolai. "Hi, I'm Becca." She smirked.

"Nice to meet you, Becca. I'm Nick." He coughed down a laugh.

"Well then, that settles it," her dad said.

They said their good-byes and walked away from the tour group, waiting to speak until they were out of earshot.

"Oh my God! Can you believe it? They practically gave us their blessing to hang out together!"

"Are you sure you're okay? That bike plowed into you pretty hard."

Becca glanced back to see the group move on to their next attraction. She and Nikolai took the steps down to the waterfront. He led her to the brick wall, and held her face with both hands.

"Seriously, Becca. Are you feeling okay?"

With a guy like Nikolai around she'd never felt better. "I'm great. How soon can we get out of here?"

"Do you want to go back to the boat and clean up?" He

looked at her scraped legs and the blood on her arm.

"I don't want to go back. What if something happens that stops us? Vicky could call ahead and say they changed their mind and they're taking me to the hospital or something insane. I want to leave now while we can."

Nikolai grinned. "Then let's go!" He kissed her quick on the lips, laced his fingers with hers, and led her to his motorcycle.

Becca clung to Nikolai's waist as they cruised down a peaceful country road, the wind whipping through her hair. He reached down and patted her leg. She rested her head against his back and enjoyed the feel of his lean, taut stomach.

At first she felt self-conscious as she climbed up and sat with her body pressed against his, but after a few terrifying minutes of Nikolai weaving through busy, traffic-laden streets of Regensburg, she relaxed and reveled in this new connection.

After several miles, he turned down a gravel road, driving through woods to a small parking area, and parked the bike in the shade.

Nikolai twisted around in his seat to see her. He removed his shades and hooked them over the neck of his T-shirt. Their bodies brushed together, their faces only inches apart. His eyes danced with joy. He seemed as happy to be free from the rest of the world as she was.

"Oh my gosh, that was amazing. Terrifying, but amazing."

He laughed. "I'm glad you liked it."

"I was so scared at first, because I've never been on the back of a motorcycle, but, I loved it!"

"You can step down, but be careful."

She held on to his shoulders as she stood and swung off. He stepped off and locked up the bike.

"So where are we?" Becca looked around. She liked how the dense trees secluded them from the rest of the world.

Nikolai unstrapped his pack from the cycle. "Well, if the guy from the bar, who drove me back last night, is correct, we're at a little known part of Crystal Lake. Apparently, this is where the locals come when they want to skinny-dip and have sex."

Becca froze. *Oh crap*. "Uh, what?"

He laughed. "I'm kidding. Relax, you're an easy mark."

She let out her breath. She should have known he was messing with her, but part of her found the idea very sexy.

He slung the pack over his shoulder, kissed her on the cheek, and guided them through a narrow path in the woods.

"How was I supposed to know you're kidding? Think about it. I'm an American girl in a foreign country, who took off with a guy I've known for barely two minutes. For all I know, you've kidnapped me and are going to sell me into slavery."

Nikolai raised an eyebrow. "You watch too much television. I've seen that movie. Don't worry. If I were going to sell you into slavery, I would have done it that first day when you got lost in Vienna."

"I wasn't lost. I was just a little turned around." She tripped on a tree root.

Nikolai caught her by the arm and held her steady. "Of course you were." He turned his head but she caught his smirk. "And do you know how to get back to Regensburg and the *Bolero*?"

She nibbled on her lip. Of course, she had no idea.

"That's what I thought. Don't worry, I'll take good care of you." He gave her a quick squeeze.

The shaded trail opened up to a wide sandy beach. The sun shone down on a crystal-blue lake; its waves lapped at the shoreline. A large outcropping of rocks lined each side, creating a secluded alcove.

"This is beautiful." She ran onto the sand. "I've been on the river for days, but never been able to actually touch the water." She kicked off her sandals, ran to the edge, and stepped into the clear lake.

"How's the water?" Nikolai asked, setting his pack near her sandals. He toed off his shoes and joined her.

"It's cool, but nice," she said, as he stepped in.

A light breeze made the warm day comfortable. They waded out until the water was knee-high. The waves had created ridges on the sandy lake bottom.

Nikolai faced her and brushed a lock of hair from her face.

"How are you feeling?" He grasped her hand, lifting her arm to inspect her injured elbow. "You took a really bad fall."

"Well, my hip and elbow are pretty sore, but otherwise, I'm fine. Other than the tread marks and the bike grease on my legs."

"We'll get that washed off." He lifted her hand to his lips, sending butterflies flitting in her stomach.

She sighed. "I've never been better."

"Me either." He leaned down and kissed her, and then pulled away. "Hungry? Want something to eat?"

"Um, sure." She'd rather stand in the lake and make out all day, but food was good, too.

"I hope you like what I brought."

"I can't believe you thought to bring food. When did you have time?"

They swished their way to shore; the water felt like silk against her legs.

"I didn't have much. I talked a guy at a local pub into giving me a ride back to my motorbike last night. I slept next to it, under a tree."

She bet not too many people would believe the Prince

of Mondovia slept outside like a homeless person. "You should have stayed on board ship with me."

"And sleep where?" He raised an eyebrow.

"Up on deck. Under the stars," she offered.

"Well, I slept under the stars, all right. Some bleating sheep woke me at dawn. I rode to Regensburg right away so I'd know where the dock was when you arrived. Then I found some breakfast and some markets."

"You barely slept."

"I don't mind. How about we take our lunch up onto that flat rock so sand stays out of everything. I don't have a towel or a blanket."

"Okay." They climbed over a few boulders and reached a large flat rock that had been warmed by the hot summer sun. She sat and peeked over the edge down to the shimmering water.

"I can't get over how gorgeous this place is. This is what we should be seeing on our tours, not more old cities with stories about people who have been dead for centuries."

Nikolai laughed and unpacked his bag. "We have bread, some cheese, strawberries, a couple of bottles of water, and a Diet Pepsi."

"Where did you get that?" She snatched the soda bottle and held it like a treasure.

"At the store, why?"

"Do you know how hard it is to find a Diet Pepsi in Europe?" She popped it open and took a long drink.

"Yes, actually, I do. I had to hit four different places before I found it."

"How did you know I like it?"

He unwrapped the bread, smoothing the paper to serve as a sort of tablecloth. "I heard you mention it in Budapest."

"Thank you." Could this guy get any more perfect?

"You're welcome." Nikolai set out the strawberries and unwrapped the cheeses.

"You have no idea how nice you are, do you?"

"I'm not nearly as nice as you think. Trust me."

She didn't know why he thought that, but she didn't believe he could be anything but kind. "This looks great."

"It's not much, but I thought it would do the trick. I've got a knife somewhere." He fished around in his backpack and pulled out a small knife.

"What all have you got in there?"

"Not much, actually. A change of clothes, a toothbrush, and a rain jacket."

"That's all you brought? How long were you planning to be gone?"

He tried to slice the bread, but squished it.

"Here, let me do it." She took the knife from his hands and deftly cut into the fresh, crusty bread.

Nikolai leaned back on his hands. "I wasn't thinking very far ahead. Things kind of came to a head and I decided to take a stand. Let's just say my people aren't very happy with me right now."

"Oh? And who are your people? You mean the citizens of Mondovia?"

He chuckled. "No. I don't think the general public cares all that much. I mean my parents, their staff and advisors, my personal secretary, the security detail."

"You have a secretary?" She pictured a sexy young woman in a tight skirt.

"Yes, but not the kind you're thinking of. Dmitri handles all my personal affairs, schedule, and appearances. I'm afraid I've put him in a bad position. My parents expected him to stop me or at least tell my security team where I was going."

"Oh." Becca laid out the bread and then went to work slicing the cheese. Her mouth watered at the savory aroma. She tried to get her head around the idea of a team of people surrounding Nikolai's every move. "Are they looking for you now?"

"I've kind of created a mess. I didn't intend to. I just needed to escape the insanity for a while. I can't live my life the way they want me to. They are so wrapped up in hundred-year-old traditions that they can't see the present."

He popped a strawberry into his mouth. "I called my little sister, Alexi, the other day. Poor kid. She had wanted me to bring her with me."

"How old is she?" Becca knew what it was like to idolize a big brother. Dylan, while often bossy and difficult, was always there when she needed him.

"Fifteen. She asked me to check in while I was gone. Of course, the second she answered her phone, they traced the call to Melk. I didn't realize a cell phone could be traced like that."

"Come on, you're Jason Bourne, you should know that." She placed a slice of cheese on the bread and took a bite. Combined with the beautiful lake setting and great company, the food tasted like paradise.

"Alexi said that everyone's having a fit about all my missed appearances, not to mention the security breach. Which is ridiculous. It's not exactly like there's someone out there trying to shoot me."

"Are you sure?" She looked around at their secluded location. A sharpshooter could easily hide in the thick foliage. Were these the kinds of things he really had to worry about?

"Relax. I'm sure. I'm more likely to be shot by a long-lens camera than a gun-toting madman. And that was part of my holdup in Melk. Someone spotted me there and tipped off the press. Between my impounded motorbike and the paparazzi, I had trouble getting out. So you can blame them that I missed our rendezvous in Passau."

"I may have to write them a strongly worded letter." She handed Nikolai a slice of bread with cheese.

"Thanks. I didn't think I'd have much press trouble. I just wanted to send my parents the message that I'm not going to be the perfect, obedient son anymore doing everything they expect. I'm not going to be another generation that soaks our people of tax dollars so I can live a pampered life of decadence disguised under the purpose of community service. It's a travesty."

"So you're going to change history?"

He picked at his piece of bread. "I don't know. I talk big, but I don't know what I can possibly do to make them change. I have a few ideas on ways to give back to the people and lessen their tax burden, but my father never listens to me. My parents are stuck in the Dark Ages. All I know is that the longer I'm away, the more I don't want to go back."

"Are you saying that you don't want to be king?"

He paused thoughtfully. "I don't know."

They snacked on the small feast Nikolai provided. The flavors of the juicy strawberries popped in her mouth while the creamy cheese seemed to melt on her tongue. "I think this is the best food I've tasted the whole trip."

"Sure hits the spot," he said.

The hot sun burned down; Becca ran her hand over her leg, marred by a long scrape from the bike accident. "The lake is so clear I can see all the way to the bottom. I'd like to wash some of this road burn off. I wish I wore my swimsuit."

"You could . . . you know," he said suggestively, looking at her shirt.

"I am *not* skinny-dipping, so you can wipe that idea from your mind right now."

"Look who's jumping to conclusions. I wasn't suggesting you skinny-dip." He delivered a sly grin. "What I was about to say is that you could swim in your underwear."

"Oh, but—"

"Ut." He held up a finger. "Let me finish. Your underwear probably covers you more than your bathing suit anyway."

She opened her mouth to speak, but then changed her mind. She knew he was secretly laughing at her.

"What? It's a great idea." He smiled devilishly.

"So, you're saying you'd strip down to your undies, right here, in broad daylight."

Nikolai stood and reached between his shoulders, pulled his T-shirt over his head, and dropped it at her feet. "You Americans are so uptight about your bodies."

Becca stared at his strong arms, lean physique, and flat stomach. He began to unbutton his shorts.

Her jaw opened. She wanted to tell him to stop, but even more, she wanted to see if he'd actually drop trou in front of her.

He did.

15

"*I* guess that answers the question of boxers or briefs," she said in disbelief as Nikolai stood before her in nothing but his navy blue underwear. They looked a bit like bike shorts.

"So, you uptight American commoner, are you going to join me or stay on this rock and bake like a turtle in the sun?"

"Well, them there sounds like fighting words where I come from." She exaggerated a hillbilly twang and tried not to look in the region of his skin-hugging underwear.

He laughed.

"You think this American hick hasn't got the guts to show off her lily-white skin?"

"No, actually, I don't." He crossed his arms.

Becca slowly rose to her feet, focusing on Nikolai, whose eyes widened just a little bit at her movement. Was it shock or excitement that she might take his challenge?

She tried to remember which bra and panties she'd put on this morning. *Please don't let it be a thong.*

Keeping her eyes glued to his, she undid the button on her shorts, lowered the zipper, and edged them off her hips until they dropped to her feet. She stepped out of them without breaking eye contact.

"You know, a gentleman would look the other way when a lady disrobes," she said.

He smirked. "Who says I'm a gentleman?"

Aw hell. No words would come and she couldn't back down.

She lifted the edge of her tank top and whipped it off fast.

Nikolai broke eye contact and stared at her lavender bra and pink leopard-print panties.

Becca felt her blush deepen, so in a final act of false bravado she stepped casually past him and jumped off the rock, saving her scream of terror until she was underwater.

"Oh my God, oh my God, that's cold," she yelled the instant she surfaced. "Well, are you coming in or not?"

Without a moment's hesitation he grinned and cannonballed off the rock, splash-landing a couple of feet away.

"*Szent szar, ez a hideg!* You weren't kidding." He swam over. "I guess you aren't an uptight American after all."

She splashed him, trying to pretend that swimming in

her underwear was normal and not an exciting new sensation. "What did you just say?"

He bobbed in the water and grinned. "Holy shit, this is cold."

Becca laughed. "What language was that before?"

"Hungarian."

Nikolai swam closer and put his hands around her waist. She felt exposed and naughty in her underwear and bra, yet her bikini actually would have been more revealing.

"How many languages do you speak?" she asked, floating beside him.

"A lot." Water dripped from his eyelashes, and his smile gleamed in the sunlight. He was so good-looking, but of course, he was a prince. It was hard not to feel like a total toad next to him.

"How many?"

"Five."

"Five! Sheesh, now I really do feel like a stupid American."

"Excuse me, that's *uptight American commoner*." He sent a small splash in her direction.

"Sorry, I forgot. I don't know how you learned all those. I barely passed high school Spanish."

"You don't learn languages in grade school?"

"I think we had a three-week unit on Spanish and French in the fifth grade."

He shook his head. "Now that is the problem with America. They were so busy trying to be a unified country, apart from the rest of the world, that they lost all the languages and traditions from their countries of origin."

"I don't know about that, but I do know that I could never learn so many languages. What all do you speak?"

"Slovak, German, Russian, Hungarian, and French."

"You left out English."

"I guess that makes six then."

"You don't speak Spanish?"

"Not fluently."

"Oh, of course not. I think I'll just float away now, back to my homeland of ignorant commoners."

"Oh, no you don't. You're staying right here." He pulled her into his arms while still treading water. "Have I told you how beautiful you are?"

"Okay, Prince Charming, stop with the pickup lines," she said even though his words sent her insides tingling.

"Can't a guy tell a girl he thinks she's beautiful?"

"Not when it's a line of bull. You just don't want me to feel bad because next to you I'm pretty uneducated. I couldn't even manage learning one language other than English."

"Hey. I don't give a shit about that. Really. Speaking a bunch of languages doesn't make someone a better person. It just means it was crammed down their throat from the time they could speak. It's not every day I meet a girl like you. Someone grounded, who knows what's important to her. You speak your mind. You stand up for what you believe in. That's a lot more noble than what I do."

"This said from a guy swimming in his underwear."

He spit water at her.

Becca dunked him and they splashed each other. They climbed out and decided to try dives into the clear, deep water. Becca went first. She popped up after her dive. "Oh my God!"

"What?" He leaned forward from the rock ledge, his hands on his knees.

She didn't want to tell him what had happened, but she couldn't exactly get out of the water this way either. "My bottoms came off when I dove in."

Nikolai covered his mouth with his hand.

"It's not funny! What am I going to do?" She wanted to curl up in a shell and hide.

"I'll have to go on a diving expedition," he said with more enthusiasm than she liked.

"Stop looking so happy." She wanted to smack the grin off his face, but was too busy praying the water wasn't so clear that he could see her bare bottom.

Nikolai entered the water like an award-winning diver. If a person could die of embarrassment, she'd be floating facedown. He popped up, sucked in some air, and went back to look some more for her leopard-print panties. She thought about trying to swim for the shore and run for cover before he came up again. Instead, she tried to cover herself while treading water.

"Got 'em!" he yelled as he sprang up, his hand held high like a synchronized swimmer, the tiny scrap of fabric in his clutches.

Relieved, she still wanted to hide. "Please, just hand them over."

Triton the sea god swam over with his coveted prize. "What do I get for saving your panties?"

Becca tried not to laugh. "Please." It seemed the safest response.

"You can do better than that," he teased, his eyes sparkling with mischief.

"What did you have in mind?" she asked, afraid of what he might say.

"A kiss."

As Nikolai came nearer, her heart raced. She treaded water nervously. Nikolai floated closer and kissed her gently. Becca had never felt so alive.

When their lips parted, he held her gaze and handed back her panties. She tried to play it cool as she scrambled into them while trying to keep her head above water. With her bottoms back on, they swam to shore and climbed the rocks, tired from swimming in the cool water.

Cold and shivering, Becca lay on the smooth, sun-warmed rock, letting the heat permeate her skin. "Oh, that feels good," she sighed, wanting to put her embarrassment behind her.

Nikolai lay a few inches away. "It does."

The sun beat down, drying their skin. "I could just close my eyes and sleep."

"I won't argue with you there," Nikolai answered, his lids closing.

Nikolai opened his eyes, chilled, as a cloud blocked out the sun. Next to him, Becca slept, her hand curled in his. She smiled in relaxed slumber.

He gently released her hand and looked around. A couple of people lounged on the distant beach and a lone man sat on the sand with a camera aimed straight at Nikolai. The hairs on the back of his neck stood up.

He turned his back to the beach and nudged her. "Becca!"

"Hmm?" She stirred.

"There's a guy on the beach and I'm pretty sure he's taking our picture."

Her eyes sprang open. "What?" She sat up and spotted the man. "You think he's paparazzi?"

"It sure isn't a random tourist aiming a long lens at us. How the hell did he know I was here?" Nikolai slid on his shorts.

"Oh crud." Becca grabbed her clothes and quickly

pulled them on. "You think he's been taking pictures of us sleeping?"

"That and more. Lord only knows how long he's been here." He didn't notice him when they were in the water, but that didn't mean he hadn't been lurking in the trees, snapping pictures.

Nikolai stuffed their leftover lunch items into his backpack. How did this camera-wielding jerk find him? Nikolai had been zigzagging up and down the Danube since he left Melk yesterday afternoon.

Dressed, with everything packed up, they headed for the motorbike. Their path unfortunately forced them to pass the creep with the camera. Nikolai pulled his baseball cap low and hid behind his sunglasses. He led the way with his head down and Becca's hand firmly in his.

"Prince Nikolai, why did you run from the palace?" The photographer, a short, heavyset man with cameras strapped across his chest, snapped pictures and moved closer.

Nikolai picked up the pace, but the man stayed with them, walking backward and taking pictures. This was no official appearance where Nikolai owed the press a friendly smile and kind word.

"Do your parents know where you are?"

He ignored him.

"Your friend is beautiful. Is she the reason you fled? What's her name?"

Nikolai bristled and fought the urge to shove the man to the ground and bust his camera. He glanced at Becca, her face pink with embarrassment. She didn't need to be targeted by this oily loser.

"Have you heard that your sister, Princess Alexi, has gone missing?"

Nikolai hesitated for an instant, but then hurried on. The man was lying. He was sure of it, and he wouldn't let this vile intruder ruin their day.

They reached the bike. He hurried and strapped on the pack and hopped on. Becca climbed up, hugging him from behind. Nikolai liked the feel of her body secure against his. It made him feel better able to protect her.

The photographer kept snapping pictures and wouldn't back off. "There are rumors that you have renounced the throne," he baited.

Nikolai stiffened, but didn't give him the satisfaction of a reaction. He started the engine.

"Where are you going next?"

"Wouldn't you like to know?" Nikolai grinned, revved the engine, and spun gravel as they raced away.

16

Thirty minutes later, Nikolai pulled up to the empty dock with Becca behind him on the bike, her arms wrapped around his waist.

"Oh my God, where's the boat?" Becca cried out.

This morning there had been five riverboats docked. Now there were none. Nikolai frowned at this new wrinkle in their day. "Upriver, I'd say by the looks of it. Any idea where your next stop is?"

"I have no idea. There was an extra tour this afternoon to some gorge," Becca said, her face stricken with panic. "I think the boat was picking up the people from that tour, someplace near there. Why didn't I pay better attention? Maybe Dylan knows."

She fished her phone out of her pocket and looked at the screen. "I have a ton of missed calls from him." She called him back. "He isn't picking up. Dylan, where the hell is the boat?" she shouted into the phone. She turned and looked at Nikolai, a hint of desperation on her face. "What are we going to do?"

"I guess we better keep going and see if we can find the *Bolero*. It's not like it can go anywhere but upriver." He patted her leg and kissed her. "We'll find it sooner or later." Nikolai put the cycle in gear and they took off.

They battled rush hour traffic on the outskirts of Regensburg. Every stoplight grated Becca's nerves. How was she going to explain missing the boat to her dad?

They cruised along the road that ran parallel to the river. Each bend gave her new hope they'd find the *Bolero* around the curve, but time and again, she only found disappointment. Just as she was about to give up hope and assume the boat had vanished forever, they entered the city of Kelheim.

"There it is!" She pointed to a couple of boats docked on the other side of the river.

Nikolai nodded, gunned the engine, and they flew down the pier. The only bridge in sight was upriver a half mile past the dock. After crossing the bridge and cruising back toward the dock, Nikolai took the turnoff and cruised past the parking lot and right onto the wide dock; there was no time to lose.

She spotted the *Bolero*, and leaning against one of the mooring pillars, Dylan.

Nikolai pulled up and turned off the bike.

"Nice of you to show," Dylan said, checking his watch. "You two have a nice day?"

Becca wasn't sure if he was angry or impressed. "Um, yeah," she answered. Nikolai nodded.

Dylan grinned. "Good. I covered for you and Nikolai. I told Vicky you were at the napkin-folding demonstration. So, I think the least you could do is return the favor."

"Oh, thank you! Yes, I'll cover for you," Becca said, thankful to be back and not in trouble.

Dylan pushed away from the mooring and waited as they stepped off the motorcycle.

"I met some students from Kiev today and they're going to hear some band at a festival tonight. I was thinking it would be pretty awesome if Nikolai wanted to trade places for the night."

Becca shot a curious glance at Nikolai, who removed his sunglasses and nodded his interest. "You want Nikolai to come aboard in your place?"

"Exactly," Dylan said.

"And how am I supposed to hide him from Dad and Vicky at dinner?"

"No problem. They ate some bad sausage today and are holed up in their private throne room. If you know what I mean." He grinned at Nikolai. "You don't have to go to dinner, at least not with them. You could always eat in the bar instead."

"I don't know. That doesn't sound like a very smart idea. Plus, how would you get back to the boat?"

A devilish smirk crossed Dylan's face. "That's where Nikolai comes in. Can I borrow your motorcycle?"

Nikolai started.

"Dylan, you can't take his cycle!"

"Why not? He'll be safely tucked away, you two can have more time together, and I'll get to go party. I'll be back in the morning, and no one will be the wiser."

Alone with Nikolai. All night. Part of her was thrilled with the idea, the other part terrified. "But what about the front desk? Don't you think they're going to notice Nikolai coming aboard, or you showing up in the morning?"

"I've got it covered. The desk clerk, Natalie, and I have an understanding. She's got my back." He grinned again.

"I don't even want to know what that's about," Becca said.

"So what do you think?" He turned to Nikolai.

A crooked smile appeared on Nikolai's face. "Sounds like fun to me." He tossed his keys to Dylan, who caught them easily.

Becca couldn't believe Dylan had just made this plan, and now she was spending the night with Nikolai. Her heart beat with nervous anticipation.

"You're the best! Now, just so we have this straight. Don't screw with my sister. Got it?" Dylan fixed Nikolai with a serious brotherly stare.

"My intentions with Becca are totally . . ."

"Honorable, yeah, whatever. Just don't make me have to mess up your pretty face. I don't want to get thrown in some dungeon by your daddy."

Nikolai laughed and unhooked his bag from the back of the cycle. "Got it. By the way, you may find some irritating paparazzi on your tail."

"I hope so. I could have some fun with that."

With her heart pounding, Becca snuck Nikolai into her room.

She tossed her room key on the dresser and turned to face him. Now that she had him here, what should she do? What did he want to do? Her eyes drifted to the bed. She turned her back to it.

Nikolai dropped his backpack on the floor near the dresser. "The paparazzi will have a hard time tracking me here when my motorbike is headed out of town."

She laughed. "You sure look satisfied with yourself."

"Come on, I couldn't have planned this better myself." Nikolai opened the sliding door and looked over the railing he'd climbed the night before.

She joined him. Outside, the crew removed the thick ropes that anchored the giant boat. "Dylan wasted no time in taking off."

"That's fine with me. I never dreamed I'd get to spend so much time with you." He rested his elbows on the railing, leaned over, and kissed Becca lightly on the lips.

The boat drifted from the dock. The engine rumble caused the room to vibrate ever so slightly.

"So what do you want to do?" He flashed his eyebrows suggestively.

Becca chewed on her lip. She liked Nikolai a lot, but she didn't know him all that well. "I don't know. What do you want to do?"

"I'm teasing, Becca."

"I know," she said, as if she hadn't been a little on edge about spending the night alone with him.

"Actually, would it be okay if I grabbed a shower and borrowed some of your brother's clothes? I've been wearing these shorts for a few days and I'd love to wash them out."

She relaxed. "Sure. It's the least Dylan can do since he basically stole your motorcycle." She went to a dresser and pulled open a drawer with clothes crammed in. "Here, pick out whatever you need. Sorry, Dylan's such a slob."

"No problem." Nikolai selected a couple of items and disappeared into the tiny bathroom.

Minutes later, he came out refreshed and traded places with Becca. She took a long shower, dried her hair, and put on makeup before she reappeared.

"You look great," he said.

"Thanks." Her cheeks heated. There was a long silence.

"So, now what? Do you want to get out of here?"

"I know Dylan said that my dad and Vicky are sick, but

I don't want to take a chance and run into them."

"You don't have to worry about that. Remember this morning, when I said I was on the *Bolero*, too?"

"I forgot about that."

"As long as they don't demand to see Dylan or burst in and find me in your room, I think we're in the clear."

"You're so smart. Must be all that princely wisdom."

He rolled his eyes and held out his hand. "Come here."

Becca joined him. He wrapped his arms around her and kissed her nice and slow. The touch of his lips ignited her. Nikolai released her, but leaned his forehead against hers. "We should go get something to eat. You are far too tempting."

She hid her disappointment; he had more control than she did. She wouldn't mind staying in the room all night and making out. Thank God he had manners, because she was a yo-yo of wanting to get closer and afraid that they'd get too close.

"Okay, do you want to brave the dining room with a hundred and eighty strangers or the lounge with only a handful of people?" she asked.

"Let's do the lounge. I'd rather not take a chance of being recognized."

"Lounge it is."

They avoided most of the guests and enjoyed a light dinner of warm buttered rolls and spicy Hungarian goulash. As the other passengers began to wander in for after-dinner drinks, she and Nikolai snuck up on deck to watch the stars pop out as the sun melted over the horizon.

They lay on side-by-side lounge chairs and held hands.

"So, your trip ends the day after tomorrow?" he asked. She heard the disappointment in his voice, and it echoed the ache in her heart.

"It does? I was thinking we had one more day." She sighed, not wanting to think about leaving him yet. Her time with Nikolai had been so perfect. How would she possibly say good-bye?

"While you were in the shower I saw the trip itinerary next to the TV. Tomorrow you dock in Nuremberg, there are tours for the day, and then you disembark the next day."

"That's too soon," she groaned. "I can't imagine never seeing you again. But wait!" She sat upright. "We're taking a side trip to Munich after the cruise."

"You want me to follow you to Munich?"

"Would you?"

"I don't know." He stared at the stars above. "I love the idea of chasing you around Europe, but at some point I need to figure out how to get my life under control, before I create an international incident."

Didn't he want to keep seeing her? She thought he liked her as much as she liked him. Maybe she was wrong. She shivered as the air cooled. "What are you going to do?"

"Come here." He scooted over and reached for her. Becca climbed into his lounge chair.

"I honestly don't know. The longer I stay away from the palace, the harsher things will be when I go back; but the longer I stay away, the less I *want* to go back."

She snuggled into his warm side, trying to imagine going home to a palace. Was it warm and lavish, or cold and lonely?

"I wish you could come home to the States with me. Except I have to start college in a few weeks, not that I even want to go." She paused. "Oh, I know! Let's run away and travel the world. We can hike, stay in hostels, and see the Seven Wonders of the World."

"I've always wanted to see the giant leatherback turtles in Costa Rica, maybe volunteer, stay in a little shack somewhere, and drink cold beer on the beach."

"Really? I think my mom spent time in Costa Rica. I've heard it's amazing." She sighed. "I wish I could run away. My dad would have a coronary if I didn't go to college. I'm not even going to a college I want. I'm going to Northwestern, but I really wanted to go to my mom's alma mater, the University of Wisconsin."

Nikolai laced his fingers with hers, linking them closer. "In a way, your life doesn't sound that different from mine."

"Except that your dad wants you in the military and that's a whole lot scarier than a college campus." She refused to picture Nikolai carrying a weapon.

"I just don't know how to stand up to him and refuse. I don't think he's capable of seeing the monarchy any differently than it's always been."

"That's crazy. The world is changing so much every day."

"I know. If my country doesn't do something to keep up, Mondovia will become obsolete."

"Maybe you're the person who's supposed to change that."

"Ha. That's funny. I can't manage to speak my mind to my own father without running away like a child. I don't see myself making any major changes to our country." He sighed.

She sensed his hopelessness and wished there was something she could do to help.

"You shouldn't be so hard on yourself. Taking off like this might be exactly what you needed to get a new perspective on things. Maybe you'll go back with a fresh approach that you haven't considered before."

He played with a lock of her hair. "If there's one thing I can say about you, it's that you're an eternal optimist."

She shrugged. "I can't help it. It's the only way I know how to get through the bad stuff."

"You know, if I were ever given the chance, I think I could make a positive difference in Mondovia. There are so many things I would change. I think the country is ready for it. It's just the leadership that isn't."

"I think you will make it a better country, when you get your chance."

"Thank you for the vote of confidence. I appreciate it." He turned to her, leaned down, and kissed her, his kisses sending her over the moon. They lay entwined on the lounge chair making out. Becca lost herself in the perfect world where a handsome prince sweeps an average American girl off her feet.

Light rain began to fall, cooling down their heated bodies.

"Come on, let's get out of here before the heavens let loose," Nikolai said.

They rushed off the deck and back to the cabin.

Becca was dreaming of meeting a prince named Nikolai and that she snuck him into her room on a river cruise vacation. A tapping noise drew her from her groggy sleep.

Her eyes popped open, and she recognized the walls of her stateroom. Becca glanced over to discover that her dream was also her reality. Nikolai lay stretched out on her brother's bed, the sheets a tangle around him, exposing his chest. He slept with one arm stretched over his head.

She bit back her smile. There was a man in her room, and not just any man. The Prince of Mondovia!

The tapping continued and she realized someone was at the door. She peeked at the clock. Eight a.m. She hesitated a moment, then realized it must be Dylan, back from his wild night.

Nikolai stirred and looked in her direction. His warm, sleepy smile greeted her.

"Good morning," she said, feeling tingly inside as she got up to check the door.

"Morning. Who's at the door?"

"It's got to be Dylan. He probably lost his key again," Becca said, looking back. She opened the door, and her heart nearly stopped.

Her dad glanced up from peering at his phone. "Good morning, Becca. Did I wake you?"

17

Becca pictured half-naked Nikolai lounging in Dylan's bed. Crap! She stepped forward and pulled the door almost closed so her dad couldn't see in the room.

"Uh, yeah. We were up really late talking." Which technically wasn't a lie.

"Vicky and I wanted to get an early start as it's our last day of the cruise. Nuremberg has a lot of World War II history, and after missing half of yesterday, we don't want to waste a minute."

She fought to keep calm and act normal, but wondered if Nikolai could hear, and if he was as panicked as she.

"Okay, well I guess Dylan and I will explore on our own."

"Before we take off, Vicky suggested I check out how you're feeling after that run-in with the biker yesterday."

He pushed the door wide open and brushed past Becca into the cabin.

Becca rushed to defuse the explosion that was about to ignite.

"Where's Dylan?" he asked, looking at the bed Nikolai had been sleeping in moments earlier.

She frantically searched the cabin, but didn't see any signs of him. "Um, ah, he's in the bathroom."

"Oh. I have a few minutes to spare." Her dad sat on Dylan's bed and looked around the cabin, taking in every detail.

Becca's eyes flashed from one corner of the room to the other. Was Nikolai in the bathroom? Or was he hanging from the rail outside the room? She even glanced up to see if he was perched on the ceiling like Spider-Man.

"You don't have to, Dad. Sometimes he's in there a long time."

"I've barely seen the two of you the last few days. You know, Vicky was really hoping that this trip would bring us all closer. I guess we're not much for family time."

What was Becca supposed to say? He hadn't made an effort to be a part of his kids' lives since her mom died. She had no interest in getting closer to Vicky. The woman was just someone her dad married to fill the void.

"Yeah, it's been a crazy trip," she offered, unsure what else to say. Then she realized Nikolai's shoes lay in plain sight. Would her dad recognize that they weren't Dylan's?

He sighed. "That it has. So are you okay after that bike crash yesterday?"

"I'm fine. Just a couple of bruises."

The longer her dad stayed the more Becca wondered what other evidence of Nikolai might be lying around. His Vienna hat lay on the dresser, his clothes were neatly folded on the chair, his backpack leaned against the dresser.

"You got some sun," her dad said.

Becca touched her cheek. She'd forgotten that a day at the lake would leave evidence. "Oh, yeah. I fell asleep up on deck."

"Well, at least you got some fresh air."

"So, where's Vicky?" Becca prompted, hoping this would help get him out of the cabin before he discovered Nikolai popping out of the bathroom.

"She forgot her lip balm and is meeting me in the lobby. We're taking the early bus into the city center. Did you know Nuremberg was totally destroyed in World War II, but all the artwork was saved? It was stored belowground in the barrel room of the breweries."

Becca stared at him dumbfounded. "Ah, no. I didn't know that. Well, I don't want to hold you up."

Suddenly the cabin door opened and Dylan strolled in with rumpled clothes and bloodshot eyes.

"I thought you were in the bathroom," her dad said.

Becca forced a smile at Dylan and tilted her head toward the bathroom.

"Ah, no. I stepped up on deck to get some early morning pictures. It's going to be another gorgeous day," he said brightly.

Their dad's eyes settled on Dylan's camera lying on the dresser next to the Vienna baseball cap. "But your camera is right here," he said.

Dylan didn't miss a beat. "Yeah, I know. I forgot it, so I used my phone. Would you like to see some? They turned out pretty good." He pulled his phone from his pocket.

"No. There will be plenty of time to look at pictures when we get home. I just stopped by to let you and Becca know that Vicky and I would like you to join us at eleven for the city tour, and then we'll catch lunch right after near the marketplace."

"Sounds good. We'll be there." Dylan dropped onto his bed and leaned back against the headboard.

"I better go. Vicky's probably waiting for me in the lobby. We'll see you in a couple of hours."

"Great." Becca hustled him toward the door. "Have fun."

The second her dad passed over the threshold, Becca shut the door. She found Nikolai cautiously peeking out from the bathroom.

"Oh. My. God," Becca said, lightly banging her head

against the wall. "I thought I was going to have an aneu-rysm."

Nikolai entered the room in his underwear, went straight to the chair, and slipped into his shorts. Dylan arched an eyebrow.

"Did you really have pictures from the top deck?" Becca asked, trying to ignore the bare-chested prince.

Dylan laughed. "Hell no. The pictures are from the concert last night and of Yuri and Andre doing shots of Russian vodka."

"So the concert was a good time?" Nikolai asked, pull-ing on his shirt.

"It was epic." Dylan pulled out the cycle keys and tossed them to Nikolai. "Thanks for the wheels. I parked it in the lot next to the dock."

"My pleasure," Nikolai said, smiling at Becca.

"Before I do anything else, I need a shower and food." Dylan dragged himself into the bathroom.

Nikolai stood dressed and prepared to leave, his expres-sion bleak.

Becca's heart ached at the thought of saying good-bye. "I can't believe this is the last day. I don't want this to end."

"I can't imagine tomorrow without you. I never knew I could fall for someone so fast." Nikolai wrapped his arms around her.

Dylan returned from the bathroom. "I'm glad to hear that, because if you two are up for it, I have a plan that might buy you a few more days."

Becca perked up. "Seriously? Dylan, you better not be kidding."

"Yuri and Andre were telling me about how they've been touring Europe and staying in hostels. They invited me to join them in Amsterdam."

"So how does that help me?" Becca asked.

"Because I figure the only way Dad and his ball and chain will let me go is if you come, too."

"To Amsterdam?"

"Or wherever you feel like going. The way I see it is that if we present this as a brother and sister wanting to join other students and backpack Europe for a few days and stay in hostels, it'll be impossible for Dad to refuse. Heck, Vicky's been pushing the idea all trip. It'll be hard for them to say no. Plus, do you really think they want to be stuck with us in Munich? I'm sure Dad is so over playing the daddy figure by now."

"So if we can get Dad to agree, then you go to Amsterdam and Nikolai and I go wherever we want?" She couldn't believe this might actually work.

Dylan nodded.

"That's so perfect. What do you think?" she asked Nikolai, anxious to see if he was as happy about it as she was.

He grinned. "I've never been to Prague, and it's only a couple of hours from here."

"Should we go?" she asked.

"Whoa, back the truck up," Dylan said. "First we have to convince them. What time are we supposed to meet Dad?"

"Eleven."

"Well then. We've got two hours to figure this out."

Becca laughed to herself as Dylan, who never kept to a schedule, arrived for the walking tour promptly at eleven and went straight to work.

"Hey, Dad. What do you think of Nuremberg?"

"Dylan. Nice to see you on time." Her father nodded. "We toured the Palace of Justice. Absolutely fascinating. You know my grandfather served here in World War II."

Dylan walked alongside him. "I knew he served, but I didn't know it was here."

Becca followed with Vicky, trying to act relaxed, when in reality she couldn't wait for Dylan to get on with it and ask about their side trip.

An hour later, their verbose guide finally finished his rambling. The tour ended in an open square with a marketplace and an ancient gold fountain. The guide stood on the steps of the fountain, dwarfed by its height. A black wrought-iron fence protected the fountain from the public.

"I hope you have enjoyed Nuremberg and are able to spend more time in this beautiful city. We end our tour here at the der Schöner Brunnen. This sixty-foot-tall fountain was originally erected in the 1300s and was replaced by this replica in 1902. Notice the gold rings attached to the wrought-iron fence. Legend says if you turn a ring three times, it will bring you good luck."

"Go ahead, Becca, give it a try," Vicky said.

Becca normally would have passed on the good-luck symbols, but if this helped get her dad to say yes to her trip, it was worth a little superstition. She grasped the three-inch ring and turned it three times, thinking of Nikolai with each turn and wondering how his morning was and what he was doing.

They waited as Vicky tried her luck, too. "I hope it works. Now how about some lunch?" she asked, leading the way. "The ship's concierge recommended a place not far from here. It's known to be the world's oldest sausage restaurant."

"I thought the place we saw yesterday was the world's oldest sausage restaurant," Becca said.

"I think they say whatever will bring in more customers. I guarantee you I won't be eating any more sausages," her father added.

The quaint restaurant featured outdoor seating under a large tree with lights dangling like icicles. Becca didn't even taste the food as she ate, because Dylan still hadn't asked their dad if they could go off on their own. Everything depended on this. If he said no, this would be her last day with Nikolai. Probably forever.

"So, Dad, I met some students from your alma mater yesterday who are backpacking through Europe." Dylan took a drink of his beer.

Finally.

"Harvard students, you don't say?" Her dad nodded approval.

Point for Dylan. Nice one!

Vicky lit up. "Backpacking through Europe is one of my favorite college memories. Every student should have that experience."

"Funny you should mention that because they actually invited me to join them."

Becca watched silently, bouncing her leg under the table.

Dylan took a bite of his pretzel and proceeded to talk with food in his mouth. "At first I told them no, I couldn't swing it. We're leaving for Munich tomorrow. But then I got to thinking, heck, we're here right now. This might be the best time to try out this whole hostel thing that Vicky keeps mentioning."

Their father stared over his glasses at Dylan and took a bite of sauerkraut. He washed it down with a swig of beer. "That's right. We have train tickets tomorrow and reservations for the next three nights."

"I know, but after learning more about World War II and that my great-grandfather served here, I was thinking that this would be a perfect chance for Becca and me to explore more of the area."

Her dad glanced at her. She tried to appear interested and positive without looking desperate.

Vicky chimed in. "You want Becca to join these students you met and travel together?"

"Exactly. Becca's going off to college soon and I'll be doing internships next summer. We may never get another chance to travel together."

"Becca, what do you have to say about this?" her dad asked.

She set down her fork. "Well, when we started this vacation, I really didn't want to come, but now that I've spent time here, I feel like I'm getting a new understanding of Europe and what the people have gone through."

She took a sip of soda, hoping her nerves didn't show. "Like the tour today, about how the whole city was destroyed and the United States helped rebuild it after the war. And to think we're related to someone who was a part of that time. It's pretty amazing. Plus, I rarely see Dylan anymore, and it would be great to have this experience with him."

"I'm glad you've improved your attitude," her dad started, "but as I said, we have tickets to depart in the morning. It makes no sense to change our plans now just because Dylan found an offer he likes better. Knowing your brother, these students have been manufactured in his head so he can go off with another skirt."

"No, Dad, I'm not lying, they do exist. They're taking the train up. There are four students, and I can introduce you to them this afternoon." He shot Becca a panicked look.

"Vicky, what do you think?" Becca asked, hoping she'd be on their side for once.

Vicky cleared her throat. "Well, I think the idea of traveling with other students is wonderful."

"See!" Dylan said.

"However, this whole trip is about family time and we haven't really enjoyed much togetherness. I think what your father is trying to say is that he'd like to spend more time with the two of you. In Munich, we have our own flat. It'll just be the four of us exploring the city together."

Vicky noticed Becca's crestfallen face. "Don't worry, there will be other trips. You're young."

Becca's time with Nikolai circled the drain. How could she have him follow her to Munich when it would be family 24/7? This meant that all she and Nikolai had left was this afternoon and tonight. It wasn't enough. She wasn't ready to say good-bye.

"So what? You're not letting us go?" Dylan asked, in disbelief.

"No, Dylan. For once in your life you can't go," their father said. "You get away with an awful lot. Vicky worked very hard on this trip to try to bring the family together.

I think you can think about someone other than yourself just this once."

Becca cringed. They hadn't been a family since her mom died. When her dad married Vicky, it did more to drive them apart than bring them together.

Dylan shoved away from the table.

"Where do you think you're going?" her dad asked.

"To tell my friends that you crapped all over our plans." Dylan stalked away from the table.

Becca grabbed her bag and followed.

"We aren't finished here, young lady," her dad commanded.

"Becca, aren't you going to join us this afternoon?" Vicky asked in a gentler voice.

"No, I think I'll spend the day with Dylan." She gave her dad a murderous glare.

18

$Nikolai$ sat in the back corner of the internet café. While Becca and Dylan negotiated with their father to stay in Nuremberg, he decided to check in on his real life.

For the most part, he'd avoided the press, but things had slowly been escalating with the paparazzi on his tail. He didn't like the comments the photographer made yesterday. It was time to find out what was really happening in Mondovia. He started broad and typed his name into the search engine.

A long trail of news stories popped onto the screen. He knew about the couple of gossip rag covers, but he had no idea the news of his disappearance had gone viral.

He scrolled down the news feed, scanning the articles. The palace confirmed that Nikolai was on holiday, but offered nothing more. It must have pained his parents to admit that much. There were reports of all the official events he'd stood up and how the palace had to scramble to send someone else, a lesser important dignitary, in his place.

There were more pictures taken by the paparazzi that he hadn't seen. Of him leaving the lot where his motorbike had been impounded in Melk, of him and Becca goofing off at the lake, jumping off the rocks, and kissing in the water. He rubbed his hand through his hair.

He really didn't want to bring sweet Becca into his mess. She had no idea how nasty it could get.

Then another headline caught his eye. *Princess Alexandra Goes Missing*. Nikolai's heart nearly stopped. He clicked on the article, desperate to know it was all lies, but it wasn't. The photographer yesterday had told the truth.

He leaned close to the monitor and read.

Princess Alexandra mysteriously disappeared Thursday night from the king's box at the Teatro Massimo's opening night performance of Rigoletto. *For three hours, security locked down the opera house and scoured over every inch. Buildings within a five-block radius were also checked. Three hours later, the princess was located at a nearby mall eating gelato.*

Nikolai wanted to wring Alexi's neck. What the heck was she thinking? Anything could have happened. But then he realized he was most likely the reason she took off. What had he started? He'd have a serious chat with Alexi when he returned. It was one thing for him to run off, but entirely different for her. She was still young and not nearly as aware of the risks.

He knew he needed to get home soon and calm this maelstrom he'd created, but he also couldn't give up the chance to spend a couple more days with Becca. Once he went back, he'd be back for good and would literally turn his life over to the crown. His gut ached at the thought.

Becca was the best thing that had happened to him in a long time. It made no sense, and yet deep down, it made all the sense in the world. She brought a lightness to his life that hadn't been there before. She saw the world through fresh eyes, gorgeous deep brown eyes that he lost himself in.

But once he said good-bye to her, it would likely be forever.

After lunch, Becca was finally able to meet up with Nikolai. He whisked her away to a park filled with lush gardens, soft grass, and a lake with small sailboats whipping about. They sat under a large shade tree.

Becca's heart ached. She leaned against Nikolai's chest, warm in his embrace. "I can't believe we have to say good-bye."

Nikolai kissed her hair. "I really thought we'd get a

couple more days together. I can't get my head around the fact that I'll never see you again."

"Don't say that. You're going to make me cry." Her throat tightened as she fought to hold back a flood of tears.

"Please don't." He stroked her hair. "You'll be starting university in a few weeks. That will keep you busy. You'll forget all about me in a matter of days."

"How can you say that? I'll never forget you. Ever. And I'm not even looking forward to college. I don't know what I want to do with my life. College seems like such a waste when I have no direction. I feel so lost."

They stared out at the shimmering lake. After a minute, Becca broke the silence. "There must be some way to see each other, isn't there?"

He didn't say anything, but she already knew the answer. They would try for a while, but the reality was that they were from different parts of the world, with very different lives.

Becca continued. "You have all my info in your new phone. We can call each other and email." She held his hand in hers and trailed her fingers over his palm, trying to remember every detail about him.

Nikolai sighed, sounding defeated. "We can try, but I'm afraid that as soon as I return to Mondovia, my parents will either put me on lockdown, or ship me off to boot camp before I create any more media problems. In either case, I won't have much access to a phone for a while. I'm afraid that I won't be leaving Mondovia again for a very long time."

He pulled her close and didn't speak. She shared his anguish.

"How can they be so cruel? Don't they realize this is your life?" His parents were taking away every option of them seeing each other again. Even if she could figure out a way to return to Europe, he'd be far from her reach.

"No, they don't see it that way. They've dedicated their lives in service to the crown. They expect me to do the same."

"That is so wrong. You have to do something. You can't let them force you to do things you don't want."

"Right. And how should I do that? Run off again, get myself an apartment, and try to find a job?"

"Sure, why not?"

"For starters, I don't have too many skills other than shaking hands, playing polo, and fencing."

"If you could do anything, what would it be?"

Nikolai played with a lock of her hair. "I'd love to live a normal life for a while, and travel on my own without advisors and security. When I took off, which I had to do because I was suffocating, I met you."

He caressed her arm with the pad of his thumb. His sad blue eyes gazed into hers. "Beautiful, feisty Becca getting lost in foreign countries and not even worried about it. You are so fearless. I couldn't have wished in a million years to meet someone as perfect as you."

Becca shook her head in disbelief. Nikolai lifted her face to his.

"I thought I was running away, but it turns out I was running to you. Becca, you've made my life worth living again and now I have to leave you. This is killing me. I've never felt this way about anyone before. Ever." He held her tighter and kissed her temple.

"How can you say that when you've been surrounded by so many girls from titled families?"

"It's probably because of that. Anytime I meet a girl, I never know if she is scheming to become the next princess of Mondovia or if she just wants to kiss a prince. You're the real deal, Becca."

Becca wanted to weep with joy. She didn't know he felt so strongly, which made saying good-bye even worse. "I must say, I rather like kissing a prince."

She tilted her face up and he obliged her. She'd never been so happy and sad at the same time. Nikolai was unlike any guy she'd ever met. He wasn't an immature kid who thought more about garage bands and souped-up cars than he did about his girlfriend. Nikolai had humor and a generous spirit. Even though he lied about his identity, she understood now how difficult it must be for him to have the world think of him only as a crown prince.

After a short ride back to the boat, Becca tried to hold

herself together as Nikolai led her toward the dock and the *Bolero*. Neither trusted themselves to speak. They'd decided to say good-bye here, tonight, and put each other out of their misery. She would be disembarking early the next morning and there would be too much chaos for more than a quick farewell.

They stopped near a light pole. Nikolai faced her, linking his fingers with hers. "God, Becca. I can't imagine tomorrow without you," he whispered and leaned his forehead against hers.

Becca fought back her tears. This was it. In another few minutes he'd be gone and she'd never set eyes on him again. He'd changed her life so much in less than a week.

"Oh, Nikolai, I don't want to leave you." She released his hands and hugged him, afraid she'd forget the touch of his body, his musky scent, and the feel of his strong arms around her.

He cradled her head against his chest then tilted her chin up and kissed her tenderly.

She sighed against him. "I know I'm not supposed to say this, but I'm going to. I've felt it for a while, but kept pretending it wasn't real. If I don't say this now, I may never get another chance.

"I love you, Nikolai. I really do." She kissed his lips. "I hope that doesn't freak you out."

Nikolai gazed at her with adoring eyes and held her

face in his hands. "Oh, Becca, I was afraid it was only me. I love you, too." He kissed her again, and then pulled her into the comfort of his arms.

Tears rolled freely from her eyes, dampening his shirt. He loved her, too! With this revelation, her pain multiplied. This was like an old fairy tale played out in modern times. The prince falls in love with a commoner, and they are ripped apart. Only this was worse, because it was happening to her.

With her face pressed against his chest, she could feel the beat of his heart. His chin rested against her cheek. The end of their world was coming and she couldn't stop it.

"Becca!" She heard her name called in the distance. Panic struck. She wasn't ready to say good-bye. "Nikolai, I can't go yet. It's too soon."

"I know," he whispered in her ear and held her close.

"Becca!" She recognized Dylan's voice.

She didn't want her brother to see her a sloppy, emotional mess. She looked at Nikolai with damp eyes. "He's not going to go away."

"It's going to be okay," Nikolai said, wiping away her tears.

She called out. "Yeah, Dylan, I'm coming. Just give me a sec." She sniffled and tried to dry her cheeks. Nikolai gazed at her with such love. How could he be so strong when his future would be so bleak?

"Hey, guys," Dylan said. "Oh, sorry." He sobered when he saw Nikolai's pained expression and Becca's tearstained face.

"Hi, Dylan," Nikolai said in a subdued voice.

"What's up?" Becca asked, drawing a calming breath.

"Dad got a call from his office. They've been trying to reach him for a couple of days. Apparently some important negotiations are falling apart, and they need him back at work right away."

"We're leaving tonight?" Could things get any worse?

"No, tomorrow. I wanted to make sure you knew in case you were hoping to meet up in Munich."

"So instead of going to Munich, we're going home?"

"That's the plan. Except Vicky couldn't get all of us on the same flight at such last-minute notice. She and Dad leave here first thing. You and I don't fly out until the afternoon."

"Then I could see you tomorrow for a while after all," Nikolai said.

More time together was definitely good news, but it was far from good enough. It was like pouring salt in the inevitable wound of saying good-bye. She forced a weak smile.

"You knew you'd have to say good-bye eventually," Dylan said.

"I know. It just sucks." She had a connection with Nikolai that she couldn't bear to break. "What time do we fly out tomorrow?"

"Four twenty in the afternoon. Why?"

Becca chewed on her bottom lip and glanced from her brother to Nikolai and back. "What if we missed the plane?"

Dylan stared at her. "Are you serious?"

"Dead serious," she said.

Her brother broke into a huge grin. "Now that's my kind of thinking! Becca, you make me proud." He fist-bumped her.

"What are you saying?" Nikolai narrowed his eyes.

She turned to him. "I'm saying that we could spend more time together if you still want to."

"Really? Because you shouldn't tease a guy like that."

"What are they going to do about it? They won't know we aren't on the plane until they get home."

Dylan laughed. "You are evil, little sister."

Becca shrugged. "Life's too short not to have fun, right?"

"I think your brother and I have been a bad influence, but I'm not going to talk you out of it."

"I can't believe we're really going to miss our plane on purpose!"

Nikolai pulled her in for a hug. "This is the best news ever. So when will you leave?"

"I don't know. What do you think, Dylan?"

"You know what they say: go big or go home. I say we stick to our original plan. I'll go to Amsterdam and you can go wherever it was you wanted to go. We can have the airline tickets rebooked for three days from tomorrow. I'll put it on my credit card."

"And I have mine, too, if we need it. This is totally going to work."

"I've got to go call my friends and see if I can still join them. I'll catch you later." Dylan walked away with a bounce in his step.

Relief washed over Becca. She gazed at Nikolai, so amazed she had just won a few more days with him. "I don't have to leave you, yet." They both grinned like a couple of idiots.

"No, you don't. Still want to go to Prague?" he asked.

"Sounds perfect."

19

The next morning, tour buses and shuttle vans pulled in and out of the drive next to the pier, carrying all of the *Bolero* passengers to their next destinations. Vicky fretted over Becca while the cab driver loaded all of Becca's and Dylan's luggage to be flown home with her dad and Vicky.

"You have everything you need for the day and the flight home in your carry-on? I figured it would be easier for you and Dylan to navigate the airport if you didn't have to deal with all your other luggage, too," Vicky said.

"I'm good. I have everything I need." Becca's bag held a change of clothes, a hoodie, and a few necessities.

"Passport? That's the most important thing, that and your money. Keep it with you at all times," Vicky reminded her.

"Got it. I will." Becca patted her handbag, wishing they would hurry up and leave.

Her father sported a jacket and dress slacks as he transitioned back to the business world.

"Dylan, don't be late to the airport. Be sure to leave with plenty of time," he said.

"Yeah, Dad. We've got it under control."

Becca stifled a giggle. Dylan was sort of telling the truth. They had it under control. Their control, not their dad's.

"I feel terrible that I couldn't get us all on the same flight, but we were lucky to get out this fast."

For a split second, Vicky's hovering concern reminded Becca of her mom. A twinge of nostalgia stabbed at her heart. She brushed it away, and let herself appreciate Vicky just a little bit for taking care of things.

"What are you going to do until you have to leave for the airport?" Vicky asked.

"Oh, I don't know. Maybe have lunch in a nice café or go through those outdoor shops we saw yesterday." Becca resisted the urge to scan their surroundings to see if Nikolai was here already and waiting for her.

"That sounds nice. Keep Dylan near you so you don't get lost."

Becca smiled weakly. Would they hurry up and leave already?

"All right then," her dad said abruptly. "Vicky, I don't want to miss our flight, we'd best get going." Her dad nodded and climbed into the car.

"We'll see you at the airport tomorrow morning." Vicky startled Becca with an affectionate hug, something she never did, and then disappeared into the taxi. Becca's own father didn't bother to hug her, which justified her decision to lie and take off with Nikolai even more.

Becca and Dylan stepped back as the cab pulled away. "I can't believe they're leaving us alone in a foreign country."

Dylan laughed. "Probably the last time they ever will."

The taxi turned the corner. Becca scanned the area for Nikolai, but didn't see him in the dispersing crowds. What if he'd been delayed again? What if he didn't show up at all?

A quick shot of panic struck, but then Becca spied him crossing the parking lot looking all tall, blond, and gorgeous. He wore an easy smile and again she wondered how she could be so lucky to fall in love with such an amazing guy.

"Good morning." He kissed her.

"Morning." Her stomach danced with excitement.

Dylan lifted his backpack onto his shoulder. "Is this awesome, or what?"

"Awesome doesn't begin to describe it," Nikolai answered with a grin.

"So are we all set? You'll have Becca back here in three days?"

"We'll be here," Nikolai reassured him. "Isn't your father going to be terribly angry when he realizes you two had this preplanned?"

"Oh yeah, he'll go ballistic. So, Becca. Don't answer their calls unless you want to deal with the drama. I'm used to dealing with the big blowhole. Also, I'll text you once I have the flight info. I'll meet you at the airport for the flight home."

"Perfect," she said.

"I've got my phone, so call if you need to. And if this guy does anything even remotely out of line, let me know. I'll come to Prague and kick his royal ass."

Becca rolled her eyes. "Ignore him, Nikolai. Can we go now?" she asked, anxious to put miles behind them.

"Whenever you're ready," Nikolai said.

"I've been ready since last night."

Dylan adjusted his backpack. "Have fun and I'll see you soon."

"Thanks, Dylan." She gave him a quick hug and couldn't help but feel a little jittery that her brother was leaving her alone with a guy neither of them knew very well.

Dylan smiled and ambled off to meet up with his friends and catch a train to Amsterdam.

Nikolai slid his arm around Becca and led her to his cycle. He flashed his sexy eyes at her as he strapped her bag next to his on the back of the bike.

Her stomach fluttered. What would the next days bring?

"Check this out." He pushed a new edition of the gossip magazine in her hands.

Becca's mouth dropped open. "Oh my God!"

She stared at a cover picture of her and Nikolai kissing at the lake—in their underwear.

"Now you're famous, too." He raised an eyebrow, took the magazine away, and stuffed it back in his pack.

She stood, shocked from seeing her image on a magazine cover with none other than the Prince of Mondovia.

"I couldn't resist showing it to you before we took off. Here. I picked up a second helmet for the trip. I need to keep you safe and I figured we should both keep our faces hidden."

Becca pulled on the bulky helmet, climbed on behind him, and settled into the seat as he started the engine. She wrapped her arms around Nikolai, still stunned and giddy to be riding off with her prince.

It wasn't yet noon as Nikolai crossed over a stone bridge into the Prague city center. The two-hour ride had gone fast. He still couldn't believe how perfectly things worked out.

He maneuvered the motorbike onto the main boulevard, Wenceslas Square. He'd done some research last night on the main attractions in Prague, and this was one of them. The square seemed a good spot for them to take a break and get their bearings.

Upscale hotels, restaurants, clubs, and stores lined the famous road. He drove to the end where an enormous statue of a man on horseback overlooked the square. He turned onto a side street that boasted more moderate pubs and shops, and parked.

Becca hopped off the bike and struggled removing her helmet.

"Let me." Nikolai nudged her hands away and worked the chin strap, his fingers brushing against her soft skin. "There you go."

She pulled the helmet off. "That was fun!" she said, her hair mussed and eyes bright.

He laughed. "It was. I thought we could stop here, grab something to eat, and figure out what we want to do next." He unstrapped their backpacks to bring along with the helmets.

"This is so beautiful," she said of the centuries-old buildings, ancient streetlamps, and cobblestone roads.

"Isn't it just like every other city you've seen this week?" He loved her unrestrained joy over the smallest things.

"I guess so, but now I'm here because I really want to be." Her amber eyes gazed at him.

Nikolai leaned over and kissed her. "Good." He'd been shocked when she'd decided at the last minute to ditch her flight and come to Prague. He felt responsible for her disobeying her father and hoped she wouldn't end up in too much trouble.

They selected a little restaurant with outdoor tables. He led her inside, away from prying eyes. "Now that it's not only my face, but yours, too, hitting all the newspapers, we need to be more careful."

On a wall in the entryway, a rack displayed tourist brochures and information. Nikolai selected a map, and after ordering lunch, spread it across the table.

"You don't expect me to read that, do you?" Becca eyed the map.

"No. I'll handle all the navigating." He winked. "I want to figure out which hostel we should try." He consulted a slip of paper with the address of three hostels that weren't too far away. They ordered chicken kebabs with roasted potatoes, and sodas.

Becca fetched the magazine from his pack. "I can't believe we're on the cover. Look, you can even see my freckles."

Nikolai grinned. Becca looked sexy as hell in the photo. "Now I'll have a picture of you in your underwear to enjoy forever."

Becca's cheeks turned rosy. "Thank God my dad didn't see this. I can't even imagine what he'd think. He'd probably never believe it. Then again, once he gets Dylan's message that we aren't going to be on the next flight, he'll probably have a coronary."

"What do you think he'll do?"

"Probably the world's longest lecture and guilt trip. 'I expected better from you.' Stuff like that."

Nikolai knew he'd get even more grief when his parents saw this new round of photos. It was bad enough to run off, but now pictures of him in nothing more than underwear and a beautiful girl in his arms . . . that would raise a whole new level of disapproval. This was one more reason he was so reluctant to go back, but his money was running low, and if he kept getting recognized, so would his time with Becca.

"So what does the headline say?" she asked, struggling to decipher the German language printed on the magazine cover.

He cringed.

"What? Tell me. It can't be that bad."

He shook his head and recited the headline. "Loosely translated, it says 'Heir He Is, Naughty Nikolai!'"

"It does not!"

"Sadly, it does."

"What are your parents going to think, or better yet, what will the king say?" She giggled.

Nikolai wished it were funny, but it really wasn't. "I assure you they won't be laughing." He felt his parents' leash tightening.

"Read some more."

He sighed, picked up the magazine, and read aloud.

"'The palace remains silent about the missing prince, but insiders say fury reigns. Prince Nikolai, the newly crowned Mondovian bad boy, has been spotted time and again celebrating an impromptu holiday. The question now is where will he pop up next? Who is the mystery girl? And when will the king put an end to Nikolai's uncharacteristic folly?'"

He tossed the magazine down.

"Yikes." Becca reached for his hand. "I'm sorry."

"It was bound to happen eventually. I just loved being anonymous for a while." He squeezed her hand.

"Now that we're in a different city and not even near the Danube, we should be safe, don't you think?"

"I hope so." But the oppressive weight of the monarchy grew near. He just needed three more days with Becca, and then he'd force himself home and beg forgiveness.

After lunch they rode to the hostel closest to Old Town, but there were no vacancies. They discovered the second hostel tucked in a neighborhood near old mansions and government buildings.

Nikolai stopped at a crossroad and did a double take. His chest tightened.

He tapped Becca's leg and pointed across the street. They both raised the face guards on their helmets so they could talk to each other.

She spoke. "Is that . . ."

He finished for her. "The Mondovian Embassy."

20

A jumble of emotions wrestled inside him as the Mondovian flag waved over the majestic building. His family coat of arms was proudly emblazoned on a bronze seal next to the double doors.

Great pride flooded over him at the sight of his country's flag. It represented everything about who he was. But deep dread also snaked toward him, threatening to put a stranglehold on him and control his life forever.

"Let's get out of here! Hurry!" Becca nudged his shoulder.

He snapped his face guard down, and sped off, struggling to stay within the speed limit.

When they were safely away, and his pulse slowed, he consulted the map and located the third hostel. It sat on a quiet side street that lacked big businesses and heavy traffic.

The building featured a stylish archway leading to a private patio. Ivy climbed the side of the building. They parked around the corner, each checking the area for onlookers. Now that they'd seen his embassy, suddenly the threat of discovery loomed closer.

"Did you know that Mondovia had an embassy here?" Becca asked.

"Yes, but I didn't expect to see it. I assumed it would be far from the tourist part of town." Nikolai helped Becca with her helmet, then removed his own.

"Well, if they're really serious about finding you, they won't have to look far." She grimaced. "Maybe we shouldn't stay in Prague."

Nikolai's shoulders tensed. "No, I don't want to ruin our plans. We'll be careful and blend in, but maybe you should do the talking when we check in." He put on his cap, pulling the bill low over his eyes.

Becca was immediately struck by the scent of stale coffee and the low rumble of chatter. They crossed the scratched wood floor, past a wall of storage lockers, posted house rules, and a list of restaurants. Nikolai hung back and concentrated on a bulletin board with lists of things to do as she approached the registration desk.

A thirty-something guy, wearing a ponytail and wire-rimmed glasses, spoke on the phone in a foreign tongue.

Becca panicked. She couldn't check them in if she couldn't speak the language. He ended his call, looked at her, and spoke rapid gibberish.

She stuttered. "Ah, um, do you maybe speak English?"

"Hi. I'm Kristoff, may I help you?" He switched languages with ease and a friendly smile.

Becca could swear she heard Nikolai chuckle. "Oh good! Hi. We'd like to check in."

"Do you have a reservation?"

"No, do we need one?"

"Not today. We still have space. How many nights do you need?"

"Two." She glanced into the next room where a handful of people hung out on couches. There were more seating areas, a wall of shelves overflowing with books, and games, and colorful paintings on the wall.

Kristoff checked his scheduling book. "Let's see. There is space in one of the coed dorms."

Becca never really thought about sleeping arrangements. Was Nikolai expecting to share a room? To sleep together? They'd shared her cabin the other night, but he'd been a total gentleman. Heck, she didn't know if she wanted to share a bed or not. Thank God the decision was out of her hands.

She glanced at Nikolai, who stood with his back to the front desk and nodded.

"Yes, that would be great."

Kristoff filled out the paperwork. Nikolai handed her his portion of the money. She didn't have a lot of cash, so she put hers on her credit card.

"Welcome to Prague House." Kristoff came out from behind the counter. "This is the common room. Lockers are over there. We encourage you to keep your valuables locked up."

They gathered their stuff and followed him.

"Breakfast is self-serve from six to nine a.m. in the room around the corner. Down the hall is the game room with a pool table and darts. You're in dorm number three on the third floor." He indicated a narrow stairway in the corner. "There's bedding in the hall closet. Once a bed is made, it's considered occupied, so only pick an unmade bed."

"Thank you," Becca said. Nikolai mumbled thanks while acting fascinated with the floorboards.

Becca couldn't imagine Nikolai being recognized with his scruffy face. He looked so different now from the magazine photos Dylan had shown her.

A couple of guys lounged on the couches, chatting with two girls who eyed Nikolai.

"How you doing?" asked a guy with shaggy dark hair and long sideburns.

"Hi." Becca smiled as they passed.

Nikolai guided her ahead and they climbed the creaky steps to the third floor. The dorm room contained six sets of metal bunk beds holding the thinnest mattresses she'd ever seen. The walls were stark white, the windows covered by ratty old blinds. They located two tiny bathrooms at the end of the hall.

"Is this what your other hostels were like?" Had the Prince of Mondovia really stayed in such lowbrow lodging?

"More or less, except I was able to stay in a single room at the last few. This ought to be fun! Do you want to be on top or bottom?" He grinned.

She shook her head and tried to frown, but a smile snuck out. "I am not going to encourage you."

They made up side-by-side lower bunk beds, washed up, and after securing their backpacks in a locker, Nikolai took her hand and they headed for Old Town.

"I feel so free!" Becca said, swinging her arms.

Nikolai put his arm around Becca and kissed her. "You and me both."

A few blocks later, they turned a bend and the volume of tourists increased. They passed street performers, and all the shops overflowed with souvenirs such as nesting dolls, T-shirts, and chess sets. Nearly every building housed an outdoor café.

On each corner, there were booths selling tours to nearby castles and classical concerts.

"Please tell me you don't want to see a concert," Nikolai said.

Becca curled her lip in disdain at the rack of pamphlets featuring tuxedoed performers holding stringed instruments. "Not if it involves an orchestra, I don't. That kind of music puts me to sleep."

Ahead, an enormous archway stretched across the road as if at one time it served as the divider of one side of the city from the other. They passed under the ancient structure and entered another world where an average girl like Becca could walk the streets of an exotic city with a prince holding her hand.

After a few more blocks, they found themselves in the Old Town Square, a wide open plaza. People of all ages and nationalities meandered the square. Becca glanced at Nikolai with his sunglasses and cap. He looked like every other tourist. This seemed the perfect place to blend in.

"Look, there's the Astronomical Clock."

Nikolai pointed to an old structure in the center of the square that towered high above all the other buildings. Clusters of people gathered in front taking pictures.

The historic clock was a large combination of dials, astronomical symbols, roman numerals, and foreign letters. "And how do you tell time on that?" Becca asked, pulling out her phone and taking a picture.

"I have no idea," he said, examining the complicated timepiece.

"Stand closer and I'll take your picture," she said.

"Only if you're in it with me. Excuse me," Nikolai asked a gray-haired man. "Would you be so kind as to take our picture?"

"Sure. I'd be happy to," he said, taking the phone. He snapped a photo. "Where are you from?"

"Chicago," Becca blurted to make sure Nikolai didn't accidentally reveal his home nation.

"We're from Cleveland, practically neighbors." The man passed the phone back to Becca.

"Thank you."

"No problem. Have a nice day," he said and wandered off.

"Do you want to climb the tower?" Nikolai asked.

"Sure."

They bought tickets and started the long trek up the stone steps. As they neared the top, the wide staircase narrowed to a spiral staircase. And for the final flight of even narrower steps, a light shone red or green, indicating when it was their turn to ascend.

Nikolai and Becca climbed the final steps to a large open area at the top. A walkway with window-like openings surrounded the tower.

"Look, you can see for miles," Becca said. They had a perfect view of the rooftops and steeples of Prague. Across the river, a spectacular castle rested upon a hilltop. "What's that, your summer home?" Becca teased, betting she wasn't far off the truth.

Nikolai put his arm around her waist and tickled her. "You're so funny."

She giggled. "So, do you have a bunch of relatives here, too?"

"If you look back far enough in anyone's ancestry, I'm sure we all have relatives everywhere, but no, not that I know of, which is one reason I know very little about Prague beyond its general history."

"Finally something you don't know." She grinned and leaned back against him. He wrapped his arms around her and tucked his chin over her head. Below, the people looked tiny, and the umbrellas at the restaurants' outdoor tables resembled miniature garnishes for tropical drinks. "Thank you," she murmured.

"For what?"

"For bringing me here. I swear this is the best time I've had in my entire life."

"Me too," he said.

After leaving the clock, and the crowds waiting for the next chiming, Nikolai and Becca wandered off the square to the smaller streets and passed a puppet shop. "Oh, that totally gives me the creeps." Becca shuddered.

"What, you don't like painted faces with fixed eyes staring at you?"

"No, they're almost as bad as clowns."

"Puppets and clowns. What did they ever do to you?"

"Nothing, they're just weird. They don't creep you out?"

"No. I actually like them. When I was little, there was a puppeteer who would come put on performances for me and my little sister. He was always nice to me. I didn't have many kids to play with, and I guess that in a way the puppets were like friends for me."

"That is so sad," Becca said.

"Don't worry. I think I turned out okay, and Alexi did, too."

"You turned out more than okay." Becca slipped her arm around his waist and hooked her thumb in his belt loop. "So, you and your sister are close?"

Nikolai draped her arm around Becca, loving how natural it felt to be with her. "Yes. She was usually the only other person around that was within two decades of my age. When I was older, I loved escaping to school, but now that's all over and I'll be leaving for the military soon."

"So you're really going?"

"I don't see how I have any other choice." He'd been racking his brain, trying to come up with a way out of it, but tradition anchored his parents' belief system, and after all the bad press he'd created, he knew they wouldn't listen to him.

"I hate that so much!" She laid her head on his shoulder.

He pulled her close. He couldn't imagine the past week without Becca in his life, and even more, he couldn't imagine how it would be after she was gone.

They walked a bit farther, and he spotted a hardware store on the corner and got an idea. "Do you mind waiting here? I want to check in that store for something."

"What do you need?"

"Just a little something. It's a surprise."

"From a hardware store? How special."

"Don't judge. You might be pleasantly surprised."

"Okay, now you have me intrigued."

"Good. I'll be right back." Nikolai left her on the corner, crossed the street, and entered the store. He checked on her from the front display window. She was digging in her shoulder bag, not spying on him. He smiled, satisfied.

He walked the aisles past nails, hinges, and tools until he spotted what he needed. Nikolai paid the cashier and slipped his purchase deep into his pocket.

As he exited, he spotted a grungy guy with dirty hair and a faded T-shirt talking to Becca. She leaned away from the stranger. Nikolai hurried his pace. Becca looked in his direction with relief in her eyes.

Suddenly, the man grabbed her shoulder bag.

Nikolai raced across the street as Becca fought to hold on to her bag. He grabbed the thief from behind. "Let her go!"

The man spun around and clocked Nikolai in the face with his elbow, knocking Nikolai to the ground.

Becca screamed.

The robber tore the bag from her hands and started to

flee. Nikolai lunged for the assailant's leg. The guy dragged Nikolai across the rough road for a few feet before kicking free and disappearing around the corner.

Nikolai lay sprawled on the ground, his hat knocked off, and sunglasses broken. "Dammit. He got away. I'm sorry." He tossed his broken sunglasses.

"Are you okay?" Becca crouched next to him. "You're bleeding!"

Nikolai touched the bridge of his nose and discovered a little blood. "I'll live. I can't believe I let him steal your bag." His face hurt from where he'd been elbowed near the eye.

"He took my wallet and all my money and . . . Oh no! Nikolai! He's got my passport!"

21

Thirty minutes later, they arrived back at the hostel. Nikolai's cheek and the bridge of his nose throbbed. Not only had he not protected Becca, he took a couple of direct hits in the process, and created a photo-worthy scene.

"I'll see if they have any ice," Becca said, approaching the registration counter.

"Okay, I'm going to grab us a couple of waters." He bought bottled water at a vending machine off the common room, carried them back, and sank onto one of the unoccupied couches.

"What happened to you?" asked one of the guys they'd seen at check-in earlier.

"Oh, just a little run-in with someone's elbow."

"Ouch," said the tall brunette girl coming over to check it out. "That sucks."

"That it does." He held the cool bottle against his eye area.

"I'm Claire," she said. "And this is Brian, James, and Andrea."

"Hi, I'm Nick." He wished he and Becca had a private room where he could hide out.

Becca joined him, holding a small plastic bag filled with ice.

"And this is Becca. Becca, this is Claire."

Claire grinned that hungry, interested smile he'd seen dozens of times before. He felt a little too exposed without his sunglasses to hide behind. "And Brian, James, and Andrea." Claire pointed to each.

"Hi." Becca handed him the ice bag, which he pressed to his nose. "There's an ice machine next to the lobby bathroom. I told the desk clerk about my stolen passport. He said the U.S. Embassy is closed for the day, but they have an emergency after-hours number."

"Someone stole your passport? That's terrible," said Andrea.

"Tell me about it," Becca answered.

"Oh no, what about your phone?" Nikolai lowered the ice bag from his face.

"No, thank God. I'd been taking pictures with it at the old clock and had slipped it into my pocket."

"Well, that's one piece of good news," Nikolai said.

With Becca's wallet stolen and his dwindling cash

supply, they'd have to be careful spending money. Thankfully, they'd both already paid for their lodging.

"So where are you guys from?" Claire asked, staring at Nikolai.

"We're from Chicago. How about you?" Becca asked, trying to pull Claire's attention away from Nikolai.

"We're from Mankato. It's in Minnesota," said Brian, a tall guy with dark hair who looked too young to be traveling alone.

"But I've been an exchange student in Germany for the past year," Claire added, looking at Nikolai again. "Which is why these guys came over. You look really familiar to me." She aimed her comment at Nikolai.

"Yeah, I get that a lot," he said, covering his face again with the ice bag.

"He does have that common kind of face, doesn't he?" Becca said.

"No, I've seen you somewhere. I'm sure of it," Claire added.

"Do you guys want to join us tonight? We're going to a pub near the river," Brian said.

"Thanks, but I think we better stay here and regroup," Nikolai said, looking at Becca with meaning.

"Yeah, thanks for the offer. Have a good time," Becca said.

"If you're sure, I guess we'll catch you later," Claire said, as their group moved toward the door.

"Do you think she recognizes you?" Becca slid closer to him on the couch.

"I don't know. She sure was trying to place me. I hope you don't mind that I told them no for dinner."

"No, of course not."

"I'm not sure how to say this, but I'm pretty low on cash, and with you losing your wallet, I think we need to be really careful." He hated that he couldn't take care of her. She must think him a poor excuse for a prince.

"Are you kidding? Don't worry about it at all. I'm good with ramen noodles."

"With what?"

"For someone so worldly and smart, you can be pretty dumb," she teased. "You know, if I had to, I could call my dad, or Vicky, to send money, but I'd like to avoid that at all costs. I really don't want them to know I lied. Maybe we could panhandle or become street performers to earn money."

"That would be bad. I am certainly not a performer, and I can't even imagine my parents' reaction to that!"

"I think it might be good to shake up the palace once in a while."

"Easy for you to say," he said, his heart heavy.

Later, they called the after-hours emergency number for the U.S. Embassy and made an appointment to get Becca's passport replaced. The embassy person insisted she file a police report so they could make the robbery official. Nikolai thought Becca should call her father or at least Dylan, but she refused. She didn't plan to call them unless she absolutely had to.

After Nikolai cleaned up and changed shirts, they walked to the closest police station. Two officers walked past them and entered the building.

Nikolai touched Becca's arm. "If you don't mind, I think I'll wait out here. Including me in the mix might raise questions we don't want to answer."

"Good idea. Hopefully this won't take too much time." Becca entered the police station feeling like she could be arrested at any moment for aiding and abetting the escaped Prince of Mondovia.

She explained to an officer that she needed to report a theft. He directed her down a corridor to another room. She couldn't believe she'd been mugged in a foreign country she wasn't even supposed to be in. She could already picture her dad's scowl of disappointment if he found out. She'd seen it directed at Dylan many times.

After filling out confusing paperwork that asked where she was staying and where she was robbed, she left the police station.

Outside, she found Nikolai on a nearby bench waiting patiently. He stood and smiled at her. She'd never grow tired of looking at him.

"Sorry it took so long. They wanted to know practically

everything about me down to my last tetanus shot."

He looked at her, confused. "You're kidding, right?"

"Yes." She leaned up and kissed him. "After all that questioning, the officer said my passport and wallet are long gone and not to expect them to turn up. What a waste of time."

"I'm sorry. I should have stopped the mugger."

"Stop blaming yourself. It's not your fault."

"Let's get out of here. There's been an officer near the building who passed by me, entered, and then came back out."

Becca spotted the man. "You mean the one on the phone?"

"That's the one. It feels like he's been watching me. I'm probably paranoid."

"Let's not take any chances." She slid her hand into his, and they headed back to the hostel. On the way, they bought cheap takeout for dinner from a small restaurant and climbed to the hostel's rooftop patio to dine alfresco.

The neglected patio featured a couple of clusters of outdoor furniture edged with rust and an occasional potted plant, struggling to survive. Still, it was a beautiful night and they enjoyed the privacy. Somewhere not far away, they heard the strains of live music as it drifted up from the street.

Becca retrieved the burgers and fries and set them on the paper takeout bag. "This smells so good and reminds me of home. I have to admit, I miss eating American food."

"I won't argue. You Americans have some good food." Nikolai popped a fry into his mouth. "I know you were traveling with your dad and stepmom, but you never told me about your mom. Is she remarried, too?"

Becca paused. "No. She died."

Nikolai looked stricken. "Oh God, I'm so sorry, Becca. I didn't know."

"It's fine. There's no way you could have known."

"What happened? If you don't mind talking about it."

People rarely asked about her mom, and her dad never talked about her anymore, as if everything about her mom had just disappeared.

Becca kept her memories of her mom locked safely away in her heart. She sipped her soda. "She had breast cancer. They didn't find it until it was really bad. She fought it as hard as she could, but she never really had a chance. She died four years ago."

Her throat tightened as she remembered her mom, and her laugh, and how she always kept her dad from getting too serious.

Nikolai moved next to her and pulled her into his arms. "That's so horrible." He caressed her hair.

"Thanks." Becca cleared her throat and fought the tears that threatened. "It's been a long time. I try not to think about it too much. It makes me miss her even more."

"I feel like such an ass. Here I've been complaining

about my parents, and you've been growing up without your mom. I knew you didn't like your stepmom, but I never imagined your mom died."

"You don't need to feel bad. Everyone's got their own stuff to deal with. Mine is having a dad who pretty much checked out of my life when Mom died. I swear sometimes that he married Vicky just so he wouldn't have to deal with Dylan and me."

"I'm sure he cares about you very much."

"I guess, but he doesn't know how to show it. This trip was the biggest joke. It was all Vicky's idea to turn us into one big, happy family. I'd like to be really mad at her about dragging me here, except that if I hadn't come, I never would have met you."

"And that would have been tragic." He held out a fry. She took a bite.

"I can't imagine not knowing you." She noticed the growing bruise under his eye. "I'm sorry you got hit today. You're probably going to end up with a black eye." She hated the idea of her perfect prince sporting a nasty bruise.

"If I'd have stopped the thief, then I could wear it as a badge of honor, but no, I let the guy escape. It's more of an embarrassment at my ineptitude."

"Stop it! I thought you were very brave." She leaned forward and kissed his bruise and then his mouth.

"That definitely makes me feel better."

They finished their dinner, and later that night, they

lay across from each other in their separate bunks. Becca tucked her hand under her cheek and smiled at Nikolai. Other people slept, so she didn't dare talk. He lifted his covers in invitation.

Are you sure? she mouthed.

Nikolai smiled and waved her over. She crawled into the narrow bunk and rolled over so they lay spooned together, his arm around her waist and her arms curled around his. They lay quietly as he caressed her arm. After a few minutes, their breathing matched and they drifted off to sleep.

The next morning, Becca enjoyed her new favorite breakfast meal, pancakes spread with Nutella. She and Nikolai sat in the far corner of the dining room, where he kept his back to the rest of the diners.

Claire, the nosy girl they met yesterday, stopped by their table anyway.

"Hi, guys, where are you off to today?" she asked, trying to get a good look at Nikolai.

Nikolai rolled his eyes at Claire's intrusion, then focused on his cereal.

Becca answered. "The U.S. Embassy to try to get a new passport."

"Oh, right. Well, afterward, if you want to join us, we're going to the Prague Castle today."

From the way Claire stared at him, Becca was pretty sure that the invite was meant for Nikolai. Becca suspected she had guessed his true identity.

"Thanks, but we've got other plans," Nikolai said dismissively, wiping his mouth and slipping on his hat.

"Okay. Well, have a good day then." Claire wandered off, clearly disappointed.

"Could she be more subtle? Jeez." Becca collected her breakfast dishes.

"I'm pretty sure the cat's out of the bag with her. Let's clear out before she comes back." He put his dishes in the bin. "Before we go, I want to check on my bike and make sure it hasn't been hauled away like in Melk."

Out on the street, they rounded the corner and Nikolai stopped abruptly. Becca ran into him.

"What?"

Nikolai stared at a man across the street and slowly stepped back. "Let's not worry about the cycle right now."

Becca followed. "What's going on? Who was that man?"

"Probably no one. I didn't get a good look at his face, but the way he's standing there, it's like he's watching, or waiting for someone. He was no average chap hanging out and having a smoke."

"Did he see you?"

"I don't know. I don't think so."

"Do you think he's paparazzi? If he is, how did he find us so fast?" She wanted to go back and see this guy for herself, but didn't dare.

"I don't know. There were people taking pictures

yesterday when your bag was stolen, Claire definitely may have recognized me, and there was that cop last night. Anyone of them may have ratted me out."

Becca didn't like the stress etched upon his face. "Maybe we better leave."

"Not a bad idea. I'm so sorry. We have so little time left together, and I don't want it ruined by the damn press."

Even though they'd been given these extra bonus days together, Becca couldn't stop the sadness of knowing she'd soon be saying good-bye.

Nikolai must have sensed her mood, for he suddenly reached for her hand. "Before we go to the embassy, there is someplace I want to take you."

After a leisurely walk, they ended up in a quiet neighborhood away from the chaotic crush of Old Town. Nikolai led her around a corner to a small bridge with a tall wrought-iron fence that overlooked a canal.

"Oh my gosh, look at that!" Becca pulled him forward. Each of the iron fence spindles was covered with dozens and dozens of padlocks. Clusters of people were taking pictures of the oddity.

"There must be hundreds, maybe thousands of locks. Why are they here?" She examined the colorful locks more closely and discovered that many had names painted or scratched onto them.

"They're called love locks. People put them here to profess their everlasting love."

"That is so awesome." She touched the thick cluster of colorful padlocks and envied the people who so openly professed their love.

"I thought you might like it. I read about it on a flyer at the hostel. Do you see any open spots?"

She checked the spindles, and ran her hands over the locks so tightly stacked. "Not really. There's so many."

Nikolai's voice softened. "I thought we should add one of our own."

Becca spun around. Nikolai held a brass-colored lock. "This is what I was getting at the hardware store." Becca's heart fluttered. She didn't know what to say.

She hoped he felt as strongly about her as she did about him. She gazed into his eyes, one marred by the black-and-blue bruise he earned trying to defend her. "Yes, I'd like that."

His face melted into a smile. "This way, when we're not together anymore, we'll always know that this lock is here as a reminder of what we've shared."

"Thank you," she whispered.

He swept her into his arms. "I love you, Becca."

"Oh, Nikolai. I love you, too."

He kissed her sweetly. Becca could never remember a happier time, yet the fact that they had to say good-bye in a couple of days loomed at the back of her mind.

He released her. "So where are we going to put it?"

"I don't know, but I guarantee that we'll find a place."

They looked up and down each spindle, trying to move the locks to eke out just enough space to hook their lock. Finally Nikolai found a spot.

"Over here, at the top. If I slide this one over, I think I can fit it."

Becca held the other locks to the side, feeling as if this were a sacred act. Nikolai slid their lock into place.

"You put our names on it."

"I did." He smiled.

"Not afraid of being discovered?"

"With you? Never." He clicked the lock closed, pulled out the key, and handed it to her.

"What do I do with it? Save it?" she asked.

A woman nearby who watched them spoke up. "No, you throw it into the canal, so your love can never be unlocked." She smiled.

"Thanks. I like that," Becca said. "Ready?" she asked Nikolai.

"Go ahead."

She kissed the key and tossed it high over the fence and into the water below. "There. Now you're stuck with me forever."

"I'd be okay with that," he said.

"Would you like me to take your picture?" the woman offered. "You should have a photo of this moment."

"Thank you, that would be great," Nikolai said.

They posed with their arms around each other in front

of their lock. At the last second Nikolai removed his cap and ruffled up his flat hair.

The woman snapped two pictures. "There you go." She handed back Becca's phone.

"Thank you so much," Becca said, showing the picture to Nikolai as he slipped his hat back on. "Look, you can see your black eye."

"Great. I forgot about that." He laughed. "We better stop for some sunglasses soon so people don't think you hit me."

Becca raised an eyebrow. "I know you think you're funny, but you're not," she teased.

A small crowd had gathered to look at the locks. She overheard a girl talking to her friend.

"I'm telling you, that's Prince Nikolai. And that's the same girl who's with him in the picture in the paper."

Becca's gut lurched. He'd been recognized. Heck, she'd been recognized, too.

"You're totally right!" her friend said, snapping a picture.

"We better get out of here. Come on." Nikolai took Becca's hand and quickly slipped through the crowd as word of his identity spread.

22

Nikolai breathed easier when they put a couple of blocks between them and the crowd on the bridge.

They arrived on a street with one foreign government building after another. He spotted a three-story building with an American flag flying high above.

Becca gazed up at the fluttering flag. She'd been away from home for so long, this was a welcome sight. "I must say, seeing the U.S. flag here in a foreign country makes me proud to be an American." She squeezed his hand.

He felt the same pride in his own country, despite all his problems. The U.S. flag reminded him of how very far away Becca lived, and that the chances of them staying connected would be nearly impossible.

"Do you want to come in, or would it be better for you to wait here?" she asked.

Nikolai noticed a figure on the corner across the

street. He looked at the embassy doors, back to the familiar man, and frowned. "You go ahead. I think I better wait here."

"Are you sure? It might take a while. You could go to a café, and I'll call you when I'm ready."

"And risk you getting lost in Prague? No. I'll be waiting right here."

"Okay. Wish me luck."

He kissed her. "Good luck."

As Becca disappeared into the embassy, Nikolai saw his father's chief security officer, Visar Shaban, walking across the street toward him.

"Good morning, Your Royal Highness," he said as he approached. "Are you enjoying your holiday?"

Nikolai tried to appear confident on this uneven ground. Here he stood, unshaven, with a bruised face, and little money.

Normally, he only encountered Visar at the palace, Nikolai's domain, or at high-level security events when it was Visar's duty to remain unseen.

"Hello, Visar," Nikolai said evenly.

"I trust you are well," the stoic man said, popping a candy into his mouth.

"You didn't need to come. I planned to return home in a couple of days." Nikolai watched the traffic go by.

"Ah, that is where you are wrong. The king is dismayed

with your recent notoriety and wishes your return to Mondovia. Immediately."

Nikolai's chest tightened. "No, Visar. That won't be possible. Not yet, anyway. I have obligations for the next two days and then I will be wherever you, or the palace, require me to be."

Visar considered Nikolai, giving away nothing. Nikolai stared, refusing to back down. Would Visar grab him here on the street and force him to leave?

What about Becca? He couldn't possibly leave without saying good-bye. Visar was only one man. Nikolai could hold him off.

Two more days were all he wanted. That wasn't asking much. He glanced at the doors to the embassy.

"I trust you aren't thinking of asking the United States Embassy for asylum."

"Don't be ridiculous," Nikolai snapped.

"I'm afraid that I am not the one who's been acting ridiculous. Prince Nikolai, come along, and let's put an end to your antics. You've become an embarrassment to the palace."

"As I said, I have other obligations. I will not return a minute sooner. Have I made myself clear?"

"Perhaps I have not explained my presence here properly. I am under direct orders from the king to return you to Mondovia, posthaste."

Nikolai fought to keep his emotions under control. Losing it wouldn't help. "I quite understand your purpose, and will ask you the kindness to relay a message back to the king."

Visar's eye twitched.

Nikolai continued. "I fully understand my future legacy and will dedicate the rest of my life to Mondovia. However, the next two days will remain mine, to be spent as I see fit."

The door to the embassy opened and Becca appeared.

"Are we understood?" Nikolai growled.

Visar nodded. "I will relay your message," he answered and walked away.

Nikolai hoped this would be the end of his father's interference.

"Who was that?" Becca asked.

"Some guy who was in the wrong place."

"Lost?"

"Yeah, you could say that. So how did it go? Are they able to get you a new passport?" He started walking in the opposite direction of Visar, but glanced back to make sure the man hadn't changed his mind and come back.

"Yes, thank God. Apparently this sort of thing happens all the time. They will have it ready tomorrow. That'll leave us plenty of time to ride to Nuremberg the next day for my flight."

Nikolai sighed and put his arms around her. "How am I possibly going to say good-bye to you?"

"I don't want to think about it or I'll start bawling. Trust me, you don't want to see that."

He smiled. "No, I don't suppose I do."

After leaving the business district, they passed through a quiet neighborhood and some retail shops. Becca spotted a small grocery store. "Let's see if they sell sunglasses."

They ducked inside and found a rack of sunglasses in the corner. While Nikolai tried on glasses, Becca picked up a few items for lunch: some grapes, crackers, and sliced cheese. They met up at the checkout. She put her items on the conveyor belt hoping they didn't cost too much. "I feel really bad that I can't help pay. Do you have enough?"

"It's all right. If I can't buy you a few meals, I'm not a very good date. I wish I could do more."

"Don't be silly, this is perfect."

A tiny older woman with long gray hair glanced at Nikolai after scanning each item. He shot Becca an uneasy look. She wished she knew a better way to hide him.

The clerk smiled. "I've never had a prince in my store before."

Nikolai grimaced. "I'm sorry, you must be mistaking me for someone else."

The woman removed a newspaper from the rack next to the checkout and laid it before them. "You are Prince Nikolai."

Dumbfounded, Becca stared at the cover of the *Daily*

Enquirer. It showed Nikolai on the ground after the mugging, with her kneeling next to him, clearly distraught.

"There weren't even that many people there. How is this possible?" Becca asked.

"Trust me, there are a lot of people eager to post their pictures online the second they take them. That explains the guy watching my bike this morning," Nikolai said.

"Haven't you seen the news lately? There are sightings of you reported on television every day," the clerk said.

"No, we haven't," Becca said. She had barely turned a television on since the trip began. "We'll take the paper, too, please." She needed to know what the article said.

The woman smiled as Nikolai pulled money from his wallet, paid for their purchases, and then slipped on his new sunglasses.

Around the corner from the store, they found a small park with old trees, a thick blanket of grass, and chirping birds.

"I don't understand how people recognize you so easily. With your unshaven face, you look more like a street person than a prince." She ran her fingers over the soft bristles.

Nikolai stretched out next to her on the grass and opened the newspaper. "It says here that I attacked the man first because he flirted with you."

"That's a total lie!"

"They write what they think will sell papers. It also

says that they still don't know who the mysterious beauty is that lured me away." He lowered his sunglasses and flashed his eyebrows at her.

"Really? You're making that up!"

"No, I'm not. It's right here. You can take it back to the hostel and have Kristoff translate it for you."

"That just proves that they make all this up."

"Au contraire." He brushed a lock of hair behind her ear. "Not only are you beautiful, but you are funny, and sexy, and have mesmerized me into following you through four countries."

Tingles danced over her skin. She wasn't used to such flowery compliments. She pointed at the article. "What else does it say?"

"The palace has finally admitted that I took off on an unapproved excursion."

"That's what we're on? An excursion?" Being together felt more like a fairy tale, and she was waiting for the clock to strike twelve.

"Apparently so." He sighed, tossed the gossip rag aside, and lay on the grass looking skyward.

Suddenly her phone rang. They looked at each other; a streak of panic ran through Becca.

She pulled out her phone. "It's Vicky!"

"Are you going to answer it?"

"No way!" Both Vicky and her dad had called multiple

times when they learned she and Dylan weren't on the next flight, but Becca had ignored them all. Dylan had said he'd deal with them.

She stared at the phone until it stopped ringing. A minute later the phone beeped that she had a message. Becca didn't want to listen to it, but worried something horrible could have happened so decided to go ahead and check it.

"She's just touching base to make sure I'm all right," Becca said, hanging up and feeling a little guilty about disobeying Vicky. She had tried to plan a nice trip for them.

"Are you going to call her back?"

"I'll text her later that everything is fine. I don't need help from her or Dad. I can handle being on my own."

"I'm afraid my parents wouldn't be calling to see if I was okay. They'd be demanding I come home on the next train."

Becca rolled closer to him, her face close to his. "I'm sorry this is so horrible for you. Actually, I'm sorry this is your life. It sucks."

He turned his head in her direction. "But you make it worth every second. I hope you know that. Before, I ran away to be free from them and escape the person I was turning into. Since I met you, I've been myself for the first time in my life, and I like this guy."

She leaned forward and kissed him slowly, repeatedly, helping him forget his troubles. Her hair cascaded around their faces, a perfect curtain of privacy. Nikolai captured her with the intensity of his deep blue eyes, as his arms slid around her. He kissed her back, their lunch forgotten.

"Okay, which way next?" Nikolai tried to keep quiet and let Becca navigate through a tangle of streets to a gift shop they'd passed yesterday. She wanted to bring something back to her brother.

"It's down this side street," she said, studying the shops and street signs. "I'm sorry this is taking so long, but it was the perfect T-shirt for Dylan. It said *Czech Mate* and had a king chess piece. Dylan played chess in high school and was really good."

They reached the end of the block. "Are you sure this is right?" he teased, admiring the way Becca scrunched up her face when she concentrated.

"Positive. Turn here."

They entered a crooked street that looked more like an alley. Signboards stood outside various shops and restaurants.

"Okay, maybe not positive." Becca nibbled the edge of her lip.

Nikolai slipped an arm around her waist and kissed her cheek. "That's all right. You'll never be lost when I'm around."

They turned the bend in the narrow street and Nikolai stopped cold. Ahead, about fifty feet, stood three men from the Mondovian guard. Even though the men were dressed in street clothes and not military detail, Nikolai would recognize them and their steely, determined eyes anywhere. They were on a mission, and that mission was him.

"Becca," he said, taking her arm. "We need to turn around and go in the other direction."

"But I know this is right. I'm sure of it."

The three men walked toward them, their eyes fixed on Nikolai. He knew he should give himself up and go quietly, but he wasn't ready. Not by a long shot.

"Becca. Don't panic, but see those men?" He spoke in a calm voice and tried to lead her away. "We need to get out of here."

She looked at the men and back to Nikolai with fear in her eyes. "Oh my God," she uttered, turning with Nikolai and rushing back the way they came.

Nikolai grabbed Becca's hand and they took off, dodging tourists. The men started running. His heart pumped and his mind raced as he tried to figure out an escape plan.

He glanced back. The men were gaining on them fast. He pulled Becca along.

She stumbled and went down. He pulled her up by the waist and kept running.

"Nikolai, who are those men?"

"My father sent them. They're here for me, not you."

Just as they reached the corner, a crowd of tourists blocked their way.

"Excuse me, pardon me." He dragged Becca through the mass.

They turned the corner and came up short against a souvenir cart of handbags and a crush of more tourists.

"Prince Nikolai!" a commanding voice called out, much too close.

Nikolai hesitated for an instant, then continued on, only to have Becca's hand ripped from his.

"Nikolai!" she screamed.

23

Rough hands grabbed Becca from behind, yanking her away from Nikolai's grasp. Even though he said the men weren't after her, she'd never been so terrified. Nikolai turned to help her as the other men caught up.

"Stand down!" Nikolai commanded with steely determination, no longer the mild-mannered guy she'd grown to love. "She has nothing to do with this!"

Instantly, the men released Becca, who ran to Nikolai. He put himself between her and the dangerous-looking men. Nikolai stared them down, daring them to make a move.

"You need to come with us now. King's orders," the taller man said.

"I've already instructed Visar that I would be more than happy to in two days' time."

Crowds of tourists gave them a wide berth, watching

with the same shock as Becca. She clung to his arm.

"Are you okay?" Nikolai asked, training his eyes on the men.

"Yeah, I'm fine."

Nikolai fired angry foreign words at the men.

Around them, cameras flashed and clicked as the crowd grew.

The taller man spoke calmly to Nikolai, again in a language she didn't recognize. Nikolai didn't relax his stance. Instead, he held up his hand, as if ordering them to stay back. He eyed the men with caution.

"Becca, I'm so sorry." He turned and cupped her face with his hand, and she saw the torment in his eyes.

"Who are they? Do you know them?" She took his hand in hers, relieved to feel his strength and steady calm.

Before he could answer, two Prague police officers pushed through the crowd of spectators. *Thank God!*

The officials looked past Nikolai to the men and nodded.

Suddenly two of the men from Mondovia stepped forward and pulled Nikolai away from her, ignoring the police presence.

Nikolai lashed out as they dragged him away. The men struggled to keep their hold. Becca experienced a stab of terror when Nikolai was knocked in the face as the men fought to control him.

"Help!" she screamed to the police who stood idle as if

they didn't want to get involved.

Without thinking, Becca ran into the fray, pounding on the back of one man as they lifted Nikolai off the ground. A strong hand shoved her away.

Suddenly her arms were pinned behind her.

Nikolai fought harder, bucking and kicking. His phone fell to the ground and was crushed by one of the assailant's boots.

The men were carrying him away.

"Nikolai!" she screamed.

"Becca!" Nikolai yelled, with blood running from his nose. "I'll find you. I promise."

Why was no one helping them? She struggled, to no avail. "Let me go! Don't you see? They're kidnapping him!"

A white, unmarked van pulled up. The men shoved Nikolai inside, jumped in after him, and slammed the door. The van sped off, as people rushed out of the way, lest they be run over.

When the van was out of sight, Becca was abruptly released. She turned to face her captor—a Prague police officer.

"What is wrong with you? Those men just abducted my boyfriend! Go after them!"

The officer glared. "Miss, you are interfering with international affairs. I advise you to return to your hotel and leave this country before you find yourself in more serious trouble."

The horrible man stood like a formidable wall. Becca turned around to find a circle of gawking tourists watching the spectacle, most with shocked expressions, others taking pictures. Becca rushed to where Nikolai had been only moments before. All that remained was his broken phone. She'd put her contact information in it so they could stay in touch.

How would he find her now?

She scooped up the pieces and looked down the street, in the direction the van had disappeared. Empty.

A glance back revealed more officers now dispersing the crowd while the mean officer watched her with an unyielding glare.

How was this possible?

Nikolai was gone.

24

Becca was lost, literally and figuratively. All she wanted was to get back to the hostel.

And after wandering aimlessly, she finally asked for assistance. A few more wrong turns and she spotted the hostel. As she approached, she remembered Nikolai's motorcycle. She ran around the corner, not sure what to expect.

Her heart lurched. The cycle was gone. Nikolai was gone. It felt like a death. She looked around, hoping to somehow find him peeking out behind the bushes, but she didn't see Nikolai or any of the terrible men from Mondovia. She was beginning to hate his country.

She entered the hostel. Kristoff was working behind the counter. He stood up, alarmed, when he noticed her defeated face.

"Miss, what has happened? Have you been hurt?"

She looked down at her dirty shorts, scraped knee. "I'm okay," she said, with a controlled breath, willing herself not to fall apart.

"Where is your friend?" he asked with concern.

"He's—gone." She didn't know if she should say anything or not. She'd been trying to hide his identity and protect him, but it hadn't mattered. He was gone, ripped from her side.

The door opened and the group from Minnesota poured in. "There she is! I told you!" Claire said.

"You're right," said Brian.

"You're on the cover of the *Daily Enquirer*!" Andrea rushed forward and pulled the paper from her handbag. "Look! There you are with Nick. I mean Prince Nikolai. Where is he?"

Becca swallowed her emotions. "He's not here."

"What do you mean not here?" Claire asked.

"He went home," Becca answered.

"Great. I finally meet someone famous and he's gone before I can prove it," Claire complained.

Kristoff came out from around the reception desk. "Why don't you come back to the office for a minute," he said, saving Becca from more of Claire's annoying comments.

Becca followed, still too shaken to know what else to do. Kristoff indicated a chair and offered her a bottle of water. He sat across from her.

"Are you sure you're all right? Because you don't look all right."

Becca gripped the water bottle. How could she explain? None of it made any sense. "I wouldn't know where to start."

"How about you tell me how you came to look so disheveled. Did someone hurt you?"

She swallowed. "Some men came and took Nikolai away. I think they were from his country."

Kristoff's eyes widened. "People from Mondovia?" he asked, wide-eyed.

She nodded silently, her eyes watering.

"Well, that's not an everyday occurrence. Is there anything I can do to help?" Kristoff asked.

"I don't know. My wallet and passport were stolen, but I pick up my new passport tomorrow."

"Do you have someone who can wire you money?"

She really didn't want to think about this right now. "Yeah, I could call my brother." She sure didn't want to alert her dad to more problems.

"I can provide you information on where he should wire it."

"That would be great, but can I get it from you later? I'd like to be alone for a while. I've got to figure some things out."

He nodded. "Please let me know if there is anything I can do. I'll be on until five this evening."

"Thank you." Becca left the office, relieved that Claire

and her friends were gone, and that the common room was empty.

Her eyes rested on the locker in the hall. She unlocked it with the key from her pocket, pulled out Nikolai's backpack, and carried the pack up to the dorm room. The other beds were bare. The guests must have moved on. She unzipped his pack and touched the clothes inside. They smelled like Nikolai, fresh and earthy.

Lying down on his bed brought back memories of last night when they'd slept snuggled together. She had woken up to his warm kisses.

Becca hugged his backpack close and stared into space. She had no money, no passport, and no Nikolai.

What was she supposed to do?

25

Nikolai arrived at the palace late that night under the cover of darkness. He'd been taken to a private plane at a landing field outside Prague, where he met Visar. Now, back in Mondovia, a car with tinted windows delivered him home.

The brightly lit majestic palace appeared all too familiar. Nikolai longed for Becca, but knew he wouldn't be seeing her any time soon. He smoothed down his hair and wiped his hands on the back of his shorts. Visar didn't allow him a moment to clean up. Instead, he escorted Nikolai down the long hallway of sculptures to his father's drawing room. The eyes on the busts of each of his ancestors seemed to follow his walk of shame.

Visar rapped firmly on the thick door. He grabbed Nikolai's arm.

Nikolai glared back at the man. "I think you've done

your job here. I am fully capable of entering a room without your *assistance*."

The head of the Mondovian security released Nikolai's arm, but held his position. Nikolai took a fortifying breath. This was not how he hoped to return. He opened the door and entered.

His parents looked icily across the room at him.

"Thank you, Visar. As always, you can be counted on to complete an assignment," his father said. "However, causing a scene on public streets was not what I had in mind. Complete discretion would have been ideal, but I'm sure my son was the cause of the disruption."

"Yes, Your Majesty." Visar nodded and disappeared, closing the door behind him.

Nikolai crossed the Aubusson rug and approached his parents. They sat in the casual seating area, each holding a cut-crystal glass of port.

His father wore a crisp button-down shirt, open at the collar, with no tie or jacket, his jaw stern with irritation. His mother wore a simple blouse and slacks, her steady expression unreadable.

They had waited up for him. Nikolai remained standing and silent. This was the moment he'd been dreading.

His mother set her port on the table and reached for a stack of newspapers and magazines. "Swimming in your underwear with random girls, public scuffles," she said with disdain at the condemning photographs as she dropped each publication to the table.

Nikolai held his tongue.

His father shook his head. "Look at yourself. You are unshaven, unwashed, with a black eye and blood on your face. You look like a homeless street beggar. Have you lost your mind? You assaulted your own guard, and in public!"

"They certainly didn't act as my guard. They assaulted me!"

His father tossed back the remains of his drink. "Clearly you are not ready to accept responsibility for this country."

Nikolai approached them. "No kidding! And as long as things stay as they are, I never will be!"

"I've heard just about enough from you." His father stood so they were matched eye to eye.

Nikolai huffed. "No, I'm afraid that's the problem. You never listen to me." He looked away, unable to hold his father's hostile stare.

As if Nikolai hadn't spoken, his father continued. "Do you realize the media storm you have created? These pictures are everywhere. The world is enjoying a good laugh over your irresponsible behavior, including your loose relations with that girl you traipsed across Europe with."

"She's not just any girl! She's very important to me."

His father turned his back on Nikolai and refilled his glass.

"And you sent your goons after me in broad daylight, putting her in the middle of it all."

"I hardly believe she's a delicate flower. From these pictures, she was half the problem." His mother slapped down a news article that must have been recently printed from the internet.

The photo showed Becca, with a fierce expression, pounding her fists against one of the guards as Nikolai was held back by three men. The photo proved Nikolai had been taken by force.

His mother read the headline aloud. "'The Prince Dukes It Out in the Battle Royale.' What were you thinking! You have disgraced your country and embarrassed the palace."

"I was reminding myself that there is more to life than protocol and public relations." All he knew was that Becca had fought for him. It made him proud, but he also worried for her.

"No wonder you ignored Visar. Your mind was on a wild girl instead of your responsibilities. What kind of girl takes off with a complete stranger? But then again, the Crown Prince of Mondovia would be an irresistible temptation to a girl like her," his mother said.

"What the hell were you thinking, Nikolai?" his father barked. "That girl better not end up pregnant!"

"It's not like that! You're the one who had me dragged off the street and locked into a van without a chance to say good-bye, let alone make sure she's okay. Because of you, that girl is stranded in a foreign country. You have to let me contact her and make sure she gets out okay."

"I think you've done quite enough. If she can stand up to the Royal Guard, she can certainly find her way to the airport," his father said.

"We will deal with the repercussions of your actions and decide on your future tomorrow."

"Go to your room and clean yourself up," his mother snapped.

Nikolai slammed the door to his suite. Nothing had changed at all. His efforts to send a message to his parents were a huge fail. If anything, he'd made things worse. He dropped onto his sofa and lay back. He covered his eyes with his arm.

Somehow, he needed to get a message to Becca before she left Prague, and the only way to do that was through the hostel. The moment in the van when he discovered his phone missing, he wanted to scream and punch something. That phone was his only link to Becca. If she left Prague before he could track her down, he didn't know how he'd find her.

Becca woke up in the hostel, alone, in Nikolai's bed. The emptiness of the vacant dorm room echoed in her heart. Somehow she hoped he'd magically appear in the night and say there had been a crazy misunderstanding. She caressed the T-shirt she'd pulled from his pack. She kept imagining Nikolai and the way he smirked whenever she said something he didn't agree with.

No wonder Nikolai wanted to be Jason Bourne. Here she'd been feeling she had so little choice in her life, being forced on this trip, and pushed to go to Northwestern. Her father was never at a lack of direction for her life, but compared to Nikolai's life, hers was a breeze.

She got up and noticed her reflection in the mirror. Mascara stained her eyes, and her hair tangled around her face due to a fitful sleep. She stood like a zombie in the shower as the water pelted her skin, and tried to digest all that had happened since meeting Nikolai.

She had started out this trip hating Europe. But then she met the most amazing guy on the planet, only to have him literally ripped from her side.

What should she do next? This was all too much. She wanted to run away and hide, but with no money, no passport, and no Nikolai, that wasn't possible.

After dressing, repacking the two backpacks, and locking them in the cabinet, she climbed the narrow stairs to the rooftop patio. The morning was crisp and bright with the sun rising over the buildings, promising a gorgeous day, a sharp contrast to her mood.

She pulled out her phone, grateful to have it after everything else she'd lost, and called her brother.

He didn't answer. She sighed and left a short message. "Hey, Dylan. Everything is falling apart here, and I desperately need your help. Please call as soon as you get this. Bye." She held her head in her hands, willing herself to hold it together.

A few tourists she hadn't seen before entered the patio. She forced a smile and went downstairs to avoid conversation. With nothing better to do, she decided to go see if her passport was ready.

Behind the counter, Kristoff read the morning paper.

"Hi," Becca said.

"Good morning." He set the newspaper aside. "You made the paper!" He held up the local news.

There on the front page was a picture of a struggling Nikolai being dragged away while Becca fought to save him.

"You are famous now, too." He grinned.

She sighed. "No. I'm not famous. I'm just a girl with no passport who needs to go home. Can you show me on the map how to get to the U.S. Embassy? I was there yesterday morning, but I'm afraid I'll get lost without a map."

"Don't look so sad. You are in the most beautiful city in the world. Things could be worse."

"I don't think they could get much worse than they already are. I also need my brother to wire me some money. Can you help me, please? Someplace close by would be best."

"Of course. There is a place near your embassy. I will show you," he said, reaching for a map.

Becca counted off the blocks until she reached the correct street. Walking by herself was lonely and kind of scary. Suddenly, her phone rang. She hoped it would be Nikolai, even though she knew he didn't have her number. It was Dylan.

"Hi," she answered with a sigh.

"I leave you alone for two days and you make international headlines," he laughed.

She stopped. "What! How did you know?"

"Becca, you're on the front page of the national paper here. Apparently, when a prince makes a public scene, it's big news."

"Dylan, it's not funny." Her voice broke with emotion.

"Aw, relax. I was just kidding."

Some workmen across the street leered at her, so she continued walking. "I know. It's just that the last day has been pretty horrible. My bag got stolen with all my money and my passport. Nikolai was paying for everything, but now he's gone, too. I'm really hungry, I've got a headache, and I think I missed the cross street for the embassy. Dammit!"

"Shit, Becs. Are you okay?"

"Yeah, but I don't like being here by myself. I just want to go home."

"What happened with Nikolai? The paper was speculating everything from terrorist abduction to his own security jumping him."

"He said it was his father's men. That's all I know. We didn't get a chance to talk much as they dragged him away."

"That sucks. Well, I'm sure he'll call you as soon as things calm down."

Her heart ached. "No, I don't think so. He dropped his phone during the fight, so he won't know how to get ahold of me."

"Aw, don't count him out yet. He's a smart guy and will figure something out."

"You think so?"

"Yeah, I do. So do you have your airline tickets or did those get stolen, too?"

"I've got them. They're just e-tickets, so I left them in my bag at the hostel. But Nikolai and I were going to ride to Nuremberg on his cycle. How am I going to get there now?" She looked at her map and at the street sign, then turned right.

"You'll have to take a train. It's not hard. And I'll figure out how to wire you money from my credit card as soon as we hang up."

"Good. I've got the information on where to pick it up."

"Okay, I'll call you back as soon as I get to a bank. Listen. I know this is hard, but you can do this, Becca."

"Thanks, Dylan." She spotted the familiar, beautiful sight of the American flag up ahead. "Oh my God, Dylan! I found the embassy!"

"See? You're going to be fine."

26

The next morning, Nikolai rose early, a pit of despair in his gut. His attempts last night to find a number for the hostel had failed. Every laptop, computer, and phone had either been removed, or access to it locked down.

A breakfast tray was delivered to his rooms. Apparently, he was under house arrest.

He didn't know if he should direct his anger at his parents or Visar and his mastermind of security experts. They must be nervous he'd sneak off again or try to get Becca to spring him out of his palace prison. They weren't far off the truth.

Today he would track down a computer, but first he needed to shave before his mother sent someone in with a straight-edge blade to do it for him. Nikolai looked in the mirror. Not much he could do about his black eye.

As he lathered shaving cream on his face, Alexi burst in.

"You're back!" She barreled across the room and into his arms. "When did you get home?"

"Late last night. Careful or you'll be covered in foam." He hugged his sister and realized how much he'd missed her.

"I don't care. You should have woken me up." She sat at the dressing table beside him.

Nikolai looked closer. He couldn't possibly be seeing a pink sparkling piercing. "Did you pierce your nose?"

"Do you like it?" She beamed with pride over her sparkly nose stud.

"How did—"

"Well, you weren't the only one having fun. A few days ago, I snuck out of the opening of the new opera. You were supposed to be there, so I had to go. Thanks for that! Mother was distracted with Lady Peregrine. I said I was going to the ladies' room, but instead I ran to the mall."

"Alexi! I read online about you taking off. Are you crazy?"

"It was only for a couple of hours, but it was totally worth it. I figured Mother and Father should know I won't be any easier." She grinned.

"You shouldn't have." He laughed and ran the razor over his cheek, creating a clean path on his face.

"I had to! They are so out of touch. They need some tough love."

He rinsed away the hair and watched as a bit of his

freedom swirled down the drain. "My escape didn't seem to change anything. Maybe you'll have better luck. I'm surprised Father hasn't demanded you take it out."

Alexi giggled. "He did, but I refused."

"And he and Mother let you get away with it?"

"When I said I wouldn't take it out, they took away my phone, my computer, all my electronics. Life has been pretty quiet, but it's so worth it. I haven't had to go to any official events because Mother doesn't want anyone to see my piercing."

Nikolai couldn't believe his sister. "I think you're gutsier than I am."

"And look at your face! You've got a black eye."

He swiped off another section of beard.

"Did that happen when you got mugged?"

"It was my friend who was mugged, but yeah, that's when it happened. How did you know about that?"

"The only way I could find out what you've been doing is to have my maid sneak the papers in. So was your trip as wild as the papers say?"

"Other than the last day, when Visar publicly dragged me away, it was great." His thoughts turned to Becca, and he worried all over again.

"And who is the girl? She's so pretty. Everyone wanted to know how you met. Are you going to see her again?"

"Her name is Becca, and she's American. Fate kept

putting us in each other's path. I realized that she was someone I was supposed to know." He smiled at the memory of all the times he ran into Becca.

"And you really like her?"

"Yeah. I do. But now she's stuck in Prague by herself. Her bag was stolen, she has no money or passport, and she's supposed to fly home out of Nuremberg tomorrow." He ran his hand through his hair. "I need to get in touch with her. I had her number, but I lost it along with my phone. I need to make sure she's okay."

"Just call the place where you were staying. She'll be there one more day, right?"

"That's what I've been trying to do, but every phone and computer around here has mysteriously disappeared." He finished shaving.

"Your rooms, too?"

"Maybe I can get Dmitri to track down her number for me."

Alexi shot him a troubled look.

"What?"

"Dmitri was fired when Father found out he gave you money. Apparently loyalty is only useful if you are the one in charge. Loyalty to you or me is considered treason," she said.

"This place is screwed up. I don't know if I can stand staying."

253

He wiped his face with a towel. But then he realized he might not be staying, he might be transferred to the military sooner than later.

"Don't worry. I've got more plans for Mother and Father. They think they can decide how I live my life, but they're wrong," Alexi said with a grin.

Becca patted her back pocket again to make sure her new passport was still safe. At this point, she couldn't relax about losing it until she was on the plane back home. She'd collected the cash that Dylan wired. Funny how having a passport and cash could wipe away a lot of her worries. Now all she had to do was wait until tomorrow morning when she could board a train for Nuremberg. She had a full, empty day ahead of her.

She followed the familiar route she and Nikolai took yesterday and came upon the horrible spot where he'd been taken. Was he okay? Was he back home?

With a heavy heart she turned a corner and caught her breath.

Before her stood the bridge with all the love locks. Was it only yesterday that they were here together?

She approached the locks with trepidation, as she feared their lock wouldn't be there. But, after a quick look, she found it right where they'd secured it, nestled snug against the others. She reached up and touched the lock, willing Nikolai to appear.

She turned to scan the tourists and passersby. No Nikolai. She sighed. He wasn't there now and never would be again.

The next morning, Becca was up and out of the hostel early. She said a silent good-bye to Prague and the memories, both good and bad.

A quick cab ride to the train station felt like a luxury after navigating the streets by herself. Upon arrival, she hoisted both her and Nikolai's backpacks over her shoulders. She refused to leave his things behind.

The station bustled with rush hour activity as people hurried to their trains. She gazed up at the lofty dome and stained-glass windows. Art Nouveau, Nikolai would have said about the beautiful building.

It took her a while to find the right ticket counter where her prepaid ticket waited, thanks to Dylan. Even though the clerk told her where to find her train, the woman spoke fast and with a heavy accent. Becca missed having Nikolai there to translate.

She approached people who looked American to ask for help, and once on board, she asked a young couple next to her if she was indeed on the right train.

The trip to Nuremberg consisted of staring out the window for two hours and missing Nikolai. As much as she wanted to go home, how was she supposed to go back to her old life now that she'd spent the most exciting week of her life with a royal prince who made her feel special and important? She really wanted to be Cinderella, where her prince would come find her, but she'd left no glass slipper, and this was reality.

For all she knew he would be entering the Mondovian military any day. She sighed and leaned her forehead against the window as the train rumbled on.

Upon arrival at the Nuremberg train station, she followed the mobs of passengers into the main terminal and easily found the ticket machine. She was relieved it had instructions in English, but she couldn't get her euros to fit in the slot of the bill feeder and wondered if she'd picked a broken machine.

"Here, you need to hit enter to confirm your order before it will accept your money," said an impatient man behind her.

She felt like an idiot. "Thank you. I figured it must be something easy."

Becca picked a forward train car so she could be one of the first off the train and into the airport. She lowered the heavy packs to the floor and settled in for the twenty-minute ride.

Travel days sucked. Every few minutes the train made a stop. She carefully tracked the progress on the map posted above the door. Just a few more stops and she'd be there. She readied her bags. Her nerves started to fray. She was so over international travel.

Finally she arrived at the airport and had to walk forever before arriving at the ticketing area. Luckily, everyone else seemed to be heading in that direction, so there was no chance to mess this up.

The line for check-in was long. She looked at her phone again. She had little over an hour to get through it. Then a text came in from Dylan: *Where are you? I'm waiting at the gate.*

She texted him back. *Stuck in line.*

Each minute dragged like ten as she watched the line crawl at a snail's pace. Finally she received her boarding pass.

Becca headed for security only to discover a sea of glum passengers waiting to make it through the line.

Dylan texted again to say they'd started boarding the plane and to hurry up.

Becca texted back: *I'm in the line from hell.* She started biting the inside of her lip.

After an eternity, Becca passed through. She grabbed her belongings and checked the direction signs for her gate. Gate 44, all the way at the end concourse.

Unbelievable!

She looked at her phone. Dylan had texted that they had called for final boarding.

Becca ran, dodging passengers, strollers, and small children. The two packs bounced heavily against her back. With each gate she passed, her fear grew to a full-out panic.

What if they left without her? She couldn't bear being stranded in Europe one more day.

She spied her gate. Out of breath, she pushed on, rounding the corner to find the waiting area empty, except for Dylan and two scowling airline employees.

"Becca!"

One look at her brother and she started to cry.

"Dylan, I was so afraid you were going to leave."

"Of course I waited. Come on." He guided her to the gangway and handed over his boarding pass. "I wasn't about to leave you behind. These women aren't too happy about it. For a minute there, I thought they were going to close the doors on us."

"Thank you," she said to the annoyed clerk as she wiped away her tears.

Once seated, the doors closed, and the flight attendants recited the safety talk.

"Don't look so miserable. You made it," Dylan said.

"I know. It's just, now that we're leaving, it guarantees even more that I'll never see Nikolai again. I'll probably never even talk to him either."

She tried not to cry, but fat tears of defeat rolled down her face.

"It's a vacation romance, Becca. Give yourself two days back home, and he'll be no more than a great memory. You'll meet lots of guys at Northwestern."

"This is different. I loved Nikolai."

Dylan raised his eyebrows.

"I know. I'm a fool. It doesn't matter how we felt for each other. I could never end up with a guy like him."

"Why not? You're just as good as he is."

But she knew better. "Our lives are totally different. He's destined to become king and serve his country. I'm just an ordinary girl from the United States trying to figure out my life."

"Becca, don't think that way."

"Whatever. It's over. Just like a fairy tale, only without a happy ending. It was more of an Aesop's fable where all the stories are evil and horrible."

"He said he'd find you."

"And how will he do that? All my info was on his phone, which I now have." She leaned her head back against the seat.

"Stop acting so negative. He must have some secret service that he can put on it."

Becca hoped Dylan was right.

27

Nikolai followed Alexi's bouncing blonde-and-pink head up another flight of steps.

"Don't you think this is a little extreme?" he asked, and he wasn't talking about her latest effort to annoy their parents by dyeing her hair pink.

"We have to be careful. For all we know there are bugs and hidden cameras in every room."

"Beyond security cameras in the public places and main corridors, I don't think we're being spied on. Now hand over the phone."

"Not till we get to the top. You don't want to get cut off because of bad reception."

He appreciated his sister's determination to help him track down the Prague hostel, but she did err on the side of the dramatic. They were on the rarely entered fifth floor of the palace where they used to tell ghost stories as children.

They'd passed room after room of stored antiquities.

Finally Alexi decided the last room before the tower stairs would be remote and secure enough.

They squeezed themselves past dusty crates and boxes to a sunny window for better reception. Nikolai looked twice at a storage crate labeled *Renoir*. He ran his finger over the letters painted on the crate. "What a shame, to keep all these priceless pieces of art locked up."

"You know Father. Lock it up, keep it safe. It's the same way he treats us. Here's a spot."

"Give me the phone already."

"Here." She handed over the phone. "You could be a little nicer about it. It wasn't easy to convince the stable hand to let me borrow it. You would not believe how paranoid everyone around here is of getting sacked."

"After Dmitri was fired for helping me, I don't blame them." He immediately searched for the hostel name and number. "Got it!" He dialed and held his breath, hoping.

Alexi climbed on top of a box marked *18th Century clock by Le Faucheur*. He could only imagine the value of her makeshift chair.

"Prague House. This is Kristoff," a voice answered.

At last! His heart soared with hope. "Hello, Kristoff! I stayed at Prague House a few days ago, and I'm trying to track down a friend who stayed there with me."

"I'll do what I can. Is your friend still here?"

"She flies out of Nuremberg today, and I don't know

what time she had to leave. Her name is Becca. I'm sorry, but I don't know her last name."

Nikolai was still frustrated that he hadn't been able to secure a phone earlier.

"I know who you mean. Becca left about an hour ago for the train station."

"Dammit," Nikolai muttered.

Alexi looked up from examining her blue nail polish with a sympathetic frown.

"Any chance you are the man pictured with her in the newspapers?"

"Yes, that's me. My name is Nikolai." Now maybe he'd be more eager to help. "So now that you know I was traveling with her, can you give me her information? I'd be forever grateful."

The phone became quiet and then Kristoff spoke. "I've never talked to a prince before. I wish I could help, Your Majesty, but the registration book went missing the same day that you did."

He couldn't believe it. More interference by Visar and his team.

"What?" Alexi asked, braiding the long pink sections of her hair.

"The registration book is mysteriously gone," Nikolai whispered.

"No way! Those dirty shits. Ask him to check the credit card receipts."

Nikolai returned to his call. "It's really important that I find her. You are my only hope. I know it's probably against the rules, but you have no idea how desperate I am. How about credit card receipts? Her signature should be on the receipt."

"I'm really not allowed to do that, but I'd be happy to make an exception for you. Just one minute."

Nikolai tapped his fingers on a storage crate while he waited.

"What's he doing?" Alexi asked.

"He's checking."

"Just think, in a minute you'll have her full name. You know she's from Chicago. It should be easy to find her now."

"Prince Nikolai?" Kristoff's voice came back over the phone.

"Yes, I'm here."

"This is very strange, but all the credit card receipts for the past week are gone. Every single one. I checked in the safe, too, but they aren't here."

"Unbelievable." He scrubbed his hand over his face.

"I can contact the night manager if you like. Perhaps he knows where they are."

"No. Thank you, Kristoff, but I'm pretty sure those receipts won't ever be seen again."

"I'm so sorry I wasn't able to help you more."

"Thank you for trying."

"She seemed very sad after you left. I hope you're able to find her."

"Thank you, Kristoff. I do, too."

He ended the call and tossed the phone on a crate next to Alexi.

"So all the records are gone," she said.

"Everything. If I didn't know better, I'd bet they cleaned the place of all her DNA, too."

"Who do you think ordered that? Father? Would he be so mean?"

"I don't know that Father would have made a direct order to wipe away all traces of Becca, but I wouldn't put it past Visar to do it on his own."

"So that was a dead end, but there are other ways to find her. We just have to think of them," Alexi said.

"I don't know her airline or flight number, not that the airline would release a passenger list."

"What other places did you go? Did she use her credit card anywhere else? What else did you do where there could be a record of her?"

"Becca always paid cash other than at the hostel. She went to the police station to report the robbery, and she went to the U.S. Embassy."

"Perfect! Try those."

"I really don't think the police station is going to release the name of a girl who was mugged."

"Well, you won't know unless you try! Are you in love with her or not?"

Nikolai grinned. "I'm on it!"

He spent the next hour contacting the U.S. Embassy, the Prague police station, and even the riverboat company. No one would help him. They all cited privacy laws, security reasons, or company policy.

Dejected, he handed the phone back to Alexi.

"It's no use. She's lost to me."

28

"*Here* goes nothing," Dylan said as they exited the gate area at the Madison airport.

"Do you think Dad will be here or just Vicky?" Becca gripped the straps of the two backpacks like lifelines. She'd never done anything as bad as when she skipped her original flight home from Nuremberg to stay with Nikolai.

"Probably just Vicky, which is good. She won't be nearly as scary. I can't imagine Dad taking time away from his precious work to welcome home his delinquent kids."

They rode the escalator down to the baggage area. Becca scanned the crowd. No familiar faces popped out. Maybe Dad and Vicky were leaving her and Dylan to fend for themselves.

But then she spotted a tall figure speaking into his phone. He had graying hair, and wore a charcoal-colored business suit.

Her stomach dropped. "Dad's here."

Dylan followed her gaze. "Well, that sucks."

Her dad noticed them as they stepped off the escalator. His calm, emotionless stare said it all. Becca had never had to deal with angering her dad before. She wasn't equipped for the outcome.

As Becca and Dylan approached, her father covered the phone with his hand. "Do you have any checked luggage?"

"No," she answered.

He resumed his phone conversation, and turned to exit the airport. She and Dylan followed without a word. When they reached her father's SUV, he popped the lock on the back as he passed to the driver's side.

After placing her two backpacks in the vehicle and closing the door, she found Dylan had taken up the entire rear seat with his carry-on bags. Becca gave him a dirty look and climbed into the front seat.

"All right, Chuck. Bring the report to the meeting in the morning." Her father hung up and slipped his phone into his suit pocket.

Becca held her breath, afraid of what he'd say. He paid the parking attendant and exited the ramp. Dylan hid safely behind their dad, out of his line of sight.

They rode in silence, but the mood in the vehicle was anything but peaceful. After a mile, she noticed her father white-knuckling the steering wheel.

"Which one of you wants to explain why you blatantly

lied to me?" he asked in a quiet, restrained voice.

At first, neither of them answered, but then Dylan spoke up. "It's my fault, Dad. Don't blame Becca."

Becca let out a breath of relief. Thank God Dylan took the hit for her.

"I'm perfectly aware that you were behind this asinine escapade." He shot Dylan an angry glare in the rearview mirror. "Sadly, this is the norm for you. What I want to know is why Becca went along with it. She knows better than to do something so stupid, yet there she was, right alongside you."

"I'm sorry, Dad," Becca said, hoping her apology would be accepted, and they could pretend everything was fine.

"Sorry? Is that all you have to say for yourself? Do you have any idea how much your little escapade cost? Airline tickets don't grow on trees. We had just changed your tickets to come home, which is what I thought you wanted all along, and then I learned the tickets were changed again!"

What could she say? She didn't want to explain that she'd really been with Nikolai instead of her brother all that time. Lord only knew what her dad would say then.

"You moped through the entire trip, and the second I gave you what you wanted, you defied me. I'm used to that type of behavior from your brother, but not you!" He swerved sharply to change lanes.

"I wasn't moping through the entire trip."

"And now isn't the time to talk back to me either. I was

trying to complete a very important negotiation when I received Dylan's message that you two . . . brats decided to stay behind. Have you any idea how much you upset Vicky? She worked very hard to put that trip together."

He fixed her with a stubborn look. "Becca, you disappoint me."

That was it. She couldn't take it anymore. "I disappoint you? Seriously? Oh my God, Dad. I can't believe you even noticed I was gone!"

He looked taken aback.

"You never pay any attention to me. Other than a couple of times on the trip, you spent the entire time schmoozing with your new rich friends. Face it. I'm no more than an afterthought. You don't notice me unless I do something less than perfect."

"That's enough!" he barked, pulling up to a stoplight.

"Hell it is! You ever think that half the reason Dylan is always causing trouble is so you have to notice him?"

Her father shot her a warning look.

"It's true! You totally use your job as an excuse to avoid us."

"My job, as you so casually put it, is what provides you with the beautiful home we live in, all your nice things, and your out-of-state college tuition."

"That's bull. It's not a home. It hasn't been since Mom died. It's a showpiece you use to impress your colleagues. And I never asked to go to an out-of-state college.

Northwestern was your decision, not mine. I wanted to stay in Madison."

"Becca, what has gotten into you?" He turned the car onto their street.

"Gee, I don't know. Maybe a backbone. I'm sick and tired of being the obedient child."

He pushed the garage door opener and pulled into the garage. "I'll tell you what it's getting you. Grounded. You can forget about any plans you had for the rest of the summer. You can sit home in that showpiece, as you put it, and think of a damn good apology. That goes for both of you!"

Becca got out of the car and slammed the door.

"Great, Dad, and how are you going to enforce it? You're never home long enough to know if we're even there."

She stormed into the house, leaving a furious father and an impressed Dylan in her wake.

Becca stared out the window at the backyard pool. She'd been home for a couple of days and still couldn't shake the blanket of depression. Her heart ached for Nikolai. She couldn't get the image out of her mind of him being dragged away.

Now that she was home, she didn't care about anything here. She didn't care that her friend, Kelly, stole her boyfriend; she didn't care about getting together with her other friends; and she couldn't care less about starting college in a few weeks.

She heard the door from the garage open. Vicky was home from work. Was it that late already?

Vicky leafed through the mail on the kitchen counter, then hung her suit jacket over a chair, and kicked off her heels. She glanced over at Becca in the living room. "I didn't see you there. How was your day?"

Becca didn't feel like talking, but she didn't really feel like getting up either. "It was fine," she answered.

"Did you get to the store and pick out bedding for your dorm room?" Vicky expertly twisted a corkscrew into a wine bottle and then smoothly pulled out the cork.

"Nah."

"I'm surprised not to see Kelly here. Haven't you called her yet?"

Becca shook her head and focused on a seam in the leather couch. Didn't Vicky remember what Kelly did? She broke the cardinal rule of friendship, stealing your best friend's guy. Then again, Vicky started dating Becca's dad less than a year after Becca's mom had died.

Vicky joined Becca, sitting in an adjacent chair and sipping her chardonnay. "You've been so unhappy since the trip. I've asked Dylan about it."

Becca's head snapped up.

"But he wouldn't tell me a word."

They sat in silence.

"Becca, I know you aren't a big fan of mine. I understand that I must seem like an outsider to you."

"No . . ." Becca started.

Vicky held up her hand. "You don't have to pretend. I understand. Your mom was a wonderful woman, and losing her was a terrible tragedy. Accepting a new person in your life must feel like a betrayal to her memory."

Becca didn't say a word, but Vicky had nailed it.

"I would never try to replace her. Ever. But I see you hurting, and it hurts me not to be able to reach out. I think your mom would have wanted you to have someone you could lean on when things are tough."

Becca looked up at her stepmother, but couldn't find the words to express herself.

Vicky took her silence as a sign to continue. "Do you want to tell me what happened in Europe?"

Becca surprised herself that she actually itched to confide in her stepmother, but knew she would only look like a lovesick teenager.

"I already know you weren't with Dylan and that you went to Prague."

They locked eyes. Becca found compassion, not judgment. "You do?"

Vicky swirled her wine and took another sip.

"After receiving a call from the credit card company, when they suspected your card was stolen, I checked all the charges on the cards for both you and Dylan. I know that neither of you were in Nuremberg. Dylan went to Amsterdam, while you went to Prague. You charged lodging at a hostel before the suspicious charges occurred."

"When I called you to check in, you texted back that you were fine. It was clear to me that you didn't want any help. But if you did, I would have been there for you."

Becca dropped her eyes and chewed on her thumbnail. "I'm sorry. I should have told you my bag was stolen, but I was afraid you'd be mad."

"The responsible thing to do would have been to call home and let us know what was going on, but then again, we expected you to be in Nuremberg, not Prague. Do you want to tell me who you were with?"

She sighed. What would Vicky think if she told her? Would she even believe her crazy story? But she wanted to share it with someone. Kelly sure wasn't the right person, and Dylan had already heard it more times than he cared to.

"Remember the guy in Regensburg who took me back to the boat after that biker ran into me?"

"Yes."

"His name is Nikolai, and he's the one I went to Prague with."

"I see. I know I was the one supporting the whole travel-on-your-own idea, but do you think it was a good idea to go off with a total stranger like that?"

"He wasn't a stranger to me. I'd been seeing him throughout the whole cruise while you and Dad were off . . . doing stuff. Plus, he's pretty well known over there."

"Oh?"

Becca bit her lip. Here goes nothing. "He's the Prince of Mondovia."

Vicky arched a skeptical eyebrow. "You're trying to tell me that you went to Prague with the Prince of Mondovia? Becca, you know I saw the magazine in your cabin. I find it a bit difficult to believe you not only met the young man, but took off with him. Why don't you tell me what really happened?"

"I know it sounds impossible, but it's not." Becca rifled through the stack of magazines next to her laptop and pulled out the bottom three. She handed Vicky the one that pictured Becca with Nikolai at the lake. "See."

Vicky examined it closely, then surprise appeared on her face. "Oh my gosh, that's him, and you! In your under-wear!"

Becca nodded.

"Why didn't you tell me?"

"I didn't know his true identity at first, and after that, I tried to help him hide from the press and his family. I didn't really think you'd have let me go off with him."

"No. Probably not."

"And then in Prague, his father's men caught up with us, and they took Nikolai back to Mondovia. He doesn't have my info, so it's not like he can even contact me. Plus, he's supposed to be entering the military. It's like the most amazing thing that ever happened to me, and it ended in the most awful way."

"Have you tried to contact him?" Vicky stared at the photo of Nikolai.

"I have, but none of the info on the Mondovian Royal Family website includes an email or phone number. It's like they live in the Dark Ages or something. All I could find was an address. I sent a letter the day after I got back."

"I hate to be a downer, but you do know that most summer romances end at the end of summer? Remember when you went to summer camp? Did you ever stay in touch with your new friends?"

"No. I always said I would, but I didn't." Becca's heart twisted to think that Vicky summed up her time with Nikolai as a summer fling.

"I'm sorry. I think you should hope for the best, but prepare yourself for the worst."

"You don't think he'll write back?"

"I don't know. We'll just have to wait and see."

Becca nodded, feeling even more miserable.

29

The photographers were waiting for Nikolai to screw up. His parents had kept him hidden for the past few days, but had now decided on a new approach on how to handle all the bad publicity he'd created.

The only way to put the gossip to rest was to show Nikolai acting the dignified, obedient prince and son.

He exited the car and walked a half step behind his father. No one upstaged the king. The heads of parliament watched their approach and nodded as they passed. Photographers captured every moment. Nikolai would have loved to crack a sarcastic joke to lighten the mood, but didn't dare.

They entered the parliament building where he spent the entire day being ignored. When he wasn't thinking about Becca and missing her till it hurt, he observed the people, listened to the speeches, and read between the political lines of everything around him.

Bottom line. His country had financial problems.

At the end of the day, he was escorted out of the building. He offered the requisite handshakes and nods to the elected officials, but knew they thought him a young fool who needed to be disciplined.

If his father expected Nikolai's presence to prove there was a strong future for the royal family, he had failed. Nikolai felt like another example of how the royal family was a drain on resources and served as no more than figureheads.

"How did your day with parliament go?" his mother asked, looking up from her afternoon tea, when he returned to the palace.

"Honestly, it was a colossal waste of time," Nikolai said, and sank into a wingback chair.

His father shook his head. "I should have known this wouldn't help."

"How can you possibly say that?" she asked.

"First off, we sat there watching the proceedings as if our presence even mattered. There are elected officials, voted in by the people, to make the decisions for our country," Nikolai said.

"And as king, I hold an important advisory position to parliament. They look to me for guidance and direction," his father said, joining his wife on the sofa.

"Do they? Or are they just being courteous to your

title?" Nikolai loosened his tie.

"Nikolai, your disrespect knows no bounds. I swear we should ship you off to the military so you can learn some discipline," his father said.

"Or is it that you want to squash my individuality and mold me into your image?" Nikolai snapped back, then stared at the ornate fireplace, not even wanting to look at his parents.

"I don't understand where all of this is coming from. You've been perfectly fine and then suddenly you sneak off to chase some girl. Is that what this is all about? A girl?" his mother asked.

"You should know me better than that. I didn't meet her until well into my trip."

"Perhaps you need a dose of true reality. Tomorrow I meet with the joint finance director. I want you there."

"Fine. I'm here to do my duty." He turned on his heel and walked away.

The next day, true to his word, Nikolai met in his father's office with the king and the finance director. Rolph Brietenburg, a middle-aged senator with a bald patch, had held his position for more than a decade.

"As you see, Your Highness, the budget for the royal family, palace, and properties is again in the red. We've dipped into the reserves for the past eight years and there is nothing left. We are cutting into important social services in order to provide for the crown."

This was news to Nikolai. He knew they were a drain on the country, but he had no idea things were this bad. His parents never let on that there was a financial problem, and they certainly didn't curtail their spending. It seemed they hosted a lavish state dinner every other month.

"I understand, Rolph, but we must find a way to designate more funds. We can't turn our back on the fiscal needs of the crown. We are the core of Mondovia."

"Yes, sir, but I need to impress upon you that the ongoing operating budget for Mersch Palace, the household and family needs alone, have escalated dramatically each year. At this rate, we're going to push the country into a recession."

"The financial situation can't be that serious." The king bristled.

"I assure you, Your Majesty, it is," said Mr. Brietenburg.

How could his father have let the situation get so out of hand? One thing Nikolai learned on his travels was how to budget his money. When things got tough after Becca's bag was stolen, he spent only the bare minimum.

"And what is it you're recommending?" the king asked, tapping his fountain pen on the table.

"Closure of the outer properties, the castles of Noraloska and Rakburg, the Turkford Estate, as well as Beaucar House and Miren Gardens." He sighed. "And that's just the beginning."

"You can't be serious," the king exclaimed.

The tension in the room doubled. Nikolai didn't see this ending well. His father did not like being told what to do. The idea of closing even one of the dozens of properties of the crown would be unconscionable in his father's eyes.

"I wish I had better news, but the revenue streams have suffered from the strained economy. In addition, we need additional social services and resources for the homeless, and the Sklos orphanage needs complete renovation due to safety issues."

"Rolph, we must support the integrity of the crown. I can accept reducing staff at a couple of properties, but even that will tarnish our image. It's a double-edged sword," the king said.

Seriously? All his father was concerned about was the crown's image?

The king turned to him. "You see, Nikolai. Running the monarchy is much more complicated than you imagined. There are difficult decisions to be made."

"Yes, I see that, but with all due respect, Father, I don't think the correct decisions are being made."

Rolph raised an eyebrow.

The king leaned back in his chair. "And what would

you suggest? Please enlighten us."

Nikolai sat straighter and cleared his throat. "Well, to start off, I agree that there are too many royal estates and properties."

His father harrumphed.

"But rather than close them down, why don't we revitalize them? Put them to other uses."

Rolph seemed intrigued.

"Yesterday at parliament, there was a lot of discussion about the need for updating our schools; and the Habsburg Museum has fallen into disrepair. The cost of renovation for these properties is high. We have the Beaucar House. It could serve as a new museum, and Turkford Estate would be perfect as a school or a senior residence."

"Go on," Rolph said.

"Rather than pour more money into the properties of the crown, or shut them down, let's turn them into something useful. Something needed now. I'm sure there is an estate that could serve as a new orphanage much better than the current one."

"Is that everything?" his father asked, probably hoping to stop him from sacrificing the crown's sacred assets.

"No, it's not. Let's become the people's crown by inviting the people to know our history better. Let's end the class system and create equality. We shouldn't boast such elitism and hit our population with more taxes."

His father remained quiet, so Nikolai continued. He might never get this opportunity again. He recalled some of what he saw while on his trip.

"The royal estates have beautiful gardens and an enormous amount of resources go into their maintenance. Let's open the properties and gardens to the public. Make them available for special events and weddings. Let the local gardening clubs study the gardens and assist with the upkeep. We could allow the symphony to put on free summer concerts."

Rolph took copious notes.

"I was up on the fifth floor of the palace the other day. Do you realize hundreds and hundreds of antiquities are stored up there?"

"Of course, they are there for safekeeping. There are pieces from the beginning of Mondovian history."

"Let's put them on display and charge admittance. Or better yet, let's display the best and put other items up for auction. There are so many things we could do. The options are endless." Nikolai leaned back and took a sip of water. He'd said his piece.

"I must say, I'm impressed," Rolph said cautiously, watching for the king's reaction.

The king tapped his fountain pen on his papers. "Nikolai, I didn't think you were paying attention yesterday."

"Father, I am always paying attention, but you've never bothered to notice."

His father leveled him with a warning look.

"I'm used to it. No one ever listens to me when I speak either," Nikolai said.

Despite his father's calm exterior, Nikolai recognized the irritation in his eyes.

"Well, I can tell you that I'm listening, and I like what I hear. Nikolai, you have a brilliant head on your young shoulders, along with a fresh perspective that is perfect for problem solving. What do you think, Your Highness?" Rolph asked.

"Perhaps I've underestimated you, Nikolai. You have made some excellent points and while the answers aren't as simple as what you propose, I see potential."

Nikolai was astonished. That was the closest thing to a compliment that he'd received from his father in years.

"Now if you'll excuse us. I'd like to speak candidly with Rolph."

"Of course." Nikolai was dismissed again. Not a big surprise. He thanked Mr. Brietenburg for his support and left.

That night, Nikolai was summoned to the garden. He met Alexi, with her bright pink hair, in the corridor and smiled. He was starting to like the look on her.

"You too?" she asked.

"Doesn't bode well for either one of us, does it."

"They had to break eventually. I guess the pink hair did it."

"At least we can face them together."

Nikolai held the door to the patio. They stepped into the warm August air, and found their parents seated in front of the Baroque fountain. A large cupid looked down from a pedestal. Nikolai wasn't sure if it smiled at him or sneered.

"Hello, Mother. Father." He nodded.

"Please sit down." His mother indicated the wrought-iron chairs adjacent to them. "It has been a very noteworthy month. Much has taken place."

So, this was going to be all about Nikolai and the trouble he'd caused.

"You have both made us aware, in your own way"—she looked at Alexi's hair and nose—"of your unhappiness. Tradition is the cornerstone of this family and of Mondovia. It is never to be dismissed or taken lightly."

Nikolai sighed, trying to stay calm.

His father stood. "That said, there are times and situations where perhaps change is necessary. Sometimes it is forced upon us during times of upheaval, war, or strife, and sometimes we can open our minds to it."

"Your father and I have been discussing this topic at length. While we are reluctant to make changes that could be detrimental to the crown, we realize that the role of the monarchy is evolving and that the world around us is changing fast."

"What are you saying?" Nikolai asked. He'd never heard his parents talk with such open-mindedness, and he didn't know what to think.

"What your mother is saying is that we've decided to rethink our stance and certain priorities."

Nikolai didn't dare hope this was something positive. "And that means?"

"It means that we want to give you and Alexandra the opportunity to make more decisions about your futures," his mother said.

His father looked out over the palace gardens and then turned to him. "What fit for the royal family in the past no longer seems appropriate. Nikolai, it has become painfully clear that you are adverse to joining our military forces."

He nodded. That life would be torture to him.

His father continued. "It has been a difficult pill to swallow, but we want to respect the man, and eventually the king, you wish to become."

"I don't have to go into the military?"

"Correct," his father said, jaw clenched.

"Thank you!" Nikolai resisted the urge to whoop with joy as he understood how difficult it was for his father to come to this conclusion.

"Alexandra, we see that you desire more freedom to be

the individual you are. We will work to make that happen," her mother said.

"Thank you," Alexi said with a pert grin, as if she always knew things would turn out this way.

Nikolai wasn't sure what exactly his parent's plans entailed, but things were looking up. Now all he needed was to figure out how to find Becca. Where did she say she was going to college?

30

Becca had been home for fifteen days with no word from Nikolai. Dylan was leaving for school in a few days and had insisted she hang out at their pool with him and his friends.

She'd gone out with her friends once, but sneaking beer down to the lake and scoping for guys on State Street was no longer her idea of a good time.

Kelly had called and begged forgiveness for going out with Ethan. The fact was, Becca didn't even care anymore. She considered telling Kelly about Nikolai, but he was so private and special that she decided to keep it to herself.

"Hey, Becca, looking good," Marcus, Dylan's best friend, said, taking a seat next to her.

"Hi, Marcus." For years when she was younger, Becca had secretly crushed on Marcus, who wore a small gold hoop earring and had his hair buzz cut. He'd never paid any attention to her. He always dated hot girls, and ignored Becca.

Marcus adjusted his aviator shades, his muscular body bronzed from an idle summer at his family's cabin.

"So, you start Northwestern next week."

"That's the plan," she said, noticing his long swim trunks. She remembered Nikolai, swimming in his underwear and almost giggled.

"That's awesome. You'll have to come by the frat house. It'll be a party every night during rush."

"I'll think about it," she lied.

"Dylan told me you had quite the awesome time in Europe, and that you were hanging out with a prince. I saw pictures online. Dang, that's crazy!"

Becca looked across the pool at Dylan, who popped open a beer for a girl from the neighborhood. He noticed Marcus with Becca, raised his bottle, and smiled.

She shook her head. Becca had never been anything more to Marcus than Dylan's annoying little sister. But now Marcus suddenly noticed her because she knew Nikolai.

"You want to go out this weekend? I've got tickets to the Badger preseason football game," Marcus asked, flicking an ant off his lawn chair.

"You know, Marcus, I really don't. But it's sweet of you to ask."

She collected her towel and Diet Pepsi, and went in the house. The poor guy looked shocked, as if he'd never been turned down before, which he probably hadn't.

If Marcus had asked her before she left for Europe, she'd have jumped at the chance. But now, Marcus was just another immature guy, more interested in the next party than anything else.

She watched Dylan's friends from the window, all laughing and goofing off. No matter how she tried, she just couldn't find that carefree mood anymore.

Instead of hanging out with friends, Becca had spent her time poring over the internet, trying to find a new way to contact Nikolai. She'd sent an official letter the second day she was home, as that was the protocol according to the Mondovian Royal Family website.

The one good thing she'd found were websites that reported on the royals, complete with articles and online photos. The palace had issued a statement downplaying Nikolai's disappearance and tabloid appearances. He'd even made a few official appearances.

In the first photos she saw, his smile seemed forced and his body rigid as he walked stoically with his father, the king. This was not the Nikolai she knew. But in the last couple of pictures, he appeared happier and was attending social events.

He even posed with a beautiful girl with glossy black hair. It was a punch in the gut, but he had explained once that most of the girls he met at social functions were distant relatives performing their royal duties, too. She hoped this was true, but each day she felt farther away from him.

Becca checked the snail mail, leafing through it quickly. There it was!

She held an official-looking envelope, complete with a Mondovian emblem, marked *International*.

"Oh my God," she whispered aloud, dropping the rest of the mail. She hugged the coveted letter. The thick, bright paper included an embossed seal for the return address. She grabbed a knife from the drawer, carefully slit open the envelope, and slid out the single sheet of paper.

Dear Miss Hanson,
Prince Nikolai wishes to thank you for your recent
letter in which you invited His Royal Highness
to make your acquaintance. He was extremely
grateful for your kind greetings.
Unfortunately, His Royal Highness is unable to
reply personally to his many requests and has asked
me to send his kind regards and best wishes.
Yours truly,
Greta Vogel
Royal Assistant

Becca flipped the page over. That's it? All that time and he couldn't even write her back? Her eyes welled. How could he let her go so fast? She dropped the letter on the kitchen counter, went to her room, and fell onto her bed. She stared at the ceiling, devastated and unwanted. Tears rolled from her eyes.

An hour later a knock sounded on her door. "Yeah," she muttered.

"Becca, it's me," Vicky called.

Becca sighed. "Come in."

The door slowly opened. "Hi," Vicky said. "How are you doing? Have you been in here by yourself all day?"

"No. Just for a while."

"I found this on the counter." She placed Becca's letter from Mondovia on the bed. "Do you want to talk about it?"

The letter symbolized everything that had gone wrong. "I feel like such a fool," Becca said, crossing her arms and hugging herself. "Everything was so perfect, and I totally fell for him. But then everything fell apart, and he hasn't even tried to reach me. Not even once."

Vicky grimaced. "I'm sorry. You must like him very much."

"I do. More than I have a right to. And now he's gone, and I'm back here. I'm supposed to start school soon and, more than ever, I don't want to go."

"I thought you were excited about Northwestern."

"Not really. I tried to be because that's where Ethan was

291

going, and I knew Dad wanted me to go there. But what's the point? I don't even know what I want to do with my life. Dad wants me to be a lawyer, but I swear it's the last thing I'll do."

"You don't need to know your future profession to attend college. There are so many wonderful experiences that are part of going to college. You'll meet great people and do amazing things."

Becca nodded. It was always easier to go with the flow. "I know. That's what everyone says. I'll go. It's fine."

"But you don't want to?" Vicky asked.

"No. I don't. It's a waste of money and time. I don't want to go 'have an experience.' I did that in Europe. I had the most amazing time of my life, and I can't imagine anything ever topping that."

Vicky smiled. "I'm glad it was so wonderful, even if it ended badly." She sat on the edge of the bed and ran her hand over the bedspread. "Have you ever thought about taking a year off?"

"I could never do that. Dad would flip out. He's still mad about me lying to him and staying in Europe."

"I'm not so sure he'd react badly. You know, Becca, some people are ready for college right away, and some people need to take time off before they settle back into school. In the UK they call it a gap year."

Becca nodded.

"Maybe you're one of those people who needs some

time off to experience more of life before you buckle down to more studies."

What was Vicky getting at?

"If you weren't going to Northwestern, what would you do?"

"I don't know, I've never thought about it."

"Think about it now. Before our trip, you wanted to stay here, at home."

Those thoughts seemed like a million years ago. "I can't imagine staying here now. It would literally kill me. I feel like a totally different person. The only thing my friends want to do is go drinking and meet guys. They're so shallow."

Vicky fought back a smile, but said nothing.

"I feel I need to escape this boring life. I really want to be with Nikolai, but everything I've tried has been a big fail. Either his people are keeping us apart, or he doesn't want anything to do with me anymore."

Vicky nodded.

"If I weren't going to school, I think I'd like to go someplace new, where no one knew me and there were no expectations. Maybe volunteer somewhere or something."

"Maybe you should do that," Vicky offered.

"Are you kidding? Dad would totally freak."

"I think I can handle your dad on this. Come with me. I want to show you something."

Becca followed Vicky downstairs to the family room.

She couldn't imagine what Vicky wanted to show her.

Vicky pulled photo albums from the bottom shelf of the bookcase. "Let me see if I can find the right one. Ah, here it is!" She handed an outdated photo album to Becca.

She recognized it immediately. "This was my mom's." Becca held it like a coveted antiquity.

"I know. When we remodeled two years ago, I reorganized down here and found it. Take a look."

Becca opened the book. The aging spine crackled. The first picture showed her mom grinning brightly and looking very young. She stood in front of a sign that read *Costa Rica*. Becca's breath hitched. "I remember this book."

After her mom's death, Becca had pored over every picture of her mother that she could find.

Becca turned the page and revealed pictures of her mom hiking in a rain forest, standing near a waterfall, and next to a giant sea turtle. "I wonder when she went to Costa Rica." Becca recalled that this was where Nikolai mentioned he wanted to escape to, if his life were different.

"Right after high school," Vicky said.

Becca looked up.

"Your mom took a year off before she started college." Vicky smiled at Becca with kind eyes.

"How did you know that?" She was seeing a new side to Vicky, one she hadn't recognized before.

"Your dad told me. He loved your mom very much and was lost after she died. I think a part of him closed off when she passed away. But there is a lot of good in your father, and I'm happy with the part he's able to share with me."

Becca had never looked at it that way before. She'd always expected her dad to be strong and deal with things. It never occurred to her that he hurt, too.

"Maybe you're like your mom and need some time before you start college."

"Is that even possible? Everything is all set. I'm already registered." Becca couldn't imagine having that option.

"Anything is possible."

Becca didn't know why Vicky was being so kind, then realized that maybe she'd never really given her stepmother a chance to get close. Her heart swelled with gratitude.

Vicky stood. "I'll leave you alone to enjoy some time with your mom."

"Vicky?"

"Yes."

"Thank you."

31

Two weeks later, Nikolai waited outside Fisk Hall at Northwestern University until every student left. Then he checked the lecture room to make sure no one remained. That was the last class on his list. Still no Becca.

He'd spent the past two days checking every class required for incoming freshman. He'd visited the dining halls and even located the freshman dorms. He asked every girl if they recognized Becca's picture. No one did.

Sadly, the only pictures he had of her were taken by paparazzi. Maybe he should be thankful for their photographic skills after all.

Nikolai sighed. If Becca were here, he'd have found her by now. He pulled out his phone and called Dmitri.

"That's it. I can't find her."

"I'm sorry, sir," Dmitri said.

After a long heart-to-heart conversation with his

parents, he'd convinced them that Dmitri was the ultimate loyal employee and the man was rehired.

"When I first met Becca, I bumped into her everywhere I turned. Now, no matter how hard I try, nothing."

"Perhaps fate only meant for you to be together for that one week. She obviously made a major impact on your life. Maybe that's why you met her. You're in a much better place than you were two months ago."

Nikolai still couldn't believe how his parents had done a one-eighty on their control of his life. They even seemed relieved at some of the new changes that were taking place in Mondovia.

"Maybe. I just can't believe it's really over. I was so sure I'd find her."

"On the bright side, now you can start your new adventure knowing you did everything you could to locate her."

While his parents said they no longer expected him to enter the military, they insisted he go to university, but in another shocking move, they said he didn't need to start until the following fall.

"I guess. I'll check in with you once I reach the airport," Nikolai said.

"Very good."

But he couldn't imagine ever feeling settled with this giant hole in his heart. As he walked back to his hotel, he saw the dining hall with students coming and going and decided to give it one final try.

After a few minutes of students barely glancing at the photo as they passed, Nikolai held out the photo to a guy with his hair buzzed short and wearing a small gold hoop earring.

"Excuse me. Do you know this girl?"

The guy glanced at the photo and suddenly stopped short. "Yeah, I do. That's Becca Hanson."

Nikolai couldn't believe it. If he'd gone straight to his hotel, he'd have missed this guy. "Oh my God, you have no idea how great this is. Do you know what dorm she's in or how I can get in touch with her?"

The guy looked at Nikolai closer. "I know you! You're that prince she was with in Europe."

Taken aback, Nikolai nodded. "Yes, I am. May I ask how you know this?"

"I'm friends with her brother."

"Dylan!" It took everything he had not to shout with joy. This was definitely a guy who knew Becca.

"Yes, I'm Marcus. How ya doing?" He held out his hand and Nikolai happily shook his meaty grip.

"It's great to meet you. I'm Nikolai. So can you take me to her dorm?"

"Actually, that would be impossible."

"Why's that?"

"She's not here. She never started school. She's off on some trip to Central America."

"Are you sure?" He'd been so certain she said she'd be attending Northwestern.

"I don't know the exact location, but I can guarantee she's not here."

Nikolai's brain kicked into high gear. If she was off in some remote country, how the heck could he find her? Would she even have cell service? "Do you happen to have her phone number?"

"Sorry, I don't. But I have her home phone and Dylan's cell." He pulled out his phone.

"That's perfect." Nikolai entered the two numbers into his phone. "Marcus, I can't thank you enough. You have no idea."

"How about a picture?" Marcus asked.

"Sure, why not." Nikolai posed beside Marcus as he held his phone before them and snapped a picture. "Dylan isn't going to believe it. Hey, we're having a party tonight. You should stop by. Everyone would totally flip out if you walked in."

He smiled. "Thanks, but I've got some calls to make and a plane to catch. It's been great meeting you."

"No problem, but if you change your mind, we're the Phi Sig house on the north edge of campus."

"I wish I could. Thanks again." Nikolai headed off, flying high. He was so much closer to being with Becca.

32

The next day, Becca walked into the tiny village store.

"*Hola*, Becca. How are you today?" asked Juan, a wrinkly-skinned Costa Rican man, who sat behind the counter of the market. His store provided everything from flashlight batteries and chewing gum, to suntan oil and flip-flops.

"*Hola*, Juan. I'm great. Another gorgeous day in paradise."

"*Pura vida*." Juan smiled, his crooked grin contagious.

"Live the pure life, indeed. *Pura vida*, Juan." She placed her Diet Pepsi on the scratched narrow counter.

"You're later than usual today," he said.

"I overslept. There was a turtle sighting just as my shift was ending at four a.m., and I couldn't possibly go to bed as that giant mama turtle laid her eggs in the sand. It's such a miracle."

"*Sí.* It is."

Becca glanced at the magazines and newspapers. A photo on the front page of an international paper caught her eye. She picked up the publication. There, in her hands, was a picture of Nikolai and his family at some sort of ribbon cutting. Her heart skipped a beat.

"I'll take this newspaper, too, please."

"I thought you didn't speak Spanish," Juan said.

"I don't, but I might as well start learning. Can you tell me what this headline says?" She pointed to the caption above Nikolai's photo.

"*Sí.* It says, 'Mondovia's Royal Family Donates Estate for Senior Living Residence.'"

"That's nice." Becca traced Nikolai's handsome silhouette. He looked so happy. It had been little more than a month, and he appeared to have moved on. She was trying, too, but Nikolai was never far from her thoughts.

"Who is this family? You know them?"

"They are from a tiny country called Mondovia. I met the son once. He was a very good person." Her heart lurched. Would it ever get easier to see Nikolai's photo, but know he was thousands of miles away?

Juan smiled, his eyes gentle and seeing into her heart. "Perhaps you will meet him again one day."

"I don't think so," she said, and paid for her purchases. "You have a great day."

"See you tomorrow, Becca. *Pura vida!*"

"*Pura vida*," she called to him.

Becca loved Costa Rica, the people were so happy, and their lives were simple. The narrow roads were peppered with potholes and confusing street signs, but the weather was always warm and sunny.

The Las Baulas preserve where she volunteered was staffed by wonderful people, and she loved being a part of saving the giant leatherback turtles. The experience was even better, knowing her mother had spent time on this same stretch of beach many years before.

Becca opened her soda and took a cool drink as she headed back to her tiny beachside room. Ahead at the intersection, she noticed a tall guy wearing sandals and cargo shorts looking at a map. His back was to her, but still, he reminded her so much of Nikolai it hurt.

She glanced at the newspaper in her hand. One more picture to save. Her only way to hang on to Nikolai was through the photos she found.

As she approached the stranger, she noticed the familiar way his shorts hung on his hips and the fit of his T-shirt across broad shoulders.

Becca stopped in her tracks. He wore a blue baseball cap.

Her body went numb. Could it possibly be? The guy glanced at his map and up at the street signs. The familiar tilt of his head was a dead giveaway, unless her eyes were playing terrible tricks on her.

She approached him, recognizing his earthy scent. A grin spread across her face. She stepped closer and said, "Excuse me, are you lost?"

He froze for a second, then slowly turned.

Their eyes locked and the disbelief on his face was palpable.

"Becca!"

She couldn't believe it. This was impossible. Nikolai's face broke into a huge grin. He pulled her into his arms, and held her close, crushing the map in the process.

"I'm not lost anymore," he murmured in her ear.

Becca savored the touch of his strong arms, the feel of his hands on her back, a sensation she never expected to know again.

"Oh, Nikolai!" Her eyes welled with tears of joy. "I never thought I'd see you again."

He held her shoulders and gazed at her. "You have no idea how hard I've been trying to find you."

She saw such relief in his eyes. He cradled her face in his hands and kissed her over and over. She laughed and hoped it would never end.

"I can't believe you're here. How did you know?"

He smiled and shook his head as if still not believing she stood before him.

"It's a long story."

"Let's get out of the middle of the road," she said. Nikolai led Becca to the side of the road, his hand a warm comfort at the small of her back. She pointed to a bench by a small park where kids kicked around a soccer ball. They sat facing each other.

"It's so good to see you." He cupped her cheek with his hand and kissed her again.

Becca felt she'd burst with joy. "How did you know I was in Costa Rica?" she asked, still in disbelief that Nikolai had found her.

"A guy at Northwestern."

"You were at Northwestern?"

"It was all I had to go on. I didn't have your last name. And I thought you lived in Chicago. I've turned into quite the detective. First I tried to get your info from the hostel in Prague, but all their records had mysteriously disappeared. Then I tried the riverboat company, but they refused to help, and then I even tried the Prague police department and the U.S. Embassy."

"Oh my God! I can't believe you did all that!"

"I told you I'd find you." He gazed at her with so much love. She still couldn't believe this was really happening.

She took his hand in hers. "I tried to find you, too. I guess, not find you, but reach you. You weren't kidding when you said Mondovia is behind the times. There isn't even an email address on the website for the royal family."

"That doesn't surprise me. Trust me, they have email, but it's not made public."

"And I wrote you a letter."

"Seriously? I never got it."

"I wondered if that's what happened. I got a reply back on formal notepaper from a Greta Vogel."

"Ah yes, she fields all unofficial mail. I'm so sorry I didn't get your letter. That would have been the simplest way to find each other." Nikolai caressed her hand with the pad of his thumb. Everything about him felt so perfect.

"But you're here now. And you still didn't tell me how you knew I'd be here."

"Sorry, I'm just so happy to see you, I can't keep my thoughts straight. Well, after all those other outlets failed, the only thing I could think of was to go to Northwestern University and try to find you."

Becca giggled. "You just showed up on campus and started looking for me?"

"More or less, yes. I hung outside the freshman-only dorms, the dining halls, and a couple of buildings that hold a lot of the required freshman classes."

Becca shook her head. She couldn't imagine the Prince of Mondovia lurking about a U.S. college campus. She linked her fingers with his. "I can't believe you did that."

Nikolai raised her hand and kissed it. "I did. On the third day, when I was about to give up, I made one more try and thank goodness I did. Some guy recognized your picture."

"Who would possibly recognize me?"

"His name was Marcus. Apparently, he's a friend of Dylan's."

"Oh my God, yes. Marcus goes to Northwestern."

"He told me you weren't on campus and gave me your home phone number. Of course, I was shocked to hear that you weren't at university, but let me tell you, I never made a call so fast in my life. Your stepmother answered."

"You talked to Vicky? I can't believe she didn't call and tell me." They'd become close these past weeks.

"I asked her not to. Vicky and I had a lovely chat, and she told me she knew about Prague and everything that happened. She told me you were down here for the next couple of months and that you wouldn't mind if I dropped in. Except I got this close and then couldn't for the life of me figure out where to go next."

Becca laughed. "Well, you did good. You dropped right into my path. But I can't believe your parents let you come. Why aren't you in the military?"

"We had a bit of a power struggle, but with my sister Alexi's help, my parents finally saw the light. It was a huge compromise on their part, and I'll always be grateful. I get to take the next year to travel and do whatever I want, and then I'll apply to university somewhere and start next fall."

She was so relieved for him. "So you're still in line for the throne?"

"Yes, but someday when it's time for me to become

king, I'll do things very differently from my father."

"That sounds really great. I'm so happy for you." She squeezed his hand.

"And you're in Costa Rica. What happened?"

"Well, as I mentioned when we were in Europe, I just wasn't feeling the college thing. I'd resigned myself to go, but after I returned home from Prague, I dreaded it even more. Vicky was really nice and we had a great talk. She told me that my mom took a year off after high school, too. She totally convinced my dad, which couldn't have been easy. I feel really bad about how difficult I was for her the last couple of years."

Nikolai brushed a lock of her hair over her shoulder. "I think she understands."

"I hope so. I'll make it up to her someday."

"I just remembered. I brought you a gift." He rifled deep into his backpack.

She wondered what he'd think when she confessed she had his old backpack and was using it here in Costa Rica.

"Close your eyes and hold out your hands," he said, with a mischievous grin.

She obeyed, her stomach tingling with excitement.

He placed something heavy into her palm. She closed her hand around a small paper bag.

"Okay, you can look."

She peered at the crumpled paper bag. "Any chance you bought this at a hardware store?"

He laughed. "How did you know?"

She reached in and pulled out a brass padlock. She locked eyes with Nikolai and fell in love with him all over again.

"Since we both have some time to travel, I thought maybe you'd like to find another bridge and add a lock."

"I can't think of anything I'd love better."

Don't miss the first book in the
JAMIESON BROTHERS TRILOGY!

1

Libby watched the cars zip by on the highway, longing for her dad's SUV with out-of-state plates to drive up and put her life back together. From her spot under an ancient oak, she spied a red SUV exiting the interstate and turning the opposite direction.

She sighed and tried to refocus on the sketch pad in her lap and the wildflowers she'd stuffed in a soda can. But instead, she traced the scars on her palm with the tip of her drawing pencil. If only she could wash the marks away along with the memories of that tragic day. She wiped her palm against her jeans, but only the pencil marks disappeared.

She focused on her drawing and rubbed the side of her pencil on the page, shading a leaf. A rumble caught her attention, and she glanced up; a large, gleaming bus turned off the exit and onto the county road toward her.

The shiny silver-and-black exterior and darkened windows of the vehicle made it look like some sort of VIP ride or maybe a tour bus.

The bus approached the nature preserve and turned in. In all the months she'd come to Parfrey's Glen, cars rarely pulled in, and she liked it that way. She thought of Parfrey's Glen as her own secret place where she could get lost in her thoughts.

The rumble grew louder as the enormous bus turned and pulled to a stop in the gravel parking lot on the far side of the clearing. She waited for the door to open and reveal the famous person within. Maybe it would be some country singer. Her mom loved country music and had always dreamt of going to a big concert. But it never happened.

A moment later the door opened, and Libby's hopes were dashed. Her quiet nature preserve had been invaded. By teenage boys.

A trio of noisy guys poured out. The first leapt from the top step and landed several feet out on the dirt, followed closely by another. The last twirled a Frisbee on his finger as he descended.

She watched them undetected from her spot under the tree, an eavesdropper on this group of loud, young strangers.

The Frisbee sailed through the warm September air as one of the guys raced to catch it. A man and woman exited the bus, their arms loaded with picnic supplies. The woman walked to a sunny spot of grass, set down her load, and spread out a couple of colorful blankets.

They were just a family; okay, a rich family. But no one famous.

Libby enjoyed a perfect view of the group. Their inter-action and happy banter reminded her of her own family and made her heartsick.

Her drawing forgotten, she soaked in their every move.

One of the boys turned around, providing her with a clean line of view. He tilted his head to the side and pushed away a lock of sun-kissed hair. A tiny thrill flipped in her stomach. He held an iPod and mini speakers, and loud music filled the air.

"Peter, turn it down," the man hollered as he set up lawn chairs.

"Dad, come on, you never let me play it loud." Peter grinned. He adjusted the volume and set the speakers down.

"Real funny. Now get out of here before I put you to work."

Peter darted through the long grass toward the other two boys, his movements swift and athletic. Libby's eyes trailed his every move.

"Garrett, over here," he yelled.

The Frisbee flew smoothly through the air. Peter leapt high and caught it. "Oh yeah, baby," he bragged, dancing as if it were a touchdown.

He flung it back, his body grace in motion, this time to the boy first out of the bus. This one appeared younger. His hair was a mop of loose dark curls and he wore a constant grin. They continued to torpedo the disk at one another and trash talk in the hot sun of early fall. Occasionally, Peter would do some crazy move to the music playing in the background. Libby stifled a giggle.

Peter suddenly glanced her way.

Uh-oh.

"Heads up," the grinning boy yelled as the Frisbee sped toward the unsuspecting Peter.

Peter ducked as it whistled by and landed not far from Libby. He looked straight at her. Every emotion she wore felt exposed. He jogged over and grabbed the Frisbee from the grass, and he whipped the disc back. He turned around and grinned as he sauntered to where she sat against the giant oak. He plopped down in the unmowed grass, his chest rising heavily.

"Hey." He looked at her with curiosity. "Whatcha doing?"

Libby's mouth went dry as this great-looking guy stretched out before her. Apparently, he expected her to respond. Her tongue felt numb.

A year ago, she would have been comfortable with him. Now, that confidence was a distant memory. These days, guys—anyone really—rarely talked to her anymore. Libby was an outsider to the kids in Rockville, which was fine

with her. She had been left in this crummy town and preferred to be alone. It was easier. She'd grown comfortable
with solitude, except for now. She prayed for her former
confidence to come back.

Libby held the sketch pad as a shield. "Uh, drawing,"
she uttered.

"Oh." He lay in the grass propped up on a muscular
arm. He watched her with casual interest, as his breath
came back. He was clearly nothing like the guys at Rockville
High School.

"Are you drawing those?" He pointed at the wildflowers sticking haphazardly out of a diet soda can.

"Yeah," she answered softly. "It's really dumb, though,"
she added, trying to sound normal and not like the inse-
cure girl she'd become. She pulled back and forth at the
pendant around her neck.

"Why's it dumb?" His deep blue eyes gazed at her.

She shrugged. "It just is. It doesn't mean anything—it's
just something to do." She pressed the pencil hard against
the pad and broke the lead.

"Can I see it?" Peter reached for the pad.

Libby's face heated. "I don't know. It's really nothing to
look at." She pulled the bound papers close; her fist gripped
the pencil tight.

When she didn't offer him the drawing, he moved next
to her. He leaned close and took the pad, and his fingers
brushed against hers. He sat so near, their legs bumped.

She wanted to reach out and touch him. His blond hair was still streaked by summer sun and hung past his eyebrows and over his eyes. He smelled good. Like shampoo and dryer sheets.

He studied the drawing, then wrinkled his brow as if it wasn't what he expected. He pushed the hair out of his eyes and looked sideways at her. She noticed a touch of razor stubble on his jaw.

"It's not of me," he said, looking embarrassed.

"Why would it be?"

"Well, you've been sitting here watching us, so I figured you must be drawing one of us, too." He handed back the drawing, a bit sheepish.

"Wow. Kind of full of yourself, aren't you?" she teased, feeling brave for a moment. "Sorry to disappoint, but it's just a bunch of wildflowers."

Libby couldn't get over this guy sitting so close. He moved right into her space as if it was no big deal, but it was. She struggled to sit still and not stare at him as her pulse raced.

He studied her, then shook his head.

"Well, it's not very good," he declared, but the corner of his mouth turned up as he fought back a grin. His eyes sparkled.

"Now you're just being mean," she teased again, surprising herself.

She scooted a few inches away to recover from the

awkwardness of being so close. Plus, this way she could sit and look straight at him. He had great eyes.

"Sorry, that's the best I could come up with. You're right. I was mean," he said. "Not a good start here. Let's begin again." He laughed, then leaned forward and held out his hand.

"Hi, I'm Peter."

She looked from his outstretched hand to his friendly face. Happiness wrapped around her like a warm blanket. She couldn't remember the last time she'd had so much fun, and this guy, Peter, with his careless good looks and confident attitude, made her stomach flip.

"Hi, Peter. I'm Libby."

They shook hands and smiled. His hand felt warm and strong.

"So, Libby, do you come here often?"

She rolled her eyes at the lame question. "Yeah, pretty often. Mostly on the weekends." Every chance she got was more like it. Anything to get away from the confines of the house.

"So you must live around here." He looked around for nearby homes.

Libby didn't want him to notice the run-down farmhouse in the distance, so she just nodded. She didn't associate herself with the house, its owner, or even the town.

"What's with the über bus? You on vacation?" She twisted her pendant on its thin leather cord.

"Not really. We live in it when we're on tour." He raised an eyebrow, aware of her not-so-smooth change of topic.

"What do you mean 'tour'? Like a vacation tour of the country?"

He laughed. "No, actually, we're on tour promoting our album, *Triple Threat*," he said with pride in his voice.

"Your family is in a band?"

"It's not my whole family, just my two brothers and me."

His demeanor changed, but she couldn't put her finger on why. She looked across the way to his brothers and furrowed her brow. "You are not. You're making it up." She could tell he was trying to impress her.

"No, really, we've had the band for over two years now."

"Sure you have." She eyed him, not believing a word. They were too young. They must all still be in high school. Plus, they looked nothing like members of a band. She didn't know exactly what guys in a band would look like, but certainly not like these guys.

"I'm telling the truth." He sat back and laughed again.

"So where do you play?" She pierced him with a stare. She'd catch him in his own lie. "You look too young for the bar scene. Do you play weddings?"

A coy expression covered Peter's face. "Uh, no, nothing like that. It's more public places."

"Like parks or fairs?" That she might believe.

"Yeah, something like that."

"Okay, if you say so." She shrugged. "Then you get to

drive around and see lots of different places? I'd do that in an instant, if I could." Anything to escape life here.

"The sights are great, but it can get claustrophobic with five people crammed in one giant tin can for days at a time. You'd hate it."

"Maybe, but I'd be willing to make the sacrifice to get outta here." A tightness in her chest occurred whenever she thought of her trapped existence.

"What's wrong with here?" He twirled a long blade of grass between his fingers.

Where to begin? Nothing about this place fit. It was all wrong. She didn't belong here and never would. But she wasn't about to explain her screwed-up life to Peter. "Just . . . everything."

"Okay, that tells me a lot." He smiled, gazing straight into her eyes. Her stomach turned upside down. "You want to elaborate?"

"No." She swallowed and looked away. "So what's the name of your band?"

"You like to change the subject." He grinned.

She noticed how his eyes sparkled each time he smiled. "So?"

"Jamieson. Our band is called Jamieson." He watched her closely, then asked, "Ever heard of us?"

"Should I have? It doesn't sound familiar."

"Really?" He wore a look of disbelief. "You've never heard of us?"

"No, do you play around here? We have a park pavilion that has groups sometimes. Is that why you stopped in Rockville?"

"No, we haven't played around here." The corner of his mouth turned up. "Don't you listen to the radio or watch TV?"

She sighed. She didn't want him to think she was an idiot. "Of course. Mostly country music, though. I don't recall ever hearing of a band called Jamieson."

"We're not country. Not even close." He shook his head. "And TV?" he asked.

Libby shook her head no. "I don't watch TV too often. Let's just say I get really good grades. And I love nature. That's why I come here so often. What's your reason for stopping?" She could tell that now he was the one having trouble believing her story.

"Whenever we drive through Wisconsin, we stop here because my mom likes how private it is. You know how moms are. Anytime she can find a spot that's surrounded by nature and not all highway, she puts it on the schedule."

Libby glossed over the mom comment. She didn't want to think of her mom. She missed her so much, her heart hurt. "You've been here before?"

"Quite a few times, actually."

Of the dozens of times she'd come to Parfrey's, she'd never seen them. How odd that today they would meet.

This news warmed her insides. She wondered how many times in this last lonely year they'd just missed each other coming and going.

"Hey, Petey, who's your girlfriend?" one of Peter's brothers yelled as he moved toward them with a cocky walk and hooded eyes. He appeared older, a little shorter than Peter, and not nearly as good-looking. He stared at her.

"That's Garrett," he said under his breath. "Ignore him. He can be a jerk."

"Lover boy, Mom said it's time to eat."

Libby pulled her knees in and hugged them. She couldn't see any resemblance between Garrett and Peter.

"I'm coming." Peter got to his feet and turned toward Libby. "I've gotta go, but maybe I'll see you later."

She smiled and nodded. She'd love to see him, more than he'd ever know.

Libby checked her watch. "Oh my God, I didn't realize how late it's getting. I've gotta go, too." If she didn't leave right now, she'd get the third degree. She flipped the sketch pad closed and gathered her belongings.

"Here." Peter extended a hand to her, his face kind and close.

"Thanks." She grasped his strong hand and stood up, relishing the touch of his skin.

"It was fun talking to you. I wish I'd bumped into you sooner," he said.

Was he actually disappointed to see her go?

"Who knows? Maybe I'll see you again someday." He smiled.

"Maybe." She couldn't imagine it happening, but for the first time in months she felt hopeful—happy, even.

"Have fun on your tour." She dumped the weeds and wildflowers onto the ground. "I've gotta go."

She hesitated for a moment, not wanting this to end. It had been a very long time since she'd relaxed and hung out with anyone, let alone a nice guy.

"Well, bye." She ran down the trail into the woods. Once in the thick of the trees, she turned back. Peter stood in the same spot, holding one of the wildflowers she'd left behind. He waved. She waved back, then disappeared into the woods.

Libby took the long way, so Peter wouldn't see where she lived.

• • •

Libby braced herself as she approached the beat-up old farmhouse. It loomed forgotten on acres of rich farmland and wooded areas. Most of the land was leased to a farmer, who benefited from the fertile soil. From what she could tell, this was her aunt's sole method of income. The rest of the property, barn, and outbuildings sat abandoned with a collection of broken-down cars littering the yard. The odor of leaking oil and rusted metal clung to the air. A vegetable garden had once flourished, but that must have been years ago.

She didn't know why her aunt had let it all fall apart, but her parents always said Aunt Marge struggled with demons early in life and never recovered from the fight. Libby heaved a sigh and inserted her key into the lock on the paint-chipped door.

Upon entering, the familiar smell of stale smoke and reeking trash filled the air. The television blared in the next room, confirming her aunt's presence. Libby hoped to sneak upstairs unnoticed.

"Don't forget to lock the door behind you. We can't be taking any chances," the gritty voice of her aunt hollered from the sickeningly sweet smoke-filled living room. "People are getting murdered in their beds every day."

"It's locked," Libby said, resigned. The house was dark, as always. Aunt Marge kept the curtains closed, as if anyone would want to watch a middle-aged woman drink and watch television all day.

"Come in here."

Libby dropped her backpack at the foot of the steps and dragged her feet as she entered the living room. Aunt Marge reclined in an upholstered chair, her feet on a mismatched ottoman. A dented TV tray served as her coffee table, cluttered with a lighter, a pack of cigarettes, a bottle of whiskey, and a dirty glass.

"What's wrong?" her aunt demanded while clenching a cigarette between her thin, stained lips.

"Nothing," she mumbled, pushing her long hair behind an ear as she tolerated the inspection.

"You're not lying to me, are you?" Aunt Marge's eyes narrowed. "I hate liars."

"No, I would never lie to you. I just have a lot of homework."

She grunted in reply. "There's groceries on the counter if you're hungry. Now get upstairs and finish your work. You know I won't tolerate laziness. You prove to those school people you're doing just fine. I don't need them snooping around here again." She picked up the television remote and started snapping it at the television, effectively dismissing her.

Libby made her way through the cluttered house into the kitchen. On the edge of the counter, next to piles of dirty dishes and old junk mail, sat a torn grocery bag. She began pulling things out. A bag of cheese popcorn, a box of granola bars, a bag of red licorice, and a warm package of sandwich meat. At the bottom she found a six-pack of soda and three candy bars.

She placed the soda and unappetizing sandwich meat on a crusty metal shelf in the refrigerator, grabbed the popcorn and a candy bar, and went upstairs with her backpack. It was always a relief to leave Aunt Marge behind. With any luck, she wouldn't hear from her again today. Hopefully, she'd drink herself into a stupor and fall asleep in her sunken chair.

Once inside her room, Libby pushed the door shut, closing out the ugliness below. She set her things on the neatly made bed. The worn bedspread featured snags and small tears, but she kept it and everything in the room as clean as possible. She'd given up on keeping the downstairs clean months ago, but here she could keep things the way she liked.

She picked up the small, framed picture of her family. Her mom, dad, and little sister, Sarah, along with a former version of herself, smiled brightly. The photo was taken while on a rafting trip out west two years earlier. Their arms hung comfortably on one another's shoulders, reminding her of the love they'd shared. Libby traced their faces with her finger and wondered when her dad would come back for her.

She returned the photo to its place on her dresser and moved to the two large windows, raising them a few inches. Cool air blew in, making her room feel better. Outside, across the fields, the rear entrance to the preserve was in perfect view. The spot she'd met Peter. She pulled a chair near the window and propped her book on her lap as she began doing homework, checking too often for Peter and the silver tour bus.

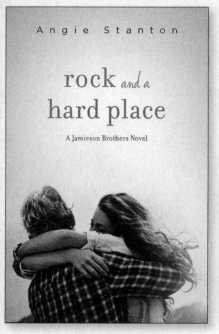
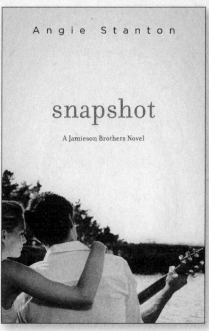